HER UNSPOKEN BLOOD

AN ABSOLUTELY GRIPPING THRILLER

J.A. CONRAD

ECLIPSE BOOKS LLC

Her Unspoken Blood
A Trent & Aria Mystery Thriller Book 2

Other books in this series:

Blood Red Winter
Blood in Truth
Flesh and Blood
Blood Is Thicker

TABLE OF CONTENTS

1

ONE YEAR AGO

bove our once green Central Texas backyard hangs a thin cloud of hazy, gray smoke. Like fog, it blankets the atmosphere and the people within, blurring my vision as my gaze strains to pierce it. I stare across the dry grass to the mostly standing pile of blackened boards. They belonged to our storage shed. Now charred studs and a jagged half-wall grin back at me like matte black teeth under the August sun. Acrid odors of sulfur, fuel, and chemicals infiltrate my nose and lungs. The airborne taste of bitter ashes cloys my tongue.

"Ms. Owen?" says the police officer beside me on the porch. His voice is kind. He's one of several from the Round Rock Police Department who responded to my 911 call.

I want to answer but can't. As I stand mute, my hand finds its way to my pounding forehead. I follow the motions of the firemen in their tan bunker gear with fluorescent yellow hazard trim around the cuffs and hems. Two men direct the high-pressure hose's jet behind the small, ruined structure where the fire tore a path to the greenbelt behind our house. A few flames still lick and dance in defiance. Succumbing at last to the unrelenting spray, they sputter and die. A puddle of molasses pools in their wake as steam and smoke billow out and add to the hovering veil. It levitates more densely now. Sticky.

Near what remains of the outbuilding, officers cluster around an indiscernible lump on the ground. I crane my neck. The authorities block my view. A few stand while several others stoop or crouch beside the unknown object. A man in a red polo shirt and khakis emerges from the huddle with a camera swinging from a lanyard around his neck. A Condor backpack hangs off his shoulder, and his left hand grips a clipboard. He steps back and writes something before walking to the other side of the seared shed, where he squats and unzips his bag.

I can't see the firetruck from here because it's parked out front. But I know it's there, cherry red with a huge, silver ladder on top, crammed obtrusively across the entire width of our little street. It's not as narrow as the country roads but could be wider since my stepmom's neighborhood isn't one of the swanky, newer ones. The engine obscured, my gaze pulls to the tense outline of the pressurized firehose. It strains from its unseen source around the side of our house to the edges of the smoldering backyard.

A chill crawls over my sweaty skin, and I resist sinking into the porch chair. The wind was in my favor. It could have pushed the blaze straight to the house, but it didn't. That's what Carol would say if she were here, but she's not the first real estate agent to work Saturdays. I remember now. I passed out on the couch after calling 911 and never even notified my stepmom about what happened.

"Are you Ms. Aria Owen?" asks the officer.

He towers over me, but I've barely looked at him. Numbness floods my every cell, much like the sooty river of firehose-water gushing toward the wild tract of land. My legs teeter, and I grip the white, wooden porch railing with hands equally as pale. "Yes. I'm sorry. I need a minute."

"All right, ma'am. Take your time," he says. He shifts his weight, and the boards creak beneath the tread of his black boots.

His boots. The sound of Ayden's heavy steps on the dusty shed floor breaks through in echoic memory. When I was alone, he entered uninvited. He told me he was my boyfriend Korey's brother. Oh God, what have I done?

My back pocket rings and my heels come off the floor. I cast an apologetic glance at the police officer. I retrieve my cell and smash it against my ear. "Carol."

"Aria! Are you all right? Red said the backyard is on fire." My stepmom's voice falters in a shrill pitch.

Red is our next-door neighbor, a woman whose house is to the left of ours if you're facing the street. "I'm okay. I'm fine. The shed caught fire when the gas can spilled, but I—I got out time. I got out in time. I called 911 right away, and the fire department already put it out. And the house is okay." My temples throb, and my face heats to a sharp crimson. Damn this heat exhaustion.

Carol lets out a breath. "Oh, thank God. I'm coming home. I'm leaving the office right now." A pause. "Aria, have you been drinking?"

"No," I say. "You know I don't drink."

"What?" she asks.

I swallow and concentrate. "Hardly ever. That's what I meant."

"Because it really sounds like you've been drinking."

I tighten my grip on the phone and risk a few paces by the porch railing—anything to ease the tension. Even when I manage to pronounce everything correctly, the cadence of my sentences rises and dips unnaturally. Well, it's no wonder putting words together feels like bathing a cat. Not only is it over one hundred degrees out here, but I hit my head pretty hard.

"I know. I know it does," I say.

In Carol's background, a car door slams. Keys jingle. "How did it happen? You said gasoline, but how did it ignite?"

I sniff, and with guilt thicker than the heat, peek at the officer. Davis, I think. I can't believe he's still waiting and not forcing me to do... something. Give a statement? Explain? Because if I were him, I'd probably be reading me my rights about now and guiding my head into the back of a cruiser. "I have to go. The police need to speak with me. He's waiting."

"Okay," she says. She loudly exhales as she starts the engine. "Okay. I'll see you soon."

We hang up. Another wave of grogginess shakes my awareness. I grab the chalky handrail again. I wonder whether the police or the medical personnel got here first. I don't know how long it's been since I called. Before I shove my mobile back into my pocket, I check. Only thirty minutes.

Besides a couple of people in blue pressed around whatever lies on the ground, I don't see anyone who looks like an EMT. My skull continues pounding, and I lift my fingers to the most painful spot. The golf-ball-sized knot on my scalp has mostly scabbed over. Sticky goo comes away at the touch. The medics have probably been administering life-saving procedures to Ayden—giving him CPR, fluids and preparing him for hospital transport. That's why no one has come to check on me yet.

The uniformed men and women huddling around the indistinct object on the ground begin to stir. The crowd parts. They reveal a mass resembling a human body covered in a white sheet.

He's dead. Ayden's dead.

Two men in black shirts with gold lettering each grab an end of the stretcher. When they lift it, the bright fabric flutters in the ascension like wisps of a ghost. The first responders briskly carry their charge away from the blackened shed, the strip of charred grass reaching toward the greenbelt, and the small gathering of emergency crew. They pass beyond view around the side of the house to the street where the vehicles are parked—the firetruck, the squad cars, the crime scene van, and probably an ambulance too. But dead men don't go to the hospital. They go to the morgue.

A hot draft of air brushes my face. The ever-present smell of gasoline twists my stomach into a knot. I grip the porch railing tighter, my trembling arms betraying the fear of falling. I've fought the dizziness this long, but now it hammers me into submission. My knees buckle, and I lose my grip. Back I go.

Officer Davis catches me under the arms and thrusts me to a standing position. "Let's get you inside."

My body jerks. "Yes," I try to say.

I force my legs to straighten beneath me. I mostly get my balance. Davis keeps a hand on my back as he directs me inside the house. I shouldn't have come out, but I couldn't help it. I had to know.

Right behind us, two EMTs make their way up the porch steps. Officer Davis holds the door, and after a few words from me, the four of us convene in the kitchen. Davis stands aside again—the man has patience—and I take a seat in a wooden chair. I stare at our brown and white tiled floor while the paramedics work me over.

The woman speaks the most. She tells me her name. It's something pretty and exotic, but it's already a blank. I focus on her accent that floats almost tangibly like strands of warm honey as she asks me questions. The man draws my blood. Then the lady cleans my head wound. She gives me something for the pain but nothing drastic. Tylenol, I think. They'll be back shortly, she says, and I wonder what for.

After they depart, for the time being, I lean on my elbows. I prop my heavy eyelids open with sheer will and a little bit of luck. I ask Officer Davis, "Would you like to sit down?"

"Thank you, no," he says. He stands with his clipboard while I finally explain what happened.

I do my best to force out every consciously available detail. Compelling my uncooperative voice to enunciate each syllable, I try not to skip anything, but I probably still do. When I finish, he thanks me. I wonder when he'll take me to jail. Shouldn't he have cuffed me by now? I've already forgotten what I told him. When the backdoor swings closed on Davis's way out, my thoughts go muddy.

I remind myself that today was because of Ayden. No, today was because of me. I did this. Ayden came here, but he died in the backyard, and now he's at the morgue. And Korey doesn't know.

The overbearing drowsiness finally wins, and my upper body sags against the table. I let my right cheek press the cool finish of the smooth wood. My eyelids flutter. I slip into blackness.

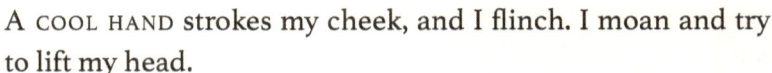

A COOL HAND strokes my cheek, and I flinch. I moan and try to lift my head.

"Aria?" says a voice. It sounds like Carol's.

I push against something soft. My body sinks into it, and my fingers curl around a fuzziness that smells like ocean breeze fabric softener. A delicious, embracing sleep wraps around me and won't loosen its hold. "Yeah?"

"Do you need help getting to bed?" my stepmom asks.

The gears in my head spin as I try to process what she's asking me. At long last, I pry my eyes open. Carol. She's here. I guess she finally made it home. With a grunt, I push myself into a sitting position on the couch. A velvety, rouge blanket slides off my shoulders. "What time is it?"

"It's a little after eight o'clock. How are you feeling?" she asks. She sits on the ottoman, her concern wrinkles pressing more deeply than usual. Her hair of frizzy brown puffs out from the ponytail behind her head.

"Eight o'clock? I thought you were heading straight here," I say. A bitter taste lingers on my tongue, and I swallow. I scan for my bottled water but don't see it. Lemonade? No, I drank that already. I wish the dizziness would stop. I swing my socked feet to the tan carpeting.

Carol gives me a sad smile. "I did. It's been quite a day. Are you feeling any better?"

My shoulders slump, my gaze finding the closed back door. At the top, one of those half-moon-shaped windows lets in a little light from the backyard.

The backyard. My core clenches, and I look back at my stepmom. "I feel..."

Carol collects a few magazines from the ottoman and sets them on the coffee table so that she can scoot over. I trace her motions with my eyes. The coffee table. There's something about that—something I should remember. I wish I knew what it was. Seconds tick by, and I stare blankly without answering her question.

"Yeah?" she asks.

"My head doesn't hurt so much. I just can't stay awake," I say. I rub my face. My sweaty palms smell like rubbing alcohol. Or is that gasoline? I don't recall getting any on me.

She chuckles. "That's okay. You need to rest. Besides, it's bedtime anyway—bedtime for both of us. Come on. I'll help you to your room."

Carol rises, takes my hands, and pulls me to my feet. I glance down to see jeans, black dress socks, and my favorite fitted blue blouse with a crinkly texture. I can't even remember getting dressed this morning.

"Thanks," I say. After taking a faltering step, something on the coffee table pulls my attention. A small, off-white glazed ceramic dish with a lid rests there. Red and pink flowers and green leaves encircle the top around a gold ball for a handle. Not really my style, but it reminds me of my grandmother. My cotton ball dish. That's the thing—the thing I was supposed to remember.

"Aria?"

"Wait," I say. "I left this here by mistake."

"I was wondering why that was out here," Carol says.

I wonder too. A sick dread tugs at me, reminding me of the terrible thing that evades my memory. But Carol doesn't seem to know either, so I won't tell her. Anyway, I can't reveal what I don't know myself.

My trembling fingers close around the decorative container. I clutch it as my stepmom guides me along as though I'm old and frail instead of twenty-four years old. Walking would be so much easier if the floor would stay still. I stumble into my room and set the dish on my nightstand. Scents of vanilla and apricot leak out of my wall diffuser.

"Do you want help changing?" Carol asks. She gives me a wink. She knows that's the last thing I want.

I manage a grin. "No, but thanks. I can do it."

We say goodnight, and she pulls the door closed. All I want is sleep. The desire fills every part of me, and I long to dive into oblivion and stay there. My bed is neat and tidy the way I left it. Its overstuffed gray comforter and marigold throw pillows beckon to me. But I can't give in yet. I have to look inside the container.

I turn and drag myself to the nightstand, where I stand rigidly with a poised hand. While I brace myself like someone about to bring a shoe down on a venomous spider, a few seconds go by with my heart hammering. Then I grasp the gold ball and whisk off the lid.

A bloody eye. I jump and slap a hand over my mouth to silence my scream. As I reel backward and get my balance, I refocus and realize that no—that's not what I'm seeing. Thank God and all that is good in the world, I didn't just find a severed human eye in my cotton ball dish. But what *is* there isn't much better. A cold, plunging sensation stabs through my chest and into the pit of my stomach.

My gaze takes in the object I misperceived—a ring. A large, gold ring, probably a man's but instead of holding a jewel setting like a college ring, there's a blue eye. It has all the trappings of the real thing—the white sclera with tiny, red capillaries, a deep blue iris, and a black pupil. Streaks of gooey red cover the surface, and beneath the gold band lies a dried puddle of Ayden's blood.

My heart hammers as I scrub my hands in the bathroom sink. I have to tell the police about this. I must. They'll need to retrieve it for evidence and submit it to the forensics lab with whatever else they got today. As I dry my hands on the towel, I swear I catch the scent of some bodily fluid—something unclean. The mild, pus-like vapor reminds me of the faint odor a cut emits when you take the bandage off. The smell comes and goes between whiffs of cucumber melon hand soap—or do I imagine that?

I don't care if I do. Grimacing, I press down on the soap dispenser and dump four globs of gel onto my palm before furiously washing my hands all over again. The ghost odor even sours my dry tongue. Different scenarios race through my mind frantically as I consider them. Or, more correctly, I half-watch them as they flick by, almost as though I'm an outsider to my own thoughts. There's only one explanation that makes sense.

The ring is a souvenir. A trophy. A reminder kept of the dark conquest that evades memory.

I dry my hands again and sit on the bed. My quivering fingers reach for my cell phone on the nightstand but withdraw. The dizziness won't quit. My head starts pounding once more, and my heart rate dizzies me. I rub my face. The metallic smell of blood adheres to my palms—I swear it does—but that's insane. I didn't touch the ring, only looked at it. I stand and readjust the floral lid.

Ring, ring! The ceramic chimes as it scrapes, and my

muscles twitch. I'm not in my right mind. Something's very wrong.

My black socks wear a path in the carpet as I pace the bedroom. Am I supposed to call the cops and tell them there's a bloody ring in my room, and I don't remember how it got there? I seat myself on the gray comforter again. If I'm going to tell the police, I'll have to do it soon. The longer I wait, the worse it will be. I hug my torso. Carol might know what to do. Or maybe she can at least help me understand what happened.

But then my stomach plunges. I can't tell Carol. I can't tell anyone.

With my body shaking hard and a cold sweat misting my face and chest, I lie on my side. I focus on my breathing, drawing air into my lungs deeply and letting it out slowly. I need to get hold of myself. I need to think. There's an answer here somewhere, and I've got to find it.

Tomorrow I'll have to face Korey. The police must have notified him, but he'll still need to hear from me about Ayden's death, whether I can remember or not. But how will I explain forgetting? I curl into the fetal position and squeeze my eyes closed.

As I rack my mind, trying to piece together the scattered, snapshot images of this broken day, all I find are more questions. And one is more important than all the others. Am I a murderer?

2

Breathless, I gulp air, sit bolt upright, and blink at the first morning light that filters through the sheer taupe curtains of my room. Deep drowsiness pulls at me, threatening to knock me unconscious again if I don't fight it. I inhale a few more deep breaths. My gut twists, and I hurl myself out of bed. I stumble across the floor in a trance. My big toe snags on the carpet, and I catch myself on the footboard but knock my elbow. It smarts.

I scan my recent memory for what happened, but it's all hazy gray or blank. A few images spring up that don't seem to fit anywhere or mean anything. Did I fall asleep? Disorientation grips me, and I don't know what day it is. I glance down to see my dusty jeans, slightly faded, blue shirt—my favorite fitted blouse that I've worn too many times—and the soft, comfortable dress socks still on my feet. A few impressions come to me slowly.

The police. There was a fire in the backyard—a dead man. A man died in our utility shed, a man whose name meant something to me when he said it. Yes, he was my boyfriend Korey's brother, Ayden Nemeth. He burned to death on our property. The police told me it wasn't my fault, but there's some reason I don't believe that. An icy fear floods my bones.

The ring. There was a bloody ring with a blue eye stone in my cotton ball dish. Ayden's ring. Ayden's blood.

Tears nip at my cheeks as reality starts to invade my addled senses. This can't be real. It just can't. I creep up on the nightstand like I don't want to lift the metaphorical shoe and see the giant, crushed spider swimming in its juices.

Please, God, don't let it be there. Don't let it be there.

The knot in my abdomen threatens to tear me apart as more dizziness rushes into my skull. I hold my breath. For an instant, only the sound of my hammering heart fills the room. My unsteady fingers get a limp grasp on the gold ball. I yank it off.

But as my gaze devours the contents of the small, shiny container, I find nothing but clean, off-white lacquer. Empty. No blood. I draw air noisily and stand up straighter. My hand flies to my heart. Unfortunately, my relief doesn't last long.

"Where is it?" I say to the walls.

With a loud exhale, I shudder as more tension flows out of my stiffened back and limbs. There's no souvenir. That's good. It's what I want but allowing myself to believe it entirely is a luxury I can't afford.

"Where the hell is it?"

"Aria, are you up?" Carol calls.

Her voice springs from the hallway and constricts my chest like she's already discovered my secret, and it's time for me to answer up. But my secret isn't here. There's no trophy. There's no dried blood or even an oozy smell—strange how I remember that odor from last night, though I can't recall much else.

I don't answer my stepmom. I pick up the dish and put it to my nose, expecting the iron-tinged reek of a used Band-Aid, but all I inhale is a mild scent of soap or cleaner. As I try to swallow the lump in my throat, I only cough.

"Are you all right?" my stepmom asks.

"Yeah," I say. My voice comes out in a harsh croak. I fling open the door. "Why didn't you wake me?"

Her too-wide smile fades. Her mousy hair is down and frizzing around her face, and she's wearing her pink robe and gray slippers. She grips the handle of her coffee mug tightly. Her gaze traces my fully dressed body. "When? Last night? I did. I helped walk you to bed."

"When? Did you come into my room again?" I ask.

She frowns. "Are you feeling worse? I can call the doctor—"

"No. No, it's not that." I lean on the doorframe and put my other hand to the lump on my scalp. It's sore but bearable. The dizziness is the worst.

Carol says, "Tell me what you need. Are you hungry?"

I shake my head. "When? When did you wake me?"

She pulls back. "Last night after you fell asleep on the couch. Aria, you don't look well, and you're not making sense. It's going to be okay. Like we talked about yesterday, if this happens, we just need to keep you calm. You need to be resting until you feel better."

Stop freaking out, is what she's trying to say. I ask, "When did we talk last night?

"After we got back from the hospital," says Carol.

I never went to the hospital. Of that, I'm certain. After the paramedics administered first aid and I spoke with the police, I fell asleep on the couch, and Carol woke me. I remember that much. All of this bothers me. And I can't keep the guilt from my voice. Does she know about my little souvenir? Did she *see*?

"Are you sure I went to the hospital?" I ask.

"I'm sure. I went to visit, but they made me stay in the waiting room." A wrinkle pinches between Carol's eyebrows. She steps back, extends an arm, and I reluctantly take the cue to follow her into the kitchen. She pours me a coffee and hands it over with a gentle, motherly motion—not her usual style. I take the mug, watching her facial creases multiply.

I shake my head. "What was I in for?"

"Oh, Aria." She stops and wrings her hands. "For what Ayden did. You have a head wound and some bruises. The doctor said it's nothing serious, but it may take a while for the headache and dizziness to go away. You don't remember any of it?"

"No." I hold my coffee cup in a tight fist. "What did I say when you woke me?"

"What?" Carol asks. Her rubber slipper bottoms swish against the tile as she goes to the pantry.

"What did I say last night when you woke me?" I finally press the mug to my lips and take a drink. The coffee is overly bitter like the pot's been on the burner too long.

"Aria, are you sure you don't want me to call the doctor?" Carol pulls the cereal box from the shelf. She takes out two bowls and places them on the counter.

"No. Carol, please. Just answer the question." I've always called my stepmom by her first name. She doesn't even blink —not about that, anyway.

Carol breaks the seal on the new box top. "Let's see. You

asked why I didn't wake you sooner. And you took the porcelain dish that you left on the coffee table."

I die inside. "Did you come into my room last night?"

"I did." The granola clinks against the glass bowl as she pours.

I wince. My nervous tone betrays me again as I ask, "And?"

Her gaze darts back and forth between her task and my face. "And you were out cold. I left you alone."

"And what else?" I ask.

"Aria, is there something you need to tell me? You can, you know. I know we must have talked for three hours last night, but after what happened, that's understandable. I'll get breakfast ready, and we can talk some more." She opens the fridge and produces a half-gallon of milk.

A hospital trip. A three-hour conversation. A missing ring in a mostly missing day. I shift my feet and stare at the floor, hoping my stepmom won't notice my reddening ears. "No, I just—only that I can't remember what happened. It's... it's making me feel crazy."

Carol nods. She gives me a sad smile. "It's okay—the doctor said that could happen, and it's not uncommon with head injuries."

My eyes ache. This must be a crueler form of shadow boxing because I guess the original kind isn't bad enough. "But what happened? What did I *do*? Or what did I tell you, or what did the police say I did?"

The full coffee mug slips from my hand. It shatters on the tile, splattering my jeans and socks with hot liquid. I swear and go for a towel, but Carol beats me to it. While she cleans it up, I peel off my socks, lean against the counter, and cover my face with my hands.

"You really can't remember any of it?" She rinses the towel and sets her hands on her hips.

"No, not really." I sigh. "Please, just tell me what I said— exactly what I said."

Carol draws a deep breath. "Well, you said pretty much the same things the police said. Ayden Nemeth attacked you, and when you fought back, it somehow started a fire with gasoline. Ayden burned to death, but you got out. He claimed to be Korey's brother, and per the police, that checked out. When I met you in the waiting room of the ER, you told me the doctor said it was nothing serious—a scalp wound that will heal on its own. You said Ayden hit you, but you stopped him from going further."

I nod and rub my arms to stem the chill. "Okay. I do remember a little of that. So... how exactly did I stop him?"

Carol whisks two clean, burgundy placements from the drawer and puts them in place. She sets down utensils one at a time before locking her gaze on me and answering. "You stabbed him."

AFTER GETTING Carol to explain her understanding of what happened, I sit at the kitchen table numbly. She wasn't here when the altercation occurred, but the police told her that Ayden trespassed on our property, attacked me in the shed and that during the struggle, I stabbed him. And that I told her a similar story last night when she and I talked. My speech was impaired, and I didn't give specifics other than that while I fought back, the building caught fire and took Ayden with it.

"What did I stab him with?" I ask. I stir my cereal, releasing aromas of apple and cinnamon, but I can't bring myself to eat.

"I don't know. They didn't tell me that," Carol says. "But most of what they told me, you supposedly told them. You can't remember any of that now?"

"I vaguely remember talking to them. I just can't remember what I said. The same with Ayden. I can see him in the shed with me and recall some of the feelings and images, but nothing specific." I set down my spoon and get up to refill our coffee mugs. "Did the police say that stabbing him is what killed him?"

Carol shakes her head. Her cereal bowl empty, she drags her knife across the butter and spreads it over warm, brown toast. Glad one of us is hungry. "They said no—that you defending yourself just stunned him. They thought it was the fire that got him."

I can't understand how the shed caught fire at all, let alone how it overtook a large man quickly enough to kill him, but I don't mention that. I sigh. I give my stepmom my untouched cereal. "Well, okay. I guess I can call the police department and ask if I can get whatever reports were filed."

When I rise, Carol stands too. She reaches out and touches my arm. "You can if you want. But it's also okay if you just want to rest now, and I really think you should. Whether you can remember or not, you haven't done anything wrong."

My stomach dips as I pad out of the kitchen. Sure. A man is dead, and I've done nothing at all besides retaining a memento of my victim, which then mysteriously vanishes.

Did I hide it in some secret, covetous place while delirium smothered my conscience?

I pace the hallway, dial Korey's number, and press the phone to my ear. I press so hard my ear aches. Korey's line rings five times before going to voicemail.

"Hi, Korey, it's me. Hey, please give me a call. We had a fire in our backyard yesterday. I'm okay, but, um, something terrible happened. I don't have all the details... it's hard to explain. Please call me right away," I say in a tremulous tone.

I'm supposed to add, "I love you." I know that. But I don't love him now. I haven't loved him in a long time, so I don't say it. After pressing the red icon to hang up, I set the phone on the bathroom counter and get in the shower.

Twenty minutes later, I emerge with my hair wrapped in a towel and check my mobile. One new call—Detective Wallak from Round Rock wants me to contact him to schedule an in-person interview at the police department. Nothing from Korey, not even a text.

My insides squirm. I breathe in the steamy, coconut-body-wash scented air and lean against the damp wall. Although Korey is all I can think about, I force myself to phone the detective. We schedule for later today. Although I've been working with my stepmom as a real estate assistant for several years now, she won't hear of me going to work after what happened. That's a shame, really, because I can't even fully grasp what "what happened" means. When I go see Wallak, I'll make sure to request a copy of the police report. Everything I need to know should be in there.

An image of Ayden's bloody ring flashes. Victims don't keep souvenirs. Only murderers do. I'm a monster. And Korey will know. He'll find out.

I wrap a bathrobe around me and pace the hall again, trying Korey's number three more times. I text him twice. Surely the police notified Ayden's family last night, and Korey would have heard by now. The hours tick by, but he never calls me back.

DRESSED and ready for the day, my head spins as I cross the threshold to the front porch. I linger outside the door for a moment as if reality and everything in it are in question. For me, I guess they are.

Behind the houses in our modest suburban neighborhood, the sun crawls over the horizon. A golden dawn breaks in smudgy tones of rose yellow like every other day before this one. I inhale the scent of fresh, dewy grass—something normal and pleasant. Then the smell of charred, smoky wood fills my nostrils, and my insides twist like a pile of worms. It's back there. Evidence of the thing I did, or what remains of it. Our blackened shed is just behind the house at the end of our long yard. I should go have a look, but I don't want to. I can't bring myself to face it, as though I won't find haphazard stacks of burned cinders and debris but a vision of myself goring a stranger and walking off with a trophy.

A gust of warm wind brings goosebumps instead of sweat, and I shudder. I go down the porch steps and shuffle across the grass toward the mailbox. My gaze sweeps all the nearby yards, the street, and the sidewalk. The idea of someone seeing me and wanting to chat makes me cringe.

Something shiny near the opposite curb draws my eye. I squint and make out the rectangular outline of a cell phone.

Great. Freaking spectacular. A mental tug of war ensues with the dark side of my conscience screaming at me to leave it— it's not my problem. Not today. Unfortunately, the human side wins. I walk across the pavement and pick up the mobile. One of the latest iPhone models, it's wrapped in a glittery, pink case. Maybe it's Sarah's. She lives at the white two-story across from us.

When I glance at her door, I learn I won't even have to bother knocking. Sarah's already emerged, and she waves at me from the stoop. I groan under my breath. I don't know her that well, only that she lives with her husband and their two middle-school-age children, and she's chatty. Chatty was okay until now.

Sarah smiles and starts walking over to me. "Aria!"

I stiffen. I wonder what she'll see when she looks at me. A burgeoning discomfort lodges in my throat, and I wish I could go back inside. It's too late now.

"Hi, Sarah," I say.

I stand by the mailbox with the phone in my hand. With the other, I adjust the little red flag more than necessary. The moisture from the grass seeps into my shoes. While I wait for Sarah to reach me, I stare at another neighbor's crape myrtle tree. The heat of the summer days is shriveling its vivid, pink blossoms—rare for such a hardy plant.

"Hey," Sarah says. She flashes me a smile as she floats over with her blonde ponytail swishing back and forth. Tight workout clothes hug her trim body—mauve shorts, a matching Adidas top, and white sneakers.

"Hey. Did you lose your phone?" I ask. I hold it up, the pink, sparkly bling catching the swelling light.

Sarah puts her hand on her heart. "Oh my gosh, yes! I've been looking for it all morning. Thank you!"

"You bet. Happy to help," I say as I hand it over.

A lady Carol's age approaches on the sidewalk, walking her boxer. I back into the yard and remain there until they pass.

"Are you afraid of dogs?" Sarah asks.

I suppress the image of Korey's bulldog Xero sinking his teeth into my leg—and other body parts. "Something like that."

Sarah and I get past a couple of pleasantries, and Sarah dives right into what I was dreading. "Dave and I saw smoke and police cars when we got home from work last night. Are you and Carol okay?"

I nod, gritting my teeth as I internally recoil. I wonder if she saw them removing Ayden in a body bag, but if so, she probably would have mentioned that. "Yeah, we're both fine. There was a fire in the shed yesterday afternoon, so I had to call the fire department. I guess even though it wasn't in the house, they sent the police and paramedics too, just in case."

"Oh." Sarah frowns, squinting at me as she studies my face. "Well, you're really okay? Were you hurt?"

"I'm fine." I shrug and force a smile. "Crazy day."

Sarah pushes out her bottom lip and puts her hands on her hips. "Oh wow, yeah. Sounds like it. Gosh, the police were here for a long time. We were worried that something horrible happened. So, this fire in the shed was pretty intense, huh?"

She tilts her head, searching my face for something. For an explanation? For the truth, I guess. She knows, or at least suspects, that I'm not giving it.

"It was," I say.

"But how did the fire start? Were you smoking, or—you don't smoke," she says. Blink, blink, go her blue eyes.

"I—we don't know how it started," I say. I flick the red mailbox flag again. Up, down. Up, down. Irritation bringing an unwelcome heat to my face, I snap open the mailbox door and reach for the stack of letters.

"Oh. Do you think it was from the heat?" Sarah asks.

I clench my jaw and withdraw the envelopes. I click the black door shut. What the hell difference does it make how the fire started? Our shed burned down. I wish she'd get on with her own life and leave mine alone.

I say, "Yeah, I mean, I'm sure the heat definitely exacerbated it. I wasn't by the shed when it happened, so I don't know." My words are flimsy. I can't remember where I was when the fire started or what part the heat played.

Sarah nods slowly. Her lips are parted, and her hands still rest on her hips. "Wow. Weird. Well, I'm glad you're okay."

"Thanks," I say.

My neighbor goes quiet for a moment, and I'm not sure if it's because she doesn't believe me or she notices how my gaze abruptly shifts toward the street at my left. A white SUV creeps toward us slowly. Korey drives a white GMC Suburban. Maybe he got my messages and wants to talk in person. Fine—but we'll chat outside, just like this. From here, I can't tell if the approaching vehicle is the same make and model as the one he drives.

The stack of mail quivers in my right hand. Maybe Sarah notices that too.

"Are you waiting for someone?" she asks.

I shift my weight. "No. I just noticed that SUV slowing down. They're probably looking for an address for a delivery or something."

She pauses before saying for the second time, "Yeah. Well, glad you're okay."

I nod absentmindedly.

"You look exhausted, Aria," Sarah says. "Take care of yourself, all right?"

"Will do," I say. I try to grin, but I think I only manage to sound sarcastic.

She returns an uncertain smile. We wave each other off, and my neighbor starts down the sidewalk on her morning jog with her huge, glittery phone shoved in the back pocket of her tight shorts.

The white SUV stops two houses down on my side of the street. No one gets out. Straining to read the plates, I make out DL7–xxxx. Not that it does me any good. I never bothered to note Korey's license plate number because why would I? I want him out of my life. After I apologize for Ayden's death—for that terrible thing that I can't remember—I'm cutting the cord for good.

But the implications of that, of what it means, and how it will play out in the real world are lost on me right now. It's too much to think about, especially trying to grasp how I'll explain what happened when I don't even know myself. And I can't mention what I found in the cotton ball dish. It's gone now, as though it never existed.

A crisp morning wind blows the hair from my face, and it dries my sweaty forehead. At the same time, the gnawing apprehension ices my bones. Rubbing my arms to banish the chill, I tell myself there's no reason to be so paranoid. That car has nothing to do with me. I turn toward the front walkway and take the mail inside. Korey will call me back, or he won't.

3

Three weeks pass. Korey doesn't call. Whenever I'm not working, I check the local media and papers. I keep wondering if anything will turn up about the fire and Ayden's shocking death. No reporters have come to see me. No one has called from the news channels. The days tick by, and no one prints a word of what happened anywhere. I guess not all crimes or strange occurrences get coverage. The reporters can't be everywhere at once.

Reading the police report doesn't help much. It's a much longer, more tedious version of what Carol told me. It cites Ayden's stab wound as "unlikely to be life-threatening." While that should quell my fears, it doesn't—because although the write-up mentions the deceased's third-degree burns, it still gives the cause of death as "accidental (unknown)." The officer's report contains nothing about a bloody ring. But then, I guess I knew that already. How could it? Besides, poring over a second-hand account isn't the same as remembering what I actually did, and there are no witnesses to jar my memory.

After the first week, I took Carol's advice and stopped blowing up Korey's phone with messages. He's grieving, she told me, and grieving people need space. I didn't do anything wrong, Carol said, and if Korey has a problem, he can go to the police. Otherwise, he'll just need to get over it in his own way.

When I'm not hunting for articles about the incident that evades my memory, I search the house for Ayden's ring. I search every nook and cranny in the bathroom. Every container, jar, or box. I scour my room, the kitchen cabinets, the pantry, the drawers of my stepmom's desk. And once the initial shock fades, I search the backyard too. I sift through the carbon-streaked boards that belonged to our shed in the hope of some answer. I don't find it. And I don't find the ring.

I'm not sad that Korey doesn't call, but it increases my guilt in a way. It clings to me like a leaden cloak. The dark part of me, the monstrous part, knows that if Korey screamed at me, I'd feel better. Oh yes, he'd get angry and throw things. Maybe he'd pound his fist against the wall. Instead, he gives me only silence.

As the days tick by, I get jumpier. My sleep suffers, and I neglect my share of the household chores. Our grass needs to be mowed. I'm usually the one who does it, but this time I pay one of the teenage boys on our street to cut the lawns.

On Saturday, exactly three weeks after Ayden's death, I drive to the HEB grocery store on University Boulevard to pick up a few things. I stop by the apples in the produce section. Scents of fresh blackberries reach me from the adjoining bin. When I glance up after setting a bag of Gala in my cart, I freeze.

With an olive complexion, dark brown hair, and near-black eyes, Korey's white, button-down shirt complements his features well. He stands about ten feet away next to a case of fruit drinks. He fingers a bottle of orange juice before plucking it from the row. When I lock my eyes on him, he straightens, and his gaze connects with mine.

My shoulders tense. I grip the handle of the cart so hard my knuckles bulge white. My legs refuse to move. I open my mouth, but nothing comes out. What am I going to do? What can I possibly say to him?

"Hey," he says. He flashes a smile full of white teeth. "Fancy meeting you here."

The cheerful greeting unnerves me. We never officially broke up, but the last time we spoke, he was angry with me. Accusatory. And that wasn't even that long ago. Now, after his brother's violent death—after which Korey wouldn't return my phone calls—he's acting like he just ran into an old buddy.

"Hi, Korey," I say.

My chest seizes up, and I can hardly breathe. Surely the authorities called him, his parents, or someone else in his immediate family. There must have been a funeral for Ayden. His death was known about, documented.

Korey stands there smiling. Beyond creepy.

I force out, "Listen, about your brother. I don't really know where to start, but I can't tell you how sorry I am, and I just want to say that I—"

"Oh no," he says. He waves his hand. "He had it coming. How are you doing? Are you all right?" Korey sets the bottle of orange juice in his red shopping basket.

My mind turns somersaults. I frown and try to stop the torrent of confusion that assaults me. He's saying what I want to hear, and it's weird—more than weird. It's abnormal behavior, and that's dangerous. That means that in handling this, I have to get clever.

I step out from behind the cart, keeping my right hand on the handle. Studying his face, I try to read his dark eyes and gauge how much he knows. I have no idea what the authorities or others told him.

"Did you hear about what happened?" I ask, my voice flatter than I intend.

Korey's smile dims. "Yeah, Aria. I heard, and I'm really sorry."

"What exactly did you hear?" I still don't want to approach him. It's strange to talk across the distance, but I don't care.

He sets the basket on the floor. A strand of dark hair falls across his forehead when he faces me again. "Ayden attacked you in your backyard. And your shed caught fire. I don't know how exactly. I guess in the struggle. But the police told me the gist of what happened. And that it wasn't your fault, that what you did was in self-defense. I was shocked at first. I didn't want to believe that Ayden had done those things. And I was really upset with you, you know. But after I thought about it, there was no possible way I could blame you. I mean, I know it was him. I may not like the facts, but they are what they are."

He looks down and sighs. When he raises his head, his gaze is far away. "I'm sorry for not calling you back. I wanted to. I just needed some time to think about things."

"Sure. I understand." I stand up straighter, my back stiffening again. I can't tell Korey I don't remember what happened. Not only will he not believe that, but it will make the situation worse. And there's a question that needs to be asked. It's indelicate, but that's life.

I steel myself against an explosion. "How did Ayden know where I live?"

Korey shakes his head. "I don't know, Aria. But that question kept me up at night. I wondered if you thought I gave him your address, and that's another reason I didn't call you. But I would never, ever give someone your address or tell anyone, even my brother, to go by your house without your permission. I know we've had our differences, but I want you to know that. There's no excuse for what Ayden did, and I'm just so sorry. You have no idea." Korey swallows, and tears collect at the corners of his eyes. He blinks them back with a sniff.

He's such an absolute, disgusting liar. If he felt bad, he would have called me right away. He would have driven to see me. My mind conjures the image of the white SUV slithering along my street. Korey's not sorry about what happened. He's sorry it didn't play out differently. And that tells me something else—he knows, or at least suspects, I did something horrible since victims don't kill people. But I won't let on. I'll play stupid like he wants. After letting go of the cart, I take a few tentative steps toward him.

"Wow, that's definitely not what I thought you would say," I reply. "I can't tell you how terrible I feel that you lost your brother, but I also can't tell you how thankful I am that you understand." Two can play at this game. I stare at him, waiting.

Korey puts on another smile, a rather sad one with the corners of his mouth downturned. He regards me beneath his thick, dark eyelashes. "I know. It is what it is, and it's not your fault. It's not your fault, Aria."

The words are too profound. Too effective. Too perfectly right for me in the wake of my guilt. My bottom lip trembles despite the need to remain detached. "Thank you."

"I don't bite," Korey says. He grins warmly and holds out his arm.

My heart hammers as I contemplate doing what he's silently asking. My mind races. How much should I play along? How far is too far?

"It's okay," he says. "If I was upset at all before, I forgive you now."

Seconds tick by, and I don't move. My feet are nailed to the floor. I want to say something. I should respond. He used to scare me a little, but now, acting the way he is, he scares me a lot. All smiles and sweet words and holding his arm out like he wants me to hug him is a bit much.

Accepting his gesture means accepting an unspoken agreement. There's not only what it will mean right at this moment, but what it will mean tomorrow and the day after that. What sort of expectations it will place upon me. And then there's the other side of the coin—what it will mean if I don't accept. If I decline, there's more to it than hurting his feelings or being rude. Refusing comes with certain implications. I may have no memory, but the consensus is that I killed his brother. Self-defense, according to some, but his brother's still dead.

The image of Ayden's bloody ring in the ceramic dish consumes my thoughts. I can almost smell it. The metallic blood so sweet, like an old penny. The oozy odor of slow decay. My nose twinges from the memory, but the only scents here are fruit and leafy greens.

"Aria?" Korey asks. His face falls, and he shifts his feet.

My heart pounds like it did when I saw the souvenir of my kill. I force a weak smile. Why hasn't Korey asked any questions about what I did? My feet drag as I shuffle over to the man who's still technically my boyfriend. Somehow, I make my body comply with this terrible decision.

"Thank you," I say finally. The words lack conviction and give away everything.

I push my body slightly beneath Korey's arm and against his side. He pulls me into a loose hug and holds me gently, carefully, the way one would cradle a small child or fragile bird. His slim torso feels like a slab of meat. It's cold, solid and devoid of feeling. My mind reels with an exit strategy. Something, anything, so I won't have to endure him after today.

Korey's cologne blasts me with the artificiality that so suits him. It's reminiscent of a pine tree dipped in battery acid. Returning his embrace with limp hands, I desperately try to hide my nervous revulsion.

"Aria, is something wrong?" He slides his hand down my back.

"No."

"I can feel you stiffening," he says. "Is there something you haven't told me?"

He knows. Oh God, he knows.

"No," I say.

He blinks. "Oh." He pulls away and searches my face. "You don't want to be with me anymore? Is that it?"

"I—I think I need some time—"

Korey staggers back like I struck him. "You need some time to think about if you want to be with me after you killed my brother?"

"I didn't—I—that's the thing. I can't remember. I can't remember what happened. I don't know that I killed him," I say, raising my voice. Big mistake, but I can't take it back now. Two women by the potato section stop dead and gape at us.

"Oh, for God's sake, Aria. I expected more from you—for you to be more responsible than that. What kind of monster rejects someone after killing his sibling?" He inflects his harsh words with a velvet-soft tone.

Pursing his lips, he crosses his arms with that crazed, overly-calm look on his face. "I think you'd regret something like that for the rest of your life. I know you're sorry now, but you would *really* be sorry."

His threat sends a wave of panic through me, but not enough to enforce his demand. What kind of monster? This kind. The kind that takes a kill trophy and then hides it from herself.

My pulse races as I backstep. "You're wrong, Korey. I'm really sorry now. I've been sorry ever since the day I met you."

Korey's mouth falls open. Lightheadedness catapults my senses upward into the dizzying heights of blatant defiance. I guess I got bored with playing along. Every second only prolonged the agony.

"Besides," I add, "monsters shouldn't dwell in pairs."

Abandoning my half-full shopping cart, I turn and march out the door.

4

Despite Korey's threat, I don't see him or talk to him again. I change my number. Four months have come and gone since I ran into him at the grocery store. Prior to Ayden's death, our relationship was a lot like the conversation in the produce section. Korey was jealous and manipulative. He worded his threats carefully so they didn't sound like threats. He knew how to "care for me" as a control mechanism. And yet, my guilt still hangs over me like the thick cloud of smoke after the fire. It's the first thing to greet me each morning and my last thought before falling asleep. But even that isn't enough to make me go back to him.

This morning, Carol and I finish up our remaining Christmas shopping. It's a bitterly cold day, with a gray, ashen sky and a biting, thirty-degree wind that finds its way between every thread in our coats. The mall parking lot is full to bursting. It forces Carol to park at the outside edge near a planter area with grass and trees. That's the best we can do.

We comb the mall for hours, and by the time we finish, it's after 6:00 p.m., and the sun is down. With shoulders hunched inside our layered clothing, we trot back to the car with shopping bags in each hand. The scent of warm pretzels and salted, hydrogenated-butter-product popcorn drifts over to us from the adjacent cinema. Before us, lines and lines of vehicles stretch like a formidable sea. Now that it's past sunset, I'm having trouble remembering where we parked.

My gaze darts between the nearest row and the right-hand one as I loop my scarf around my neck. I can make out a section of trees under the streetlamps farther down. I ask my stepmom, "Do you think we're one more over?"

Carol sets her bags on the pavement and pulls her gloves from her pockets. She hastily tugs them on. "I think it's this one, but all the way in back."

Shivering, we clutch the handles of our bags and walk briskly through the rows, the steel car bodies floating by in our peripheral vision. The farther we get from the mall entrance, the fewer people there are. This is especially true because of the cold weather—no one wants to be out here a second longer than necessary.

At least the parking lot is well lit, and there are plenty of drivers on the road encircling the mall. However, there isn't much foot traffic in our little corner. Many of the cars parked along the outskirts of the lot belong to employees. Their employers make them park there so customers can pick from the better spots near the building.

My stepmom's dress boots clickety-click over the asphalt as we near the end of the row. Our bags swish and sway from our bustling. I scan for Carol's blue Ford Expedition but don't see it.

From the corner of my eye, I glimpse motion. Maybe someone walking parallel to us in the row at our left. I look, and he's gone. Did I imagine a guy skulking rather than walking, prowling along, hunched over with his head turned slightly in our direction? It's dark. Plus, I'm paranoid, which is something that happens when you're an amnesiac murderer and your creep ex-boyfriend knows.

Increasing my pace, I think back a few seconds. Yeah, I saw someone, just for an instant. And I can't be certain, but I swear he ducked from sight when he saw me turn. My stomach drops as I wonder how long the person was there before I noticed.

I can't help but think of Korey. Not only because of the grocery store but before that. Only a few hours before Ayden turned up in my stepmom's shed, Korey went ballistic during our fight. It was one of the worst. He had an absolute melt-down when I told him I wanted a break from his accusations and jealousy about a nonexistent affair.

"You're a liar, Aria," he said. He narrowed his eyes to dark slits while working his mouth into a puckered grimace. "I know you're hiding something. You manipulative little bitch. Who is he?"

"There's no other man. There never was." I didn't expect Korey to listen. He never accused me of anything real, just heaped on the incessant shaming for my imaginary whoring and fictitious secrets.

Korey picked up a glass and hurled it against the living room wall five feet from me. It crashed and shattered, my body jerking as though the shards imploded inside me. I continued edging my way to the bedroom for my overnight bag.

"Liar! Who is he, I said? Now you tell me. You've been

screwing around on me. I know you have." Korey's loud breathing engulfed the room as he stalked toward me with clenched fists. A string of spittle ran down his bottom lip. But by the time I left a few minutes later, he was calm again—the disturbing calm that was even worse than the yelling.

In the cold mall parking lot, I shut out the memory and crane my neck to scan the stretch of vehicles. If someone was trailing us, it seems they're gone now. It's funny how your mind tries to fill in the gaps with too many details when you're nervous. I try to shrug off my paranoia. Even if Korey were here, or if some thug is preparing to rob us, he'll have to try it underneath the glaring light of the streetlamps. There are cameras everywhere, and the mall employs extra security guards for the holiday season. I don't know how many of them are watching nearby, but I saw one of their vehicles pass earlier. I fill my lungs with the harsh winter air and try to focus.

"I think you were right," Carol says as she looks both ways. "We're in the next row over."

After stealing a glance at the location of the imagined movement, I turn and start walking the opposite way, to the right. I pass all my bags to my left hand. With the other, I press my coat more tightly against my chest.

"You okay?" Carol asks. She increases her pace, bringing her body beside mine.

"I'm fine," I say. "I just don't like being so far away from the building after dark."

"There it is," Carol says. She points at her blue SUV just up ahead. A brisk draft of December air buffets my face, and my nose starts to run. Carol digs into her purse for her keys. She swears quietly under her breath. With the keychain in her hand, she stops and sets her bags down to rifle through them.

"What's wrong?" I ask.

"I think I forgot that small Hallmark bag in Macy's. I set it on the counter when we were checking out." She furrows her brow as she digs.

"Why don't you warm up the car, and I'll go get it real quick. Maybe you can pull up by the door and pick me up there?" I say.

Some of the tension leaves Carol's face. She's probably thinking of blasting the heater. She straightens and grins at me. "Well, if you insist. Thanks, Aria."

"Sure," I say. I smile and hand her my bags before turning to go back into the mall.

Already being on edge, I don't walk but jog to the end of the row, and when I near the entrance, I learn I won't need to go into Macy's after all. Carol's small, brown Hallmark bag full of Christmas cards lies right there on the grassy median. Maybe it slipped out when she was putting on her gloves. I lean over and snatch it up with triumphant fingers before turning and walking swiftly toward Carol's SUV.

Something brushes my right shoulder. I jump. Some indefinite sound escapes my lips as I whirl—but no one's here. Who touched me? I felt it. I know I did.

I surge into a breakneck run. "Carol! Carol!"

As I increase my pace, my feet pound the pavement, and the cold air pummels my face with its tiny fists. My heart races in desperate panic as I anticipate something. A striking. A grabbing. A blow.

I glance behind me again. Still no one. I look over my other shoulder and sidestep, trotting a couple of paces before I spin around once more. Am I going crazy, or is

Korey here toying with me, just like I imagined? My gaze flitters in a dozen directions, but I don't see him.

"Carol!" I call. She must be inside the car already.

And then, as I turn and push myself into a run again, I see Korey. He's right there in front of me like he materialized from winter chill and parking lot dust. Braced in readiness, he locks his dark eyes on me, hunter to prey.

He's holding something—a spray bottle—and he shoves it toward me. He squeezes the trigger, releasing a heavy stream of liquid at my face. It assaults my senses. It's strong and sharp like alcohol with scents of gasoline tinged with brown sugar. Hot, sweet-tasting saliva pools in my mouth. Already the substance overtakes me, and my legs go buttery.

I know I scream, but it gets lost somewhere as though I'm crying out inside the plastic bottle. The sound tunnels into nothingness, and no one can hear me. I'm succumbing to the effects of the chemical. Ether? A derivative or something similar?

My eyes and nose sear like fire, and I bury my face in my hands. Red-hot tears gush unnaturally down my cheeks. I take one staggering step. My eyes flutter.

Run, damn it, run.

I have to run. I have to, I know I do, because if I don't, this may be the last thing I ever know. I retreat from Korey and stumble a few steps before my legs buckle. My stomach erupts with nausea and my remaining thread of bodily control snaps. I can't run. I can't hold myself up. I can't stay awake.

As I go completely limp and prepare to faceplant on the dirty parking lot asphalt, Korey sweeps his arms around me and scoops me up like a little girl.

MY EYES SNAP open to thick, black darkness. I gulp air in short, shallow breaths, sucking in smells of old, rotten wood and dust. It's an ancient dust, the kind that gathers with mildew, cooking ashes, and crumbling photographs. The parking lot incident tears through my mind in erratic flashes. My heart races, and my head hangs heavy with dizziness though I lie still. At least, I think I'm not physically moving. A part of me reels, and the ground tilts me back and forth. I'm nauseous. My temples pound. And though I'm not yet fully aware of myself or my surroundings, I know something worse happened while I was knocked out. Something bad. Something's very wrong.

I blink a few more times, my headache increasing and pressure building around my eyes. As I try to move my arms and legs to get some bearing on where I am, I learn I'm lying on my side with my hands tied behind my back. My feet are also bound, but not only to themselves. When I try to extend my legs, which are bent at the knees, something catches against whatever binds my wrists.

Korey. Korey did this.

I groan, but there's something stuffed in my mouth. Maybe paper. It feels both dry and wet at the same time. Drool leaks from the corners of my lips, and a bitter, newsprint taste leaches onto my tongue. I can't spit out the uncomfortable wad. Something blocks it. Tape? An adhesive strip clamped across my mouth and cheeks. When I chomp down on the paper, it activates my gag reflex, and I almost wretch. I swallow a few times and force the bile down. I can't throw up like this—I'll choke.

My groaning increases to a frantic muffled whimpering.

Where is Carol? She was in her car. I said I'd wait by the mall entrance for her to pick me up, but I didn't because I didn't even get that far before finding her bag. I tried to go back to her, knowing she barely started the engine. She probably didn't see Korey take me. Maybe she's out looking for me now, calling my cell. Wondering why I'm not answering. Calling the police.

I whine loudly, trying to make as much noise as I can so she'll hear me if she's nearby. A coldness bites against my skin, but I don't feel any wind. From the little I'm able to move, it seems I'm still wearing all my layers of winter clothing—my coat, sweater, two shirts, jeans, and tall boots. But I don't know for sure. All I know is that through all that, my hip still aches against the hard surface beneath me.

For about fifteen minutes, I struggle wildly. I exert all my energy to try and break free from my bindings. I strain my muscles with my back and neck screaming in protest. In all my life, I've never experienced such discomfort as this horrible position—this impossible, tight, hogtied knot in which my limbs are used against me.

I wonder how long I was unconscious and how long I've been tied like this because every part of me cries out with soreness. I'm incapacitated. A helpless animal awaiting the slaughter. I can't scream. And it's so dark. So utterly black I wonder if I've been locked away in a basement. There aren't many in Central Texas, but there are a few. Maybe this is one of them, and that's where I am.

Time passes. I don't know how much. I sob because it's all I can do. No one comes in response to my muted, guttural noises, and my surroundings return few sounds apart from an occasional gust of wind or the creak of wood. What I imagine to be hours elapses. My urge to urinate builds, and my bladder expands to overfilled pain, but I resist. After a while, the burning pressure recedes. Then it's gone, and my mouth aches with thirst. The thirst grows until it fills every part of me, my desire for water second only to my longing for escape.

Sleep never happens. It can't. I lie here and run probably a hundred different scenarios through my mind. Where I might be, where Carol is, what Korey's planning on doing with me. How I might bargain for my life. What may happen if I fail to do that. I've already failed, and this is the price of that failure. I wonder where he stashed my purse and cell phone. And strangest of all is the question of why he isn't with me now. He captured me, tied me, and left me in this dark place until... what? Until it's time for worse things.

After more long, lonely hours that slither by the way spilled ink seeps across paper, the pale, sickly light of dawn peaks in from unseen windows. There's still no sign of Korey or anyone else. I decide to flip myself over. I can kind of kneel, and I can scoot. With stabs of pain shooting through my lower back, I grunt and twist my body. As my shoulder and hip bang sharply on the hardwood floor, I finally learn where Carol is.

There, a few feet away, lies my stepmother, tied and gagged just like me. She's on her side with her knees bent, her arms pulled behind her. Whether unconscious or dead, she's not moving. She's been here the entire time.

All my groaning, struggling, and now flipping didn't wake her. I scoot closer, watching Carol's chest to see if it rises and falls. She's taking shallow breaths, but she's alive. Korey clamped silver duct tape over her mouth, but it's also partially blocking her nose. She probably isn't getting enough air. Maybe by positioning my body with my back to her, I can get my fingers around the tape.

I strain my stomach, back, and neck and manage to right myself. Since my feet are attached to the cords at my wrists, correctly placing myself proves a combination of contortion and gymnastics. I need to maintain the awkward position without falling over. And I have to do it without kicking my stepmom in the face. As I balance on my kneecaps, they crunch against the floor. Grimacing from the pain, I make a few wobbly attempts before I find the gag with my fingers and tug it off as gently as I can. My knees teeter unstably, but I stay upright.

Carol begins to stir. Murmuring inaudibly, her lips twitch. Her eyes flutter. By balancing a little longer, I wiggle my fingers into her mouth and pull out the large, soggy wad of newspaper Korey shoved inside.

While Carol comes around, I get a look at my surroundings—not a basement, but an old house. The walls of the room were probably white once, but now they're stained cigarette-smoke yellow. Two windows with frames full of broken glass let in the weak winter light. In front of me is a stack of dusty cardboard boxes. Grimy hardwood coated in crusted-over dirt and grunge resembling hard wax covers the floor. By continuing to scoot along, I find the walls of the small space cluttered with odds and ends and old junk. Scattered around me are an old television, some type of couch with a wooden frame, a rickety rocking chair, more boxes, and a broken lamp.

Whatever Korey used to knock us unconscious seemed to have a worse effect on Carol than it did on me. Although still woozy and my head is pounding, I'm coherent, but Carol's disorientation hangs on.

"Muh," she says. Her lips and cheeks are red from the tape.

I don't know what she's trying to say, and I can't answer.

"Ma. Muh?" says my stepmom. "No."

Even though I removed her gag, she can't speak much. I drag myself behind her to examine the cords tied around her wrists. She's restrained with a combination of rope and zip ties. I can undo the knots in the rope, but I'll need something to cut the plastic. There might be something sharp enough in this very room, but I'll have to find it.

I want Carol to remove my mouth tape like I did for her but being gagged like this, I can't ask. Normally, she would have thought of it on her own. Now, she only gazes at her environment with wide, frantic eyes. She doesn't try to raise her head, and despite her awful backbend, she doesn't struggle much.

As I scuttle among the broken items and discard piles in search of anything with an edge I can use to free us, a door creaks open. A sick churning in my gut tells me Korey has returned.

The first day of the worst three weeks of my life has begun. In these three weeks, I learn what pain is. I also learn the meaning of "alone."

PRESENT DAY

It's been eight months since Trent Lemend found me in the house on County Road 140, chained to the wall like a bloody voodoo doll and left for dead. Now, I sit cross-legged, shoes off in the stuffed leather chair across from my counselor. Despite an upsetting phone call earlier, I try to focus on Norma's last question. Maybe it will help.

"Aria," she says gently. "I know it's hard, but we'll work through this together. Can you remember what Korey said when he took out the knife?"

I shake my head, glancing at the lemon verbena candle that flickers on the table beside her. "I'm trying."

Since my rescue, I didn't think I had trouble talking about what Korey did to my stepmom and me. I talked about it with the police. I talked about it with Trent, who's become my closest friend. I explained how I was starved, beaten, raped, and stabbed before strung up and abandoned to die. And though I described all of it in what I thought was painstaking detail, my therapist Norma has a way of asking questions that necessitates re-experiencing the incident to dig out an answer. Although this is difficult, she tells me it's important because drawing out the specifics will ultimately help free the negative emotional hold Korey's words have upon me.

"Can you see the knife now in your mind?" she asks.

I nod. "He shows it to me first."

Norma knows Korey was arrested and sentenced to life behind bars. These sessions help me focus on healing. Each day, in counseling and life, I do my best to put the trauma behind me. It might not be possible in every sense. There are parts of my body that will never be the same, that will never really heal completely. Not to mention the intrinsic part of myself, the spiritual essence that makes me human. Will *I* ever heal completely? I'm not sure. But I can still try, and I will, so long as there's life in me.

"And what does he do next?" Norma asks.

She's a pleasant, smartly dressed lady in her fifties, with straight, blonde hair that hangs neatly to her shoulders. She sits attentively with her ankles crossed and gazes at me through her black-rimmed glasses. As I try to come up with an answer, I stare listlessly at the beaded necklace that hangs over Norma's beige blouse.

I grip the arms of the chair and draw a breath as I concentrate. Sometimes I can recite the details like it happened yesterday. At other times, I only draw a blank, like I'm peering into the blackness the night I woke up tied and gagged. "I can't remember. I'm not sure. I think he might have said something about liars. Something about me being a liar."

"All right," Norma says. Her voice is soft and kind. "What was he saying you lied about?"

I shake my head. "I don't know. He would never say. I

don't think he ever told me what I had supposedly lied about the whole time he kept me locked in there. But before that, when we were seeing each other, he always thought there was another man."

"I see. Did he ever mention anything about what happened with his brother?" Norma asks.

My belly tenses. My pulse quickens, and I wipe my palms on my slacks. *What happened with his brother*. It's the one memory I can't get to resurface, no matter how much therapy I get. Of course, Norma doesn't know about the bloody ring. Neither does Trent. But someone knows. He called me this morning. Swallowing, I shove the thought aside.

I've already pondered how Ayden's death factored into my torture more than Norma could possibly know. But no matter how much I dive into my misery inside the abandoned house, I can't find Ayden's name even once.

"No, never," I say. "I could never figure out whether Korey didn't really care about Ayden, or he assumed I knew that I was being punished for killing him. But Korey never mentioned him. He talked about other things. He said I screwed him over, that he knew I was unfaithful, that I had no right to treat him that way and leave him. But those things never happened, except the leaving him part. It still makes my head spin trying to figure it out."

Norma says, "I understand. Aria, I want you to know that you don't have to figure anything out. Korey's words and actions didn't make sense, and they never will. All I want is for you to uncover enough so that you can let go of some of it."

I nod. I turn my inner eye toward the black abyss of memory and try again. I picture Korey standing over me with the knife. My neck muscles clench into a tight knot, and I press my back against the bulky chair.

"He said, 'You're a liar, and I'm going to bleed you like a hog.' Then he started to explain the ancient practice of bloodletting—how when it started in Egypt, it was used to release evil spirits. He talked about how this was going to be part of my purification." I shudder and hold out my left arm, running a finger along the crook where a puffy, pink scar gleams faintly.

I tell Norma what else I remember—things I've told her many times, but I tell her again anyway. I mention how the newspaper articles covering the County Road 140 case all talk about my being stabbed. It's true that I was stabbed, but not in the traditional sense of someone doing it with the intention of killing me—of puncturing vital organs. First of all, by the time Korey got around to it, I was so weak and emaciated I could barely struggle. He removed the gag from my mouth. I think he took pleasure in hearing me beg, apologize, and cry when I had the strength.

That was when Korey put me in the white dress. While I lay on the filthy floor, slipping in and out of consciousness, he stripped me naked before roughly tugging the garment over my body. He told me the purpose of the white dress, but it's one of the things I haven't been able to recall. Not yet, anyway. But once I was wearing it, Korey drew a long hunting knife from his back pocket. He leaned over me, his hair greasy and unwashed and hanging in his face. Korey grabbed my limp arm and drove the knife into the big vein at the bend. I screamed. I tried to pull away as warm, sticky blood oozed out. He cut me like this five more times to other parts of my body.

The irony is that Korey's freakish bloodletting procedure

is probably why I lived, besides Trent finding me when I lay at death's door. None of my vital organs were damaged. The worst wound is near my right shoulder. My physical therapist told me I may always have trouble with that arm because the muscle tissue hasn't grown back properly after the inflammation and infection.

Pulling myself from the nightmarish images, I look up at Norma. "You're right that it doesn't make sense. I never understood why he stabbed me near the shoulder. I don't even know if he could see a vein there, like on the other parts of my body he cut. If he truly wanted to bleed me, he could have gone for my carotid artery."

I snort. "But then, he always tried to confuse me. To make me wonder, just like when we were together."

I manage a weak smile and exhale, then blinking a few times as I dart my gaze around the room like I've just "come back." Warm daylight streams in the sheer-curtained window framing downtown Round Rock. On the walls are photographs of flowers, bluebonnets in some and daisies in others. Light gray carpeting covers the recently vacuumed floor, and in front of the chair where I sit is a glass coffee table. On it rests my water bottle. Beside Norma, the pale-yellow candle flickers and exudes a pleasant, citrus scent.

"How are you doing now?" Norma asks.

"Better," I say. "I remembered more that time."

My counselor smiles. "Very good. I'm so glad to hear it."

I think she's getting ready to conclude our session for the day when I remember something else. "Norma, I meant to tell you about the license plate—Korey's license plate number. The day after Ayden died, I saw a white SUV slowing down and parking on my street. I couldn't tell if it was Korey's or not, but I noticed the license plate. Well, this is the terrible part, but after I was rescued, I checked. That had been his SUV that day, idling not far from my house."

I frown and shake my head as I pick up my purse from the floor. "I never should have spoken to him in the grocery store. And I made a nasty comment—I can't stop thinking that maybe if I wouldn't have called him a monster, he wouldn't have abducted us. I knew it wasn't smart. I *knew*."

"Thanks for telling me, but the abduction wasn't your fault, Aria," Norma says.

I nod, but my inner voice says otherwise. What if it was? What if what I did to Ayden wasn't in self-defense at all, and I killed him in cold blood? Maybe I set him on fire myself.

"Did you want to say something?" my counselor asks.

I stall, pushing my socked feet against the gray carpeting. "It's just that... even though I've remembered more in our sessions, I still can't remember what happened with Ayden. I just don't understand."

"I know," Norma says, "but like we've talked about, that's often the mind's way of protecting itself from traumatic experiences. You've read the police report. Do you have any reason to believe it's incomplete?"

Only that Ayden's ring turned up in my house, but other than that, no. No reason at all. Yet when I awoke the day after the fire, the ceramic dish was clean and empty—no blood.

"Not really," I say, which isn't true at all. But even Norma, who I'd trust with my life, can't be trusted with that memory. At best, I could go to jail. At worst, I'll be locked up in a psych ward somewhere for hallucinating murder tokens.

I add, "It's just that I remember most of what Korey did to us. I should be able to remember the incident with Ayden."

"Don't worry about that. We'll get to the bottom of it in

due course when you're ready for it. Are you feeling better for the time being?" This is her way of asking if it's okay to end off. Norma is an alternative counselor who was recommended to me by one of my housemates, and we don't always talk for the same amount of time each visit. It depends on how I'm doing.

I take another deep breath. "Yes, definitely better. Thank you."

We both stand up, and I stretch my back.

Norma smiles as she asks, "You said you're meeting Trent for dinner tonight?"

"I am." The grin dies on my face.

Thinking of Trent usually makes me happy, but not today. I clench my jaw and rub my sweaty palms on my slacks for the third time before hooking my purse strap over my shoulder. I snatch my bottled water. As I move off toward the door, guilt gnaws a hole in my chest. There's something else I haven't told Norma—something that happened just this morning, and it's my reason for wanting to see Trent even more than usual.

I tell Norma goodbye, go out to my car, and lock myself in. Sitting with the windows up and the A/C blasting, I know I can't keep my secret much longer. Not if I want Trent's help or at least his understanding. Unfortunately, revealing this one thing will probably push Trent away forever.

6

The person who found me in that house on County Road 140, stabbed, chained to the wall, and left for dead, is a thirty-one-year-old man named Trent Lemend. I lost Carol, but for some reason, God, or the universe, sent him to me. I'd like to think my torture fulfilled some penance. That I'm now supposed to live out the rest of my days as best I can with the person who's dearer to me than life itself. Too bad it doesn't feel like that. It's August now, and besides the brutal heat of Texas summer stirring up the memory of Ayden's burning, I received a strange call at work this morning. Strange and oddly specific.

After leaving Median Realty for the day, I sit across from Trent at Jack Allen's Kitchen in Round Rock. In the open dining room divided down the middle by long, brown curtains hanging from the ceiling, spicy aromas of grilled catfish drift up from my plate. I explain to Trent what I know about Ayden's death a year ago, including that I have almost no memory of the incident itself. For now, I leave out what I found later. My hands shake so hard I have to tuck them between my thighs occasionally. Beneath the suspended strands of golden lights, I study Trent's brown gaze while he listens.

He holds his drink but doesn't put it to his lips. Confusion hardens his face. Maybe he doesn't believe me. Maybe he thinks I'm suffering from post-traumatic stress disorder from the abduction. Or that I'm desperate for attention since he knows I want a relationship with him. Maybe it's something else. Am I burdening him with one more thing? All I know is Trent sets his glass down and stares at it. His eyes go distant in the long silence before he replies.

"Aria," he says, mopping the puddle under his Coke with a napkin. "Why did you never tell me about this before?" He lags before looking up like he might be angry with me.

"Well, probably several reasons." I poke at my mashed potatoes with my fork. "For one thing, I'm ashamed of it. And secondly, I thought you might not understand. I don't understand myself. Tell me what you're thinking."

Trent scowls. "Aria, with something that important, you should have told me as soon as possible. Why did you wait so long?"

My face heats. I shove a strand of hair out of my face and squint at him. "It's been a year since it happened. Ayden is dead. Dead men can't come back to haunt us—I mean, not in the flesh, anyway." I swallow and look down at my plate. "This wasn't something I would have told you at that coffee shop in Georgetown the first time I saw you after being released from the hospital. All I could think about was what happened with Korey." I pause. "'Great to see you, Trent, and by the way, I think I killed a guy a year ago?'"

Trent inhales and leans back. He heaves out a heavy sigh and rubs his face. His voice is more solemn when he replies.

"Well, I guess that's understandable. Did it get any news coverage?"

"No. Not even an article," I say.

"And Korey knew about it? You told him?" He picks up his cola and takes a sip.

"He knew, but I couldn't remember enough to tell him. He found out from the cops. But the last time I saw him before he kidnapped me, he didn't ask for my side of the story—not one question," I say. "And after he took me, he never mentioned his brother's name one time."

An image of the foul, urine-covered floor of the County Road 140 house flashes into my mind. Carol's emaciated body lies like a skeletal ragdoll below me. Then, the same as I always do, I shove those images in a vault and lock the door.

Trent shakes his head, his frown making a deep line between his eyebrows. "Okay. It sounds like what you did was fully in self-defense. He had it coming. And the police must have investigated, and the case is closed. So, what made you decide to tell me now? I don't mean that as a criticism—I'm interested."

I shift in my seat, feeling like a liar. How will he react when I tell him the reason? It's been a year, Korey's in jail, and there's no reason it should be on my mind. I set my fork down and lean my arms against the edge of the table.

"This morning, I got a weird phone call at work. At first, all I heard was a lot of background noise and static. Terrible reception. But I was able to make out a few things the caller said. First, he mentioned something about being interested in a building, but I couldn't hear where. I just heard 'building,' or maybe 'buildings.' That part wasn't strange. Then there was a gap, like papers shuffling or wind. After that, he said, 'What you did is as good as murder.'"

I watch Trent's face. Unable to gauge his degree of belief or lack thereof, I continue. "The man who called also said, 'sometimes it's the things we don't say that hurt us the most.' After that, there was more static. The last thing I heard was something like 'just because'... then something about 'property' and 'you acted in your best interest doesn't make it right.'"

Trent puts a hand to his forehead. Running his fingers through his dark hair, he exhales. "Aria, are you absolutely sure that's what he said? I don't suppose you wrote any of this down."

I snort softly. "Of course I did. I have it right here." I reach into my purse for the small notepad. After tugging it out, I flip open the green cover and find the last written-on page. I hand it to him.

Trent takes it. His gaze traces the words on the page. "This was smart. I should have known you'd make a record."

I know that's his way of apologizing for assuming I didn't.

Trent says, "You said 'he.' Did you notice anything about his voice? Anything that stood out?"

"He sounded older. Maybe close to sixty. His voice was kind of... I don't know, haughty? Like he was full of himself. And he also seemed irritated. Not angry, really, but irritated at me." Without realizing it, I've leaned forward and clasped my hands over my plate. I drop them to my lap and push my back against the chair.

Trent scans the numbered lines of my notes a second time.

"God, why now?" he asks, more to himself than to me. He huffs and avoids eye contact. His attention has turned inward to that dark, distant place he seeks when something pains him.

I can already hear the questions he isn't asking. My ears burn. "I don't know anyone, Trent. I don't even have many friends besides you and Kyle, a few acquaintances at the office, and my housemates. Obviously, my family is gone. Korey is in prison. He has family, but they know what happened because I spoke to them after Ayden died. They were grieving, but they understood that his death was accidental. They never pressed charges. So, I don't have any answers. I don't know who would want to unearth what happened or why."

I pick up my fork and make sharp furrows across the mashed potatoes. Trying to keep my hand from shaking, I force a bite into my mouth. I focus on the taste of buttery starch. Since being rescued, the eight months of safety have been so wonderful, like a chance to start over. Now that pretense is being taken away. I haven't paid my dues yet. Murderers are irredeemable.

"Korey's family never took you to court?" Trent's jaw muscles tighten.

"No. My stepmom thought we should get a lawyer, but we never needed one. I remember that Korey's mother was distraught, but she didn't accuse me of anything. His father didn't speak to me much. But I did apologize to them both, over and over. The police said my statements, the evidence, and their investigation showed that I acted in self-defense. I never meant to kill anyone." I swallow the golf ball in my throat.

Trent takes a bite of his fish tacos, which are probably cold by now. He wipes his hands on the cloth napkin and stares at the notepad.

I ask, "What do you think?"

"Well, I don't know what to think. Did the caller sound like Ayden's father?" he asks. He picks up the notepad and passes it back to me.

"No, the guy who called was too old. And his voice was different. Softer."

The hunch of Trent's shoulders tells me he's on edge. Grasping his fork with stiff fingers, he shovels black beans into his mouth. He barely chews. "I guess right now we don't know enough. I'm not sure what to make of this. Have you contacted Crime Victims Services yet?"

"Yes. And Jeffrey Spade at the Austin Police Department," I say.

Trent flinches at the name. Officer Spade was his late fiancée's contact in Austin as well. Despite police assistance, Elizabeth was still murdered and deposited on Trent's porch for him to find. Knowing this, I wouldn't have brought up Spade without reason.

"Well," Trent says, keeping his eyes from me. "It sounds like you've done what you can."

Pressure builds behind my eyes, hot and unwelcome. I clench my teeth and resolve that I won't cry at Jack Allen's in the middle of dinner rush. It's demoralizing enough as it is. "But you do have some opinion. I can't help but feel you don't believe me. Is there something you want to say?"

Trent sniffs. He checks the time on his cell phone before answering. "Aria, I do believe you. What you've told me is disturbing, and I'm confused at this guy's timing. But I don't have enough information yet."

You don't know how disturbing it is. You really don't. Trent returns to eating his tacos and looks up at me intermittently. A draft of cold air blasts me from the A/C duct. The resulting chill sends a virtual ice storm down my arms. I wriggle into my jacket, something I always bring to restaurants for this very reason. I warm my hands between my knees.

I say, "I feel the same way. And I don't expect you to do anything about it. I just wanted to tell you."

Trent nods. "I know. Well, thanks for telling me. I'll think about it and maybe get a bright idea of what we should do."

We chew our food, a thick, awkward silence hanging over us despite our immersion in the noisy restaurant. A group of young people laugh and drink at the nearest table. Someone's child throws a tantrum on the other side of the room. Servers clink glasses and deposit trays of dishes in the kitchen. When the waitress comes by to drop off the bill, I jump. I put on a smile and thank her.

"So, how are things going at work?" Trent asks.

I manage a chuckle. I guess this is a good time to change the subject. "Fine, besides that phone call. Business as usual. How's the police academy?"

Trent grins. "It's been going well. I never thought I would learn to be so proficient with a weapon. But given what's happened to you and me, it's probably the best skill I could have."

I nod. Trent knows how I feel about his newly chosen line of work. He's the only person I'm close to now, and instead of keeping himself safe, he's intentionally pursuing a career that will put his life in danger every day.

"Well, I'm glad. I'm glad you're enjoying yourself." That came out harsher than I intended, but I'm still a bit miffed about his earlier reaction. I can't help but think there's something else he wants to tell me—or is that just my guilt for not disclosing all?

"I don't know if I'd call it enjoyment," Trent says. "Of course, I want to do something more with my life than muck out stalls and fix fences. For once, I have a way to create a future for myself. A real future, through a real career. It's a chance to start over."

"I respect that," I say. "And I think it's commendable. But there's also nothing wrong with working on a ranch in Texas. I'm sure a lot of people would love to do that kind of work every day. Some people are stuck behind a desk for eight hours. And the ranch is safe. Doesn't that sense of security appeal to you?"

Trent laughs stiffly. "Aria, I was nearly killed working there earlier this year. It was a matter of months ago. And no, I guess that sense of security doesn't appeal to me all that much. The work I did for Tim isn't a real job. It's not the type of thing a guy in his thirties should be doing. I barely made over minimum wage. And it was fine for a while. I was able to sustain myself, and I was able to rent my house. But my work on Corbin Ranch has seen its day. It's time for me to move into something respectable. A career for life that matters, and one that I can eventually retire from."

"Well, that makes sense," I say.

Seeing how I can't argue his logic, Trent flashes a fleeting smile. Then he clears his throat and frowns. "Aria, there's something I need to tell you too."

I blink at him. So, I was right—something's irking him about my story of Ayden and the strange phone call, and now he's finally going to say it.

"Like I've told you, once I finish my training, I'm going to be a deputy sheriff for Williamson County. I know that my being enrolled at the police academy has been stressful for you. You're worried about what might happen to me, which also makes you worried about the future. And just as you understand my need to improve my life and make something of myself, I completely understand your concerns about my taking such a dangerous job." He pauses, watching for my reaction.

"Yeah?" I've stopped eating.

"Because of this, and because of the unnecessary stress it's causing you, I think it might be a good idea for you and me to take a break."

7

Trent puts his hands up. "Aria, I am by no means trying to shove you away or saying you can't be in my life. I'm in no way saying that, and I want to make sure you understand that. But it might do you some good to be away from me for a while. To just stay home with your female friends, relax, and get your mind off things like police training and daily use of firearms. I can't stand to see how much it's been upsetting you lately."

I shake my head. The ice-cold air from the vents magnifies the chill running down my back. So, this is what he was withholding. I thought his odd facial expressions and withdrawn behavior were due to what happened with Ayden—the parts I told him, anyway. But they weren't about that at all. Trent wanted to drop this bomb on me, but then I went and ruined his timing by telling him someone may want revenge. More revenge, apparently, as though what Korey did to me wasn't enough.

I say, "It isn't stressing me out. I'm glad you're pursuing your chosen career, especially since you weren't able to finish college like you wanted. Like you said, this is your chance to start over. Yes, it does worry me at times, but I'm still behind you." The strain in my voice detracts from any conviction.

Trent pushes his plate away and folds his hands. "Well, thank you. I appreciate that. But I have to be honest. All the discussions we've had about it, some of them in the middle of the night, are getting to be pretty hard on me. It's nothing against you. I like having you with me. But both of us have been losing sleep, and I can't justify putting you through this. And as unhappy as it's making you now, imagine when I start my new job. That's why I think it might be a good idea to have a little time apart. You should think about it. And you should think about the fact that it isn't healthy for you to worry so much about what I'm doing."

I slowly nod as I conceptualize his statements. There's what they mean for the immediate future. Then there's what they mean for our future, period. The idea of not visiting Trent at home, of not sitting on the couch with him or having dinner with him like we're doing now leaves a hollow, aching pain in my chest. I don't want to impose, but the thought of being alone in actuality, right now in real life, terrifies me more than the possibility of losing him to the job.

"How about if I just don't bring it up anymore?" I ask. But what if that's not what's really bothering him after all? I shouldn't have told him about Ayden.

"Aria, that isn't fair to you. It's like saying you don't have a right to communicate your thoughts," Trent says.

"But, if what I've been communicating is getting burden-some and making you crazy, then I won't. I can keep it to myself." And I can keep other things to myself too, like burn victims and bloody souvenirs.

Trent shakes his head. "Aria, I'm sorry, but no. I think you need a break from me, a real break. And I need one too. Not because I don't care, but because I do. And because it isn't healthy for either one of us to be up half the night discussing me getting killed by criminals."

Biting my tongue, I know Trent's probably being generous. During the wee hours, we don't only discuss the possibility of him getting offed while on duty. I also have horrible nightmares. Sometimes I wake up screaming. Occasionally I sleepwalk, and once when I regained consciousness, I found myself sitting on the kitchen floor wearing nothing but my shoes. It must be hard on him those nights I stay over. But he's always such a good sport about it, and I appreciate his kindness so much. Trent has been there for me all the way these last eight months. I'm beyond grateful.

Trent's eyes widen beneath his dark brows, his frown indicating he's preparing for my imminent freak-out. I'm not going to. I'm not angry, but the diving of my stomach and the pace of my heart tells me I'm sure not happy about it. What an awful surprise after I got threatened at work.

I blink too many times and lower my voice. "Is it really because of what I told you—because of Ayden?"

"Of course not." He rubs his chin.

"It is. Are you afraid of me?" You shouldn't be, because I'm a nice person. But you should be because I'm also a monster. Simple.

Trent shakes his head vigorously. "Aria, no, it has nothing to do with that. And all I'm proposing is a break. We're still friends. We'll always be friends."

And something more. Or maybe less. Nothing at all, yet something deep and unnamable, that's what we are.

Silent, I gawp at him. He shoves his dirty plate aside and reaches for my hands across the table. I'm unprepared, and I twitch. The warmth of his skin against mine makes my heart all fluttery. Then the feeling is gone. My chest aches. He doesn't want to be with me, and he probably never will.

"All right, then," I say in a soft, even voice. "We'll take a break."

I pull my hands from his. Trent scratches his head and glances toward the other side of the restaurant. He sniffs. "Okay. Well, thanks. Thanks for understanding. Do you have any other questions for me?"

Yeah. Why would someone take my hands after asking for time apart? And how does a dead man's jewelry disappear without a trace? "No, none that I can think of. Since we've already paid and I'm done eating, I should get going."

Trent pushes back against the table. "Oh. Okay, Aria, sure. And hey, if you need to call me, or if you need anything, feel free to let me know."

My core smolders with the familiar, dull hurt, but I keep it to myself. I grab my purse, slide out of the booth, and stand up.

"Thanks." It falls flat like my smile.

Before I can say another word, my feet get moving beneath me. They carry me toward the front doors of Jack Allen's and out to the parking lot. The warm air and sunlight of the bright August day are a shocking contrast to the frigid air conditioning. Wriggling out of the jacket as I squint from the glare, the sunlight turns my vision to silver cotton fuzz. Reality is too bright to face. Bright and damn lonely.

I white-knuckle the steering wheel on the drive home.

I'm so used to being afraid all the time that I've become accustomed to it. But after getting that call and now being "freed" from Trent, my fear has taken on a new layer. Since Korey was jailed, I haven't considered the possibility of anything else happening to me. True, there's the lingering post-trauma of it all, and its invisible cloak is hard to shed. It seems natural to carry it for a while—probably years, if not for life. But receiving a threat out of nowhere eight months later, from a caller I don't know, is something I never anticipated.

When I experience stress or a threat of loss, I'm plagued by intermittent flashbacks of my time in the County Road 140 house. Their severity depends on the external stimuli, I guess, but there are also times I've had them with no stimuli at all. My therapist told me this happens to many people who've experienced something like I have.

This first week away from Trent is no exception. A bleak fear looms over me like dark, brooding rain clouds that never break. Rain means relief, means water, means survival. While Carol and I were imprisoned, water was such a problem. Occasionally, I got Korey to give us some if I begged and did certain things for him. The dry heat outside is like a mirror to my soul.

By day seven of no contact with Trent, the bad memories just won't let up. In my cozy room, I block them out the best I can with a poetry book—Songs of Innocence and Experience by William Blake—and a bit of wine. That's saying a lot because I don't drink much. After two glasses of pinot noir, I lie in bed thinking of my last conversation with the man who saved my life. I wish there were a way to get inside his head, to find out what he's thinking without him filtering his words for me. As I toss and turn, the eighteenth-century author's words stay with me.

In the universe, there are things that are known, and things that are unknown, and in between, there are doors.

Maybe I can find a door. It's terribly awful of me, but that's beside the point.

EVERY SATURDAY NIGHT, Trent goes out for a drink with his best friend, Kyle, who is also my boss. I've even tagged along a few times. The Tex-Mex bar called "Chupacabra" on 6th Street in Austin is their usual haunt, and this weekend is no exception.

I get there early and find a parking space not far from the brick building on the corner. After choosing a table near the bar, since they seem to prefer that when it's the two of them, I sit with my back facing the door. My hair is put up and hidden beneath a black cowboy hat. I order water and nachos. While I wait, I knot my straw wrapper and take in the atmospheric aromas of sweet drinks, lime, and spicy, grilled beef.

A little after seven, my stomach dives when I hear the guys' voices behind me. From the corner of my eye, I watch them step up to the green stools at the bar. They make themselves comfortable in the yellow glow of the overhead lights and order drinks. They half-watch the television screens as they talk. For the first ten minutes, it's chit-chat about work. Then Kyle asks about me.

"She's having a hard time. It's—I don't know, it's become too much. I don't know what to do," Trent says.

Under his Longhorns baseball cap, Kyle peers at Trent while he lifts a whisky glass to his lips. I didn't hear what he ordered, but it looks like Jack and Coke. "Well, have you talked to her about it?"

Trent swigs his own drink, his old favorite Corona Extra. "Kind of. In the past, she's told me point blank she knows we're not in a relationship, and I don't owe her anything. But I'm not sure I did the right thing. I told her we should take a break because she's so stressed out. I didn't mean no contact at all, mostly no staying over. But I haven't heard from her in a week."

Kyle nods. He's young, clean-shaven, and his UT hat hides his short, blond hair. "Okay. Well, how far into it are you? Have you..." Sometimes, he's too polite to be blunt.

"Have we screwed?" Trent snaps. "My God, man, no. Are you kidding me?" Trent's face breaks from its stoic mold, and he cracks a smile. They both laugh.

"Just wondering," Kyle says. "Okay, so why don't you explain it to me more. What problem are you trying to solve?"

Trent sighs. "She was coming over about five times a week, almost every day after work. Sometimes she made dinner and would leave in the evening. Other times she fell asleep on the couch. And sometimes she slept in bed with me."

"Okay," Kyle says. "Well, was there physical stuff?"

I shift my legs, studying the tan and black granite tabletop inlay as I strain to hear Trent's response. He says, "Eh, stuff like sitting on the couch together, holding hands, hugging. Things like that. But not all the time. Just sometimes."

Kyle asks, "So you're more than friends, but not into anything deep."

Trent sighs. "Honestly, I have no idea what we are."

"Because it's so soon? Or because you just don't like her?" Kyle asks.

"I do like her. It's the too-soon part, mostly. And it's the fact that I just can't get past what happened to her and how fragile she is. It's like I see it on replay, flashbacks of that day I looked in the back room of the house on County Road 140. I see her strung up there, hanging from the wall. But now there's more. Earlier in the week, she told me she killed someone in self-defense a year ago. And she said she got a phone call from someone who seemed to have a connection to what happened. Maybe a guy who knew the man she killed. She said he threatened her."

Kyle raises an eyebrow. "Wow. Did she call the police?"

"Yeah," Trent says. "She said she did. I want to believe her. There's no reason for her to lie, but she just seems so *fragile*. Sometimes I don't know what's going on in her head."

"You used to tell me how strong she was, but now you're saying the opposite. She doesn't act fragile. Recovering, maybe, but not easily broken," Kyle says. The waitress drops by with a sizzling plate—probably fajitas. He thanks her.

"Well, no, not in front of you at work. And I think about Elizabeth." Trent stops and stares across the bar at the myriad-colored bottles of alcohol against their mirrored backdrop.

Kyle nods. "It hasn't been that long. I don't blame you. But you know, you've both been through some traumatic shit. Things that most people don't live to tell. It might be good for you and Aria not to be alone. If she's cool with the arrangement and you like her, then what's the problem?"

"Kyle, Elizabeth's been dead for less than a year. Even having Aria around feels wrong. I should have gone with my original gut feeling and not got involved with her at all."

"I'm not so sure," says Kyle. "I think you're looking at this too one-dimensionally. You can be close friends who care and help each other get back to normal again. And if you need to hold hands sometimes, or if you both want to do more, then do it."

"So, you're saying the remedy is 'friends with benefits?' Thank you, Doctor Phil," Trent says. He pulls a face like he's mildly ill.

Kyle laughs and drains the last of his bourbon. "Maybe more like friends with exclusive benefits. But I'm serious. Besides, when you were hospitalized after your ordeal with Durham, Aria was with you every day until your discharge. You told me you wouldn't have made it without her. That's a true friend. What changed since then?"

Trent shakes his head. "I guess I wasn't prepared for the rest of it. She started coming over without asking. It was nice at first. It helped. But it got weird. She's in such bad shape. She screams in her sleep."

"Well, yeah. That sicko tortured her," Kyle says. "I'm amazed at how well she does at work. She doesn't give any outward signs of what happened."

"Maybe not, but she doesn't hold back with me. One time I got up in the middle of the night and found her sitting hunched under the kitchen table. She said she had a nightmare and didn't want to wake me. But it wasn't just strange. It was creepy. Another time I woke up, and she was standing next to the bed, just staring at me."

"Trent, she needs help. Is she still going to counseling?" Kyle asks.

"Yeah. She's been seeing someone. Some kind of alternative therapist," Trent says. "Even so, standing over me at night? That's too much."

Kyle frowns, considering his empty glass. He tilts it and lets the ice clink around. "Maybe she just wanted to make sure you were okay. She probably feels protective of you."

"I don't expect you to get it," Trent says, shrugging.

"Okay," Kyle says. "So, your girl has some issues. Give it time. If you care about her at all, don't push her away, and I bet after a while, she'll come out of it. It's probably going to take time, but she will."

"I do care about her, and I'm not. I told her she could call if she needs anything."

"Not what?" Kyle asks.

"Pushing her away," Trent says.

But from the look on his face, I can tell he wants to. Korey was my monster. Maybe I'm Trent's.

I hunch over my plate of nachos and turn my head, so my cowboy hat obscures my face from their view. I don't have a drink to sip like Trent and Kyle do, and that's my preference. But undiluted, Trent's words are harsh. And at the same time, even though I don't like what he said, I understand where he's coming from, and not every word was bad. Still, it hurts. My chest aches with a new, raw wound because while Trent may not have wanted to be completely honest with me, he's telling Kyle the truth.

I pay the waitress and quietly thank her. Still keeping my head down beneath the black brim of my hat, I rise and head out into the warm summer night. The outside air in this section of downtown Austin smells like beer, flowers, and the occasional puff of cigarette smoke. I turn right at the corner of Trinity Street, where I parked. I can just make out the white Camry not far ahead. It's past the restaurant's covered outdoor eating area, across from a white two-story building by the alley behind Chupacabra. But there's something else too—a quick sweep of motion near the passenger's side door.

8

Someone's there, lingering near my car. I stop and hold my body still as I strain to see in the evening light. It's after eight o'clock now, too dark to distinguish if the person is male or female. There's about thirty feet between me and the car. That doesn't help either. If I try to gauge the person's height, I'd say he or she isn't much taller than I am. Beyond that, I can't tell much.

Quietly, without dragging my feet, I edge over to the fence bordering Chupacabra's outdoor tables. Brown canvas which covers the top and sides of the enclosure obscures me from the customers. Warm lighting shows the silhouettes within. People raise drinks in their hands or eat, chat, and laugh. I doubt anyone will notice me. Catching a draft of lime margaritas, I press my shoulder against the chain link. Hopefully, the darkness will give me a few uninterrupted minutes to observe the person by my sedan.

He or she is wearing a dark jacket with a hood. This is odd right off because it's still over eighty degrees outside. The person leans toward the passenger's side window and peers in. I squint, straining to pick up anything I can about the person's appearance or build. Besides the wrong clothing choice for the Texas heat, there's nothing noticeable about the person's size. They aren't apparently thin or heavy. The person isn't obviously male or female. They seem more androgynous, a nameless, human silhouette snooping around my vehicle. The person briefly goes around to the driver's side and then departs, passing the white building and heading into the adjacent parking lot where the food trucks are stationed. I wait, watching as the figure disappears.

Thinking of the phone call and my last conversation with Trent when I told him about Ayden, my heart pounds. But it gets worse. I consider going back into Chupacabra to tell the guys what I just observed. Ridiculous. I shove the idea away and instead keep my vision keen and taking in my surroundings. As I start toward my Camry, I make sure to take light steps. My sneakers press quietly against the pavement as I walk, and I don't need to go dashing to my car in a pounding, panic-stricken run and let the creep know I'm here.

Gripping my keys tightly so they won't jingle as I pull them from my purse, I increase my pace slightly as I near the car. I think about inspecting the exterior, but that would mean stopping and being obvious—the less time outside, the better. I swing around to the driver's side from behind the sedan. My racing heart spurring me on, I snatch an irresistible glance near the food trucks where the hooded guy went. No one's there now. He must have passed through that parking lot, and the other building obscures him now. I unlock the door as naturally as I can, but my gaze darts around like a frightened rabbit.

I swiftly pull the door closed and lock myself inside. My

stomach clenches and flips, and my chest shakes with every contraction of my heart. Trent once told me about the time someone planted an IED in his truck, and I'll never forget it. My mind spins out of control. Images of bright orange flames consume my consciousness as they would my vehicle. With tense fingers, I turn the key in the ignition anyway, and the engine turns over. It rumbles to life like usual. I inhale. I try to steady my rapid breathing as I put the car in gear. I take stock of the parking lot again, but it remains empty. A few cars pass before I back up into Trinity Street.

Keeping my eyes on the road with effort, I work my way through downtown Austin to the Interstate 35 access road. My glances find every pedestrian, scanning them to see if they fit the appearance of the figure I saw. Not one of them has on a hoodie, but I gawk at them all the same. While doing so, my thoughts echo the guys' conversation from Chupacabra.

"I don't expect you to get it," Trent said while I eavesdropped.

I can't speak for Kyle, but I do get it. Trent has his own demons to fight. I'm a train wreck, and even with everything he knows about me, he still doesn't know the worst.

AFTER WORK ON MONDAY, I buy a new mountain bike. With it strapped to a rack behind the trunk of the Camry, I envision my first ride around our neighborhood as I thread my way through rush hour traffic on 35 North. I came to this purchase decision last night while lying in bed staring at the ceiling. If Trent's no longer going to be a part of my life, I need something proactive to pass the time. Something to keep me from diving into dark crevices where the memories, grim and cruel, swallow me up and spit me out as someone else. Something else.

Since leaving protective police custody earlier in the year, I've been renting a room in a newer home in Round Rock. The neighborhood is a nice one off East New Hope Drive, and it's where I stay when I'm not visiting Trent. I guess that will be all the time now. The house is a modest two-story covered in white stone façade. Its small front lawn bears a single maple tree near the curb. A planter area under the windows is sectioned off with railroad ties and mulch, but we've never done much with it. Maybe I'll get ambitious and put some flowers there.

I share the house with three other renters—Margarita, Rebecca, and Ann. My room is on the second floor, toward the back. It overlooks a sunny backyard with a gray stone birdbath in the center. Lilies, yellow wildflowers, and purple sage bushes nestle in colorful patterns around the chain-link fence and along the walkway leading back to the utility shed. The place is cheery and safe enough. Although I haven't been a socializer since my abduction, it's nice not to live alone.

When I pull into the driveway, my car is the only one here. None of my housemates must be home yet. My stomach flips, and I tell myself to knock it off. Just because I got a creepy phone call is no reason to be afraid now. Just because some weirdo was snooping around my car. Just because I used to be a prisoner. Right. Who the hell do I think I'm kidding?

Glancing at the western horizon, I estimate there's about thirty minutes of daylight left. Going biking now would be cutting it too close for me. I'll store the bike in the shed overnight and take it to work with me tomorrow. I can ride at Zilker Park every day, and by the time I wrap up, I'll have missed all the traffic on my drive back to Round Rock.

I untie my bike from the rack and steer it along the walkway. After I lift the latch and swing open the gate, I pause before stepping into the backyard. Birds call from the two maple trees at the rear of the property. Beyond the privacy fence to my right, I hear the neighbor's kids playing. A little boy laughs.

"No, you're not, no, you're not," he says.

"I am, I am," his friend answers back.

I have no idea what their conversation is about. I peek over at the other neighbor's yard to my left, but no one's out today. The light is fading, a golden warmth falling over the flowers and shrubs around the birdbath. Seems I'm ensconced in suburbia. There's nothing to fear.

Walking my bike toward the shed, I listen to the rhythmic click of the bicycle chain as the wheels turn. We keep the storage building locked, but all the renters have a key. As the all-terrain tires roll over the grassy yard, my head whirls with lightheadedness. I slow, choosing my steps more carefully. I lean my bike against the side of the shed and reach into my pocket for my keychain.

With shaking fingers, I fumble for the smallest key. I glance around as though the small, wooden structure might spontaneously combust. Images of blackened two by fours flash by. But as I remove the lock and open the door, nothing happens. The hinges creak, and smells of wood, paint, and faint traces of mildew linger in the background. I stand here, arms at my sides, and listen. There's nothing but bird calls and the laughter of children.

After taking a deep breath and pushing my hair out of

my face, I grab my bike from the exterior wall and wheel it inside. I tuck it in the back corner near some of my house-mates' bikes. I exit the shed and lock it up, waiting for my heart to ease up its frantic pounding. Well, I guess I've conquered one tiny thing in my life. My mind's eye produces a headline—"Crazy girl gets over fear of sheds."

Tonight, I'm supposed to do some research on the Lamar buildings for Kyle and have it ready for him tomorrow. This is a property that's been on the market forever, and we've finally found a potential buyer. Our client, Rance Epstein, has been poring over the inspection report and blueprints we gave him but wants more information on any renovations done, especially those performed without a permit. He called at the end of the day, and I told Kyle I didn't mind getting started on his request tonight since we were hoping to close on the property soon. So, I'll email Martin Thomas, the current owner, and check online with the Development Services Department for any permits pulled. That will be a start, anyway. My laptop is inside its case in the car, and I'll need it.

I close the gate behind me and head back to my Camry in the driveway. When I grab the door handle, someone touches my arm. A lightning bolt of pure terror rips through me. First, I go rigid. My bones ice over, and I can't move. Then I jump so hard I nearly tumble over backward. My heels skid on the concrete, and my scream silences the birds.

I jerk my head up to see Margarita. She's one of my housemates, a woman in her early thirties who rents a room on the first floor. I should have noticed her car in the drive-way, but I didn't because I was thinking about work.

My breath comes out in short, little pants while I wonder

what possessed her to touch me unannounced. I glare at her. "You shouldn't do that."

"I called out to you twice. Didn't you hear me?" she asks.

"No," I say. I push my back against the car body to stabilize myself.

"I'm sorry," she says. She frowns like she means it. "When it looked like you were going to leave, I wanted to catch you in time."

My heart hammers. I press my fingers against the warm Camry door. "Okay. What's up?"

"I'm going over to my sister's tonight, and she's having some friends over. I was wondering if you'd like to tag along." She gives me a small, hopeful grin. In a royal blue satin top with black leggings and heels, she's dressed to kill. Her black hair of considerable length cascades around her shoulders in thick waves.

This isn't the first time Margarita, or one of the other renters, has asked me to participate in some enjoyable activity. It's charitable and all, but each of us has a different definition of "fun." Mine is staying inside where it's safe unless I happen to be hanging out with Trent—which I'm not now.

As I lag for an answer, she adds, "It might be good to get out. We worry about you staying cooped up in your room after work."

She must have noticed that I didn't go to Trent's last week. My housemates know my history, and they have a rough idea of my relationship with my rescuer.

"Thanks, Margarita, but I'm supposed to do a little work for Kyle tonight." My racing pulse slows, and I catch my breath. I open the car door and scan for my laptop case. Not seeing it, I lean in and feel along the floor and in the back seat.

"Crap," I say. "I think I left my computer at work. I'll have to go back for it."

Margarita tilts her head and gives me that sympathetic look I hate. "You work too much. Can't you ask Kyle if you can do it tomorrow?"

I try to chuckle, but it comes out like a snort. "Does this have something to do with guys? Are you trying to encourage me to get out there and meet people?"

Margarita's face breaks into a smile instantly. She laughs. "Yes, but not like that—not like the dating scene. I know you like Trent, and there's nothing wrong with that. But there's also nothing wrong with meeting other people too."

I sigh. "How could you possibly think I want to meet people? The thought of it makes me cringe."

Her face falls. "No, I know you've said you're not looking for a relationship. It's just—you were spending so much time with Trent, I thought—"

"I was spending time with him, but I'm not right now. And Trent is the man who rescued me. That's different. If not for him, I wouldn't be alive right now. But I don't want to be around guys—new guys. And anyway, I can't because I have to drive back to Austin to get my computer." I should go easy on her. She means well, but it's hard to muster the strength for social graces after being startled.

"But what about the traffic?" Her smile is barely hanging on, but she's doing a better job than I am. "By the time you get back, it will be so late. Maybe you can ask your boss if you can do it tomorrow, and then you can come hang out with me. You don't even have to talk to anyone. You can just get out and unwind. Not a long time, maybe just like an hour."

"No! I don't want to unwind!" I slam the car door.

Margarita flinches.

Get your shit together, monster. "Sorry."

She rubs her arm. No smile now. "It's okay."

"What I meant to say was there won't be any traffic heading to the office or on the way back either because it's after seven. And the work won't take all that long, but I promised Kyle I would do it. I don't want to bail on him," I say, even though I know I don't have to explain it to her.

"Well, okay," Margarita says. Sober now in her going-out clothes, a wrinkle springs up between her eyebrows.

"Thanks for inviting me, though."

"Sure. Maybe another time. I worry about you," says Margarita.

"Thanks," I say. "See you later tonight after we both get home."

"See you later," she says. She steps back and waves as I get into my car.

She worries about me. That's cute. She wouldn't worry about me if she knew what I am or what follows me.

MEDIAN REALTY IS DARK INSIDE, but the porch light came on since I left earlier. The real estate office where I work is a quaint, dark gray house with a red door and cream trim—a residence that was remodeled and rezoned for commercial use. Since it's located on Bluebonnet Lane in South Austin, I won't have any trouble riding my bike to Zilker Park after work every day.

I let myself in, then turning off the alarm using the keypad near the door. The place smells like lavender. It must be the floor cleaner from the company I hired to come once a week. After clicking on the lights, I find my laptop bag right where I left it on the seat of my chair. I sling the strap over my shoulder, reset the alarm, go out the front door, and close it.

As an orange sunset seeps below the housetops, I wiggle my key into the gold lock and turn it. It'll be dark soon, and I want to be long gone by then. When I face the street, I start and swear under my breath. The strap of the bag slides down my arm. I grab it just in time.

A man stands at the end of the parking lot, near the street. Not a young man. He's probably close to sixty, and while remembering the strange phone call, I take a good look at him. The man has a slender build. His dark hair is beginning to thin on top. He's clipped his sunglasses onto the breast pocket of his dark gray dress shirt. To his right is a black Mercedes sedan. Its high hood ornament stands out even in the fading light. The man gazes up at me intently as I peer back from our low cement porch.

The stranger gives me one of those tight-lipped, closed-mouth smiles. The kind you make when you think someone's reaction is awkwardly childish or unprofessional in some way. He flutters his eyelids a few times. What a jerk. Can't he see that he startled me?

"May I help you?" I ask in a cold voice.

"I certainly hope so." His annoyed smile evaporates. He replaces it with detached regard. "My name is Nick Pearlman. I was hoping to speak with someone about the commercial property for sale on Lamar."

"Oh," I say. "For what address?"

"1515 South Lamar," he says.

Those are the same warehouses for which Kyle is having me pull more info—the whole reason behind my inconvenient trip back to the office. A chill races up my arms at his timing.

"Sure, let me give you our number. Kyle and I will both be in the office tomorrow." I dig into my purse for the pocket where I keep my business cards. I tug one out and hold it between my fingers, noticing my hand still shakes.

Taking a few steps toward him, I say, "This has the office hours on it too."

Nick huffs, taking my meaning. "Thanks. But I was hoping to speak with someone tonight."

He reaches into the pocket of his shirt and draws out his own card. I take it.

"I see." I nod. "I can go ahead and give Kyle a call if you like, but you should know that we already have a sale pending on that property."

"I know," he says. "That's what I wanted to talk to you about. I also know that Rance Epstein is the buyer, and I was wondering if you'd be willing to discuss it with me over coffee. You won't understand it yet, but I need your help. It's very important you sell the property to me instead."

Now it's my turn to stare and blink. My gaze rivets to that cold, pasty-white face. I don't want to talk about the Lamar property over coffee. If he made a better first impression, it might be different. But turning up after hours with me here alone creeps me out. Then there's his voice—it sounds like the caller's.

I say, "I'm sorry, but I really can't tonight. Also, Kyle has most of the information. He's the agent overseeing the sale. But if you drop by the office tomorrow, or if you give Kyle a call, I'm sure he'd be happy to talk to you. That property has been on the market for such a long time. I'm surprised to have two people interested within a few months."

He narrows his eyes, and the look he gives me makes me uncomfortable. Mentally, I note down his measurements to the best of my ability. I put him at five foot six, maybe one hundred and fifty pounds. Can't see his eye color. Yeah, he's probably in his early sixties, like I first thought. My mind flashes with a snapshot image of the snooping person in the hoody by my Camry the other night. His silhouette fits, though that proves nothing. Still, I notice.

After a long pause, Nick says, "I would have bought it sooner, but I didn't know I needed it. I can explain. How about we just talk about it right here?"

The last traces of burnt orange touch the cityscape to the west, and the sky above it rapidly darkens to dusty blue. My pulse quickens. I sidestep, edging my way to the car.

"I wouldn't mind if it were earlier, but I don't think it's safe to stand out here at night." I glance over at the shabby convenience store in the adjacent lot, hoping he'll get the idea. "If you give us a call tomorrow, we'd be happy to arrange something."

Nick Pearlman does that pompous eye-flutter thing again. Like he's a distinguished captain of industry, and I'm a waitress who got his order wrong.

"Which is why I suggested we meet somewhere for coffee. You can pick the place. This won't take long. Please. I really need your help." He follows me, stepping closer—too close. He places his body about a foot from mine.

He's blocking the way to my car. I wonder if I have enough nerve to run around him in hopes he doesn't grab me. I'm not sure that I do. I can tell by how overtly he plants himself that he isn't sure I do either. His positioning seems intentional.

Nick scowls and says, "I would have bought the property

a long time ago had I known what I know now, but there's still time. Selling to Epstein is a big mistake. And it might be a good idea to investigate your clients more thoroughly before doing business with them." He presses his lips into a thin line.

With my heart slamming against my chest, I look him straight in the eyes and smile stiffly. "All right, then. Definitely give us a call tomorrow. Thanks."

I dart past him, brushing against his arm with my shoulder. I run around to the driver's side of my car. After unlocking it with my remote, I yank open the door. I steal a glance back. Nick hasn't followed. He hasn't moved and watches me with the same aloof expression from earlier.

"I know what you did," he calls after me as I start lowering myself to the car seat.

I freeze in place with my hand on the door.

As I hesitate, he says, "Yes, that's right. I can see the question you're not asking. Well, here's your answer. I know what you did in the shed when you thought no one was looking. Are we clear now?"

9

N ick Pearlman's message couldn't be any clearer if he handed me Ayden's bloody ring in a gift-wrapped box. A frigid chill dashes up my spine and radiates down my arms. It's like being punched in the soul. He's the caller. Without a doubt, it has to be him.

I slam the door, start the engine, and back up into the street. The headlights make Nick's pale face even whiter, his pallor and his straight line of a mouth the last things I see before I peel out. Burnt rubber smell invades the car as I fly down Bluebonnet Lane. There's no traffic at this hour. The rearview shows no car following.

My pulse increases to a frantic fluttering, and my hands start to sweat. There's no question now that he knows. He told me he did. As I work my way toward Barton Springs Road to get on the Mopac Expressway, I shake my head. Maybe Nick is related to Korey, an extended family member set on vengeance. Or he might have been friends with Ayden. Maybe asking about the Lamar property was just an excuse to speak to me, but why choose that place? And why doesn't he want us to sell to Mr. Epstein?

But he said something else, too. *Please. I really need your help.* What if he wasn't trying to threaten me? What if he has a legitimate concern and truly needs to fill me in? But if so, his way of going about it was too off-putting. He could have called or stopped by the office and sat down with Kyle and me during the day. Neither of us would have objected. In fact, we would have been happy to. We talk to people who have questions and concerns all day long. But his last statements blow that idea all to hell.

...when you thought no one was looking. He saw. He knows.

IT DOESN'T MAKE a bit of sense why Nick Pearlman, my stalker, gave me his card. Before starting business this morning, Kyle faces me across his desk as I sit and explain. Trees shiver in the morning breeze outside the window behind him as he leans forward, digesting my paraphrased account of what happened. Naturally, I gave him the short, sterilized version. But it's important that he know someone threatened me right here at work.

"I'm sorry trouble seems to follow wherever I go," I say. "I never meant to bring this to your door. What happened with Korey's brother was years ago, and I don't understand why it's suddenly rearing its ugly head. Why now?"

"Nonsense," Kyle says. "You haven't done anything. The guy was being a creep, and we don't need to do business with him. I don't care what he was saying. If he has some problem with Median or with you, he can get a lawyer. Otherwise, we're not touching this."

He makes a copy of Nick's business card and hands it back to me. The card lists a name and number only, with no address or company. Not very helpful, but maybe it's something.

Kyle is twenty-eight, but he doesn't really look it. With his short, blond hair and a babyface, he almost seems too young to be so successful. At times I envy his life, one that's gone according to his plans. But it's hard to be sour when he always extends me such kindness.

I nod, drawing a breath. "Thank you."

"When are you planning on going to the Austin Police Department?" Kyle asks.

"I spoke to Victims Services earlier, and I was told to check in with Mr. Jeffrey Spade. I gave him a call, and he said I can send him an email or go in and file something in writing. I could take a long lunch today and do it then if it's all right. I don't know if I have enough to report, or maybe what I do have isn't enough to link anything to Nick Pearlman. But I don't want to wait around and see what happens."

"Yes, absolutely go today. And you do have enough, Aria. After what you've been through, if you see a shadow out of place, the police should investigate it," Kyle says.

I smile. "It means a lot that you believe me."

"Of course. You're an honest person, and those are hard to come by these days. Besides, why wouldn't I believe you?" he asks.

Maybe because I'm not so honest. And because Trent doesn't believe me. I scream in the night, and once, he caught me standing over him while he was sleeping. What he doesn't know was that I woke up from a nightmare, and I just wanted to make sure he was there. Seeing him reassured me, something even amnesiac murderers need. But I keep all of this to myself.

"Well, I really appreciate it. I wonder if Nick will have the nerve to come here today after last night," I reply.

Kyle lifts a corner of his mouth. He shakes his head, barely. "I seriously doubt it. He was probably just trying to scare you, and now he's too embarrassed to show up. Also, if he was really going to do something, it's doubtful he would have given you his card. But if I see this guy, I'm going to forbid him from the office. So, you have nothing to worry about. We'll just keep our eyes open."

I don't mention it to my concerned boss, but the methods of control-hungry men happen to be an area of knowledge in which I'm intimately familiar. If Nick decides to make another appearance, it will probably be when I least expect it—and when I'm alone.

THE NEAREST POLICE department on 8th Street is only about fifteen minutes from Median Realty. Ironically, it's also not far from Chupacabra, where that shady person—perhaps Nick—was snooping around my Toyota. Cranking up my A/C to combat the morning sun baking the car interior, I drive along South Lamar. My gaze flicks over to the property of interest as the buildings pass outside the window.

As usual, there are no cars outside. The two adjoining warehouses in front are most visible, baring their rusted, corrugated aluminum exteriors and dark, broken windows. In most places, the metal siding looks redder than silver. The slightly newer portion, the annex building toward the back of the parking lot, has spots of bare wood exposed through the peeling, white paint. Weather and time beat it to hell. However, I know from the inspection report that the structure itself is mostly sound.

The lot outside isn't even paved but covered in white gravel. With but a few patches of dry, withered grass on the entire property, the piece of real estate reminds me of an old aircraft hangar in the desert.

When I push open the glass door at the station, I restrain a smile. That crisp, papery smell that all offices have intermingles with scents of coffee and donuts. Cops need their caffeine and sugar like everyone else, right? I banish my impending giggle. My black high heels click across the white floor tile as I step up to the front desk.

After the receptionist directs me where to go, I head down a hallway and poke around the third door on the right. A man types at the keyboard at his desk. I knock on the door frame. "Good afternoon. I'm here to see Mr. Jeffrey Spade."

"That's me," says the imposing man who glances up. He gets to his feet and grins.

"Aria Owen," I say.

We exchange a hearty handshake. Although I've spoken to him over the phone before, I've not met him until now. Spade has dark brown skin, buzzed black hair, and stands probably six foot five. The guy is solid muscle. With that physique, it's a wonder he's working on my case instead of patrolling the streets and busting criminals. Glancing down at his desk, I find the reason. Looks like Spade made detective.

"Thank you for fitting me in," I say.

"You bet. I'm glad you came to see me, Ms. Owen," he

replies as he sits back down. "You seem surprised, but I want you to know we take this very seriously. Since the first time we spoke two weeks ago, I've been doing some reading on the run-in you had with Ayden Nemeth a year back. I've also been doing some checking in our database and elsewhere on Nick Pearlman."

My belly flutters as I take a seat. "Were you able to find anything?"

"Yes, and no. I found many entries for the name he gave you, but the only Nick Pearlman who meets an early sixties age description died over a year ago. We might assume that that isn't his real name, but that's only an assumption, not a fact. I have to do more digging. Having a cell number for him, though, that's good. Since we have probable cause, I should be able to obtain a warrant to track and tap the phone he's using. He may not keep the same number for long, but we can still monitor what he says if he calls you."

I nod. "So, based on everything I've told you so far, you do believe Nick wants some sort of revenge for Ayden's death?"

He pushes a stack of papers aside. "I can only tell you that's what it looks like. Like I said, because you were the victim of violent crimes by both Ayden Nemeth and his brother Korey, we're taking this very seriously. Not doing so would only be committing another crime, and we're not about to do that. We're on your side."

I exhale and hope he's right about the Ayden part. Maybe I *was* a victim. Maybe I didn't find his bloody trinket in my cotton ball dish later—I imagined it. I try to smile. "I can't tell you how glad I am to hear that."

We discuss what I should do if confronted by Nick again and how I should behave if he calls me. After speaking with

Detective Spade for about half an hour, I fill out the paper-work he needs. Most of the butterflies in my stomach have stilled.

"I do have one last question," the detective says. He holds an open manilla folder in his hands.

"Yes?" I set my purse on my lap.

"If we want to get a lock on this guy as soon as possible, and we do, we need to think like he thinks. Is there anything else you can tell me about the incident with Ayden Nemeth? Any other details—something that only someone who was there would know?"

AFTER WORK, Detective Spade's words nip at my ears as I stop at Los Potrillos Restaurant on the interstate. When he stared at me intently in the fluorescent lighting, he may as well have been peering into my soul. My answer was "no." I then told myself I wasn't lying because there's no way to know if the bloody ring was real or not since I've never found it again. There's that unwavering honesty Kyle mentioned.

I'm wolf hungry and want to get home, so I devour my dinner at one of the honey-colored tables underneath a longhorn skull on the wall. The tastes of cilantro and grilled shrimp linger on my tongue as I finish up. I toss my crum-pled napkin on the empty plate. As I make my way to the door, my gaze keeps flicking to a couple at a booth. They weren't there when I came in, so they must have arrived after.

I walk a few more paces. Now I can see the man clearly. Trent. Only the back of the woman's head is visible from here—a thick, blonde ponytail. My stomach clenches like an iron vise, and I increase my pace. I'll slip by unnoticed.

"Aria?" Trent calls.

Disbelief flows heavily through his voice. It's ripe with everything he's not saying. Like, "Did you know I was here?" And almost, "Are you following me?" Trent and his companion are about fifteen feet away in the booth closest to the door. The decorations on the knee wall must have obscured my view earlier, especially the wooden keg holding a western saddle with a plastic palm tree beside it. The woman turns around in her seat to have a look at me.

My feet slide to a halt against my will, and I stand awkwardly with my fingers laced. "Hey. I was just grabbing a bite. And... heading out."

I smile with my mouth closed and take a few more steps toward the door, bringing myself nearer to the booth in the process. I have to pass by it to leave. No choice.

Trent nods. "Oh. Well, great, I—"

The woman cuts him off. She asks quietly, "Is that her?"

She's a twenty-something and attractive, with a thin nose and blue eyes. As she glances between Trent and me, her gaze lights up with curiosity.

"Yeah," Trent answers. "Naomi, I'd like you to meet my... really good friend, Aria. Aria, this is Naomi. She's a fellow cadet at the academy."

My gut sinks when he refers to me as his "really good friend." But were I in his position, I don't know if I would do any better. I stride up to their table and force a smile.

"Hi, Naomi. It's nice to meet you." I extend my hand, and she wiggles out of the booth to stand as per proper introduction protocol.

"Likewise," she says, returning my handshake with a firm grip.

Slim and muscular from her police training, Naomi smiles warmly. She smells faintly of gun oil, leather, and something sweet like herbal tea. Her eyes are about level with mine. The locks of her ponytail fall beside her neck as she grins at me.

"Trent has told me so much about you," Naomi adds.

"I bet," I say. I glance at Trent with mock sarcasm, but all I can think of is how he likes me, sort of, but I creep him out.

"All good things, of course," Trent says. He chuckles.

Naomi laughs. "Yes, definitely all good things. It's an honor to meet you. After what you've been through, you're an inspiration to a lot of people. You're certainly an inspiration to me. Not only did you survive, but you found the strength to keep going. I was following your story in the Statesmen. So many people were praying for you."

I pause, puzzled as to how I did anything inspirational. "Well, thank you. A person's gotta keep going, right?"

"Aria," Trent says. "Would you like to join us? Sit and chat for a while?"

I frown at him. Wasn't he the one who told me he wanted a break? Although recalling the conversation at Chupacabra, perhaps Kyle got Trent to change his mind. This might be his chance to remedy his "pushing me away" without it seeming contradictory.

"Yes," Naomi says. She extends a hand toward the booth. "Please join us."

A lead ball drops into my stomach. I shift my feet and fiddle with my purse strap while I stall for an answer. It might be nice to run into Trent under other circumstances, but I find it hard to believe he isn't interested in this woman. They may already be engaged in some torrid, whirlwind romance for all I know. My chest aches. All I want is to bolt for the door.

"Thanks," I say. "But I'm beat after work today, and I just want to get home."

"We understand. Well, it was great meeting you," Naomi says.

"You too. Catch you guys later." I begin walking away as we call out our goodbyes.

Trent gawks after me with his mouth open like he wants to ask a question, but I'm already moving off at a good clip. If he has something to say, he can call. My high heels plink in crisp notes across the floor, and I push open the heavy door of the restaurant. Not the most graceful exit, maybe, but I have to get out of here. I emerge in the stuffy heat of late afternoon, squinting in the bright sun of the parking lot.

When I slide into the car, my cell rings. My muscles twitch. I curse as I dig my phone out of my purse. Silly ideas about Trent calling to apologize spring to mind. Silly and unreal. When I see the caller, I draw a loud breath.

It's Nick. I entered his number yesterday, not wanting to be caught unawares if this happened. I also installed an app to record phone calls. After all, Spade hasn't tapped the line yet. He needs a warrant first. I sigh, answer the call, quickly open the app, and press "record."

"This is Aria," I say.

"This is Nick Pearlman," he says. "Don't hang up. I need you to—"

"I know who this is, and I'm not taking orders from you," I say through clenched teeth. Just took his head right off. I'm so rattled at Trent that I'm directing my anger at my stalker now. Nice.

"Now look," Nick says, his voice dropping in pitch. "I told you I needed your help. Just stop and listen for a minute. Whether you like it or not, the Lamar property is your problem now, and so am I."

"Not true. We won't be doing business with you at all. I just came from the police department, and I told them everything. The property is as good as sold, and I'm not obligated to do anything with you," I say.

"There's more to this than the acquisition of real estate. I already told you that I know the buyer. There are other things I need to tell you—important things. But I'm not going to do it over the phone."

"If you have something to say, then you can send us an email with the information. And if you needed my help, you should have thought of that before you threatened me. That isn't the best way to get someone's cooperation. I did what I had to do to protect myself," I say.

"I didn't threaten you," Nick says.

"What would you call it then?" I ask.

Nick snorts. "You should have thought of the consequences of your actions. I guess it's easy not to give a shit when it's not your life. But you can redeem yourself. Meet with me alone, and we'll get this sorted out."

I shake my head, gripping the steering wheel with my left hand to try and make myself stop trembling. Redeem myself, indeed. My heart races, and I'm lightheaded, but I've secured a minor victory by recording the call.

I ask, "And what if I don't meet with you?"

"If you don't, things are going to get ugly, Ms. Owen. Don't force me to play the bad guy. It's a role I don't want to assume, but I will if I have to. Meet me at Maudie's Too on

South Lamar tomorrow at noon. It's in your best interest to come alone."

I huff. I wonder if he would dare order Kyle like that. Well, my answer is the fact that he hasn't contacted Kyle at all—even though Nick supposedly has an interest in the Lamar warehouse property, and Kyle is the agent.

Ignoring his instruction, I ask, "How the hell do you know about what happened in the shed?"

"I was there. I saw everything. And I've had my eye on your activities for longer than you know."

My hand clutching the mobile goes rigid, and I nearly drop the phone. I don't reply, but it doesn't matter because Nick hangs up. As I sit here quivering, running my fingers through my hair and trying to gain my composure, I replay his words.

I was there. I saw everything.

Nick reaffirmed what he said outside the office last night. He was there. The creep was *there* when Korey's brother burned to death. If that be the case, then he must have seen what I did to Ayden—the horrible thing I can't remember.

10

S tanding Nick Pearlman up for lunch is the nice, big middle finger he deserves. I forward the recording of the phone conversation to Detective Spade in Austin. I buy a small, easy-to-use switchblade knife and a can of pepper spray, both of which I keep on me at all times. I reflect that had I hidden them on my person before Korey knocked me out, my time as his prisoner in the County Road 140 house might have played out quite differently. I can't go back in time, but it's nice to have weapons now.

Additionally, I'm sick of being afraid all the time, so I've also started taking shooting lessons at a range not far from my house. I practice with a small handgun I rent, deciding that I'll buy my own soon.

A week has passed without incident. I worried Nick would punish me for not showing up, but he didn't call, didn't come by the office—and no surprise, he didn't contact Kyle. That would have taken actual balls.

It's Friday, and Kyle and I are meeting with Rance Epstein in our small conference room. This was once the dining area, as evidenced by the chair rail running horizontally along the middle of the wall, with chestnut-stained wainscoting underneath. Above that, the walls are painted a warm parchment color. The floor is still the original, varnished hardwood floor. It's been kept immaculately well over the years, and we always get compliments on it. Next to the door sits a large fiddle leaf fig plant in a blue pot. Since I've pulled the heavy fabric of the ivory curtains back to reveal the window, the morning sunlight illuminates the room without making a glare. It's a downright cozy place to do business.

I laid out the contract and all the paperwork beforehand. I sit on one side of the long table and wait for Kyle and our clients to arrive. Fidgeting with my pen, I think of Nick Pearlman's words, among them his caution about Rance Epstein. As though someone's dirty laundry is any of our concern. I listen to the tick of our copper-rimmed wall clock. After turning and glancing out the window, I see a boy ride by on his bike—hopefully, that will be me later today. The minivan in the driveway across the street starts backing out, and its white brake lights flash. I've always liked the fact that I work in a suburban neighborhood. Green grass, pedestrians, and kids are more hospitable than being trapped inside some sterile high-rise building all day.

It's almost 9:00 a.m. Footsteps thud against the floorboards, and the front door closes, followed by Kyle's voice. He says something like, "All right, if you're ready, we'll go ahead."

I strain to hear the reply, my stomach twinging and doing a little dip. A man clears his throat. "Yeah, sounds good."

That was Rance.

Another voice answers, "Great."

That has to be the seller, Martin Thomas. So, everyone is here.

I stand up as Kyle, Rance, and Martin come in through the wide doorway to the conference room. Kyle wears his usual facial expression of pleasant optimism and extends his hand for our clients to enter. "You've both met Aria."

I smile. "Good to see you. This is an exciting day."

"Hell yes, it is," Martin says. "And good morning to you too!"

A heavyset, fortyish man in a red polo shirt, he looks at me and laughs. His grin lingers like he's just made out in the stock market. I laugh back and glance at Rance, but he says nothing. His aspect reminds me of a funeral-goer. As he steps inside behind the seller, with him comes a strong, spicy fragrance. I take him in with a new pair of eyes. Probably in his early sixties like Nick, Rance has light brown hair clipped very short. It's neatly trimmed at the sideburns and edges. Narrow glasses rest over an aquiline nose. Wearing a light blue button-down shirt under a black blazer, he carries a briefcase of dark brown leather. He's clean-shaven. If I had to pick one word to describe him, it would be "meticulous."

"How do you do, Ms. Owen?" Mr. Epstein says at last. His eyes sweep over my body briefly.

I have on my usual business attire for work—a gray pants suit with a high-necked, white blouse and heels. Nothing to see here. "Very well, thank you. Please make yourself comfortable."

I motion toward the seat opposite me. Kyle will sit at the head of the table, with me on one side and Martin and Rance on the other. That way, we'll each be able to speak easily with the clients while they're looking through documents.

"Would you like some coffee?" I ask. The coffee maker, accessories, and glass mugs bearing our logo rest on a small, mahogany table in the corner behind me.

"I'm good," Martin says, plopping down in a chair and rubbing his hands together. He smiles at Kyle and glances down at the papers I laid on the table.

"No, thank you," Rance says. His face hasn't broken its plaster cast once yet.

Giving me a genial grin, my boss Kyle takes a seat and reaches for the first set of papers to review.

I take my seat and fold my hands on the table. When needed, I assist, producing a document, an addendum, or mentioning an extra detail that Kyle may have omitted. Martin sits up straight and never lets go of his pen. He doesn't say much unless he's asked a question. Besides Rance's rigid posture and emotionless face, everything goes the way it always does.

"I did want to check back on the information I requested yesterday," Mr. Epstein says after about twenty minutes. "Were you able to find out about any renovations I hadn't been aware of?"

"Yes," I say. "A new roof was put on in 2001. There was also some electrical work done in the early eighties and a walk-in closet installed. I have copies of those permits here. That's all the city had, and I also checked with Mr. Thomas." I nod at Martin. "He said there's been no work done at the property since the roof."

Martin chuckles. "And I only did it because I had to. The old one was damn near ready to cave in."

Epstein glares at me, shifting in his chair. "All right. But are you absolutely certain there was no additional work done in the smaller building? I'm still concerned about the annex area in back."

"I'm certain of it," Martin says. "The annex only has some basic electrical and was mostly used for storage. It got a new roof when we did the rest, but nothing else."

"May I see the permits?" Rance asks.

"Of course." I tug them out of a tabbed stack of papers and pass them across the table.

We watch Rance study the pages and switch back and forth between them. He tilts his head as he scans each sheet. He coughs. He flips pages again, allowing his gaze to linger on one of the electrical permits the longest.

I wonder what he's worried about since he saw every inch of the add-on during the walk-through. I recall he was interested in that area then, too. When Kyle and I first viewed the real estate, the annex area was the most unremarkable part of the entire property. Still, Nick's criticism must have colored my thoughts because there's really nothing strange about Rance's questions. Buyers always want to know as much as possible.

Mr. Epstein glances between Kyle, Mr. Thomas, and me. He frowns and opens his mouth, then shuts it again.

"I'm happy to answer any questions," says Martin. "I know with all the work the buildings already need, you don't want any surprises. I can tell you with certainty that 1984, the year listed on that permit there," he says, pointing toward the paper in front of Rance, "was the last time we did any major work in that area. I know it was a long time ago, but I remember because we'd installed a walk-in closet and needed some lights in there. We also converted that main room to a locker room for our guys, and I got a few recessed lights put in. So, don't worry. I hope that puts your mind at ease." He grins and folds his chubby hands on the table.

For the first time since he came in, Mr. Epstein tips up the corners of his mouth. He barely moves, and he still focuses his eyes on the city documents, but it occurs to me he's making an effort to smile. He glances at Mr. Thomas before gathering the permits into a stack and setting them aside. "Fair enough. Thank you."

Kyle smiles. "Very good. Mr. Epstein, do you have any more questions, or are we good to proceed?"

"No further questions," he says, sitting up straighter. "Yes, let's continue."

Mr. Thomas's face lights up, and he exhales slowly and leans back in his chair. Restraining a further display of happiness, he keeps his expression to that of polite regard. He rests his crossed arms on his ample belly.

We proceed to wade through documents, and two and a half hours later, everything's signed. The property is sold.

"Well, I certainly thank you," Mr. Thomas says. Now he grins and extends his hand to Mr. Epstein. "Been a pleasure doing business."

"Likewise," says Rance. He stands up briskly, returning Martin's grip with his manicured hand. He addresses Kyle and me. "Thank you all for your time."

"You bet," Kyle says. "We're glad to do it. Give us a call if you need anything."

Mr. Epstein takes the keys to his new property and grasps the handle of his briefcase. He departs, moving through the wide conference room door swiftly. Mr. Thomas leaves less quickly, saying a few more words of thanks and how thrilled he is "to have finally sold that place."

To me, it was a closing like any other closing. Nothing

odd about it. But after observing Rance for these couple of hours, a tense uneasiness clings to me. As I gather papers and pens off the table, my gaze flicks sideways to Kyle. "Maybe it's just me, but did you find anything about Rance's behavior odd?"

Kyle turns down the corners of his mouth and considers. "Nah. He has a conservative personality, so he's cautious. He did wait until the day before closing to look into permits and renovations, but he probably hadn't thought of it sooner since he's a first-time commercial buyer. I guess I've been at this so long and heard so many questions that Rance couldn't have been more normal if he tried." He laughs.

I nod. At twenty-five, I'm only three years younger than my boss, so it's hard for me to believe Kyle has "been at this so long." But he's probably right. I hate to admit it, but I know my perception of Rance Epstein was tainted before this last meeting. It's only natural that someone buying old warehouse buildings would want to know about previous remodeling or electrical work. I need to get out more. I'll put my new bike to use today.

AFTER GRABBING a quick dinner alone at the nearby Chipotle, I drive back to the office. I retrieve my mountain bike from the back porch, where I chained it beneath the awning. It's still strange not to be darting off to Trent's house as soon as I get off work. It hurts. If not for making myself exercise every day, the loneliness would probably kill me.

I head northeast toward Zilker Park, peddling in the bicycle lane along Bluebonnet. The day is still bright and hot, and some of the lawns are beginning to brown. Water restrictions have probably gone into effect. I try to look around and take in the suburban scenery when I smell something burning. The farther I go, the stronger the burnt carbon odor. Trying to place its direction, I turn right at the corner on Collier Street, which heads away from the park.

The first thing I notice is the smoke. Opaque gray and black, the thick mass reaches up to the late afternoon sky. I can't see the buildings, not yet, but the first thing I think of is the Lamar property. My mind races with "what if." I pedal harder.

11

Smoke billows from Lamar Boulevard in charcoal and slate gray clouds. My legs pump the bike's pedals faster, and I keep to the right of the street as much as possible to avoid parked cars. Keeping my eyes on the road just enough to make sure I don't run into anything, I strain to find the source of the smoke. I increase speed again, and as I follow the turn onto Lamar, I make out part of an Austin fire truck. Traffic is backing up. People are starting to get out of their cars. A group of pedestrians walks along the sidewalk where bystanders cluster to see the show, whatever it is.

My stomach cartwheels and I press the hand brakes to slow down. Police cars form a line, the red and blue lights from multiple vehicles dancing erratically. I watch the towers of smoke, denser and blacker now as they pour from the source. I draw closer. When I finally figure out what's happening, my core clenches. Is this a joke? It's not funny. 1515 South Lamar—the property we closed on a matter of hours ago—is burning. I pedal more slowly but don't stop yet. I want to get close enough to see how bad it is.

My nerve wavers in anticipation. My arms and legs
tremble as I steer the mountain bike, but with so many cops
and other emergency professionals around, the fear is bearable. For now. The police created a barricade with their
cruisers perpendicular to the yellow and white road lines.
Behind it, personnel shout. The firemen give one another
instructions I can't make out. But I recognize their bulky, tan
bunker gear with neon green safety stripes and yellow
helmets. Several of them move steadily in a line, their work
boots grinding into the white gravel as they carry a thick,
mustard-colored hose from its attachment to the fire hydrant
outside the new condos across the street.

I press my brakes completely, and the tires skid to a halt.
I swing off my bike and walk it the remaining way to the
group of onlookers. The smell of burning wood and smoke
hangs heavy in the stuffy summer air. Behind that, I catch
the faint scent of chlorinated water. As the firemen spray the
building with the high-pressure hose, steam plumes out
from the roof. I still can't find a flame. Not one. But then,
during a gap in the vapor, I see fire. It licks venomously at
the sky, and am I imagining it, or can I feel its brutal heat all
the way back here?

One of the firemen yells something. The team adjusts
the angle of the hose, arcing the stream upward. I glance
across the street near the other curb where they're running a
second hose from Engine Number 4. My mind goes wild
with scenes of Nick Pearlman holding a can of gasoline,
dowsing the ugly, metal buildings before tossing an incendi-
ary. That scenario is too obvious to be true. It sure fits,
though.

A blue Ford Taurus with a dent behind the rear fender
noses past the line of cars, driving in the wrong lane until it

can't go any farther due to the barricade. It jerks to a stop with a brief squeak of tires. The driver's side door flies open. A man wearing a black jacket and tan slacks launches out. He has short-cropped hair, glasses, and a hard-set face. Rance Epstein.

But his face doesn't stay set for long. He grimaces, shakes his head, and pounds his palm on the hood of the car. He stalks forward, putting his back to me.

"Fuck!" The word sounds strange coming from his prim mouth, just as the well-used, modest car he drives doesn't suit him. Rance grips something in his left hand. I can't tell what it is. He turns before raising his right fist as he restrains the urge to slam it on the sedan. Instead, Epstein runs his hand over the top of his semi-shaved head.

Part of me wants to go to him and say something. Anything. His property catching fire is the last thing I wanted to happen. But as I listen to him swear, I scan the crowd for Nick Pearlman. My pulse increases. The moths in my stomach knock themselves senseless. Coming here wasn't a good idea—but how could I have known?

Taking the handlebars and swinging my leg over the seat of my bike, I turn the front wheel to head back to the office.

"Hey," Rance calls over my right shoulder.

Great. I look up, pretending I've only now seen him. "Mr. Epstein."

"What happened? Did you know about this?" he asks. His forehead is all knotted up, his mouth twisted in disgust. He might lose his dinner on the white line.

Did I know about this? Is he serious?

"No. I saw the smoke and rode over to see what it was. I'm so sorry, and I still can't believe it." But I know the last part isn't entirely true. I was mildly if only half-sarcastically, expecting it from the first moment I saw the black clouds rising over the city, but I attributed those thoughts to my cynicism.

"How long have you been there?" he asks. He glares at me with his free hand on his hip.

"Just a few minutes," I say. "Why?"

"We just closed on the property today, and now it's on fire!" he says. Now I see it's a water bottle he clutches in his left hand. Shouting more profanity, with a lot of force for someone so tightly wound, Epstein throws his Ozarka at the black asphalt. The cap pops off, and water splatters out in an angry ribbon.

I'm not going to get into some heated discussion over whether I "knew about this." But then the fervent moths in my belly start clambering up to my esophagus. I can't help thinking about Nick Pearlman. What if Rance is in danger? If he is, he has a right to know. Will telling him make it worse? Or will not telling him be the greater evil?

I can hear myself now. Yeah, so Mr. Epstein, this creep named Nick Pearlman has been threatening me, and he was saying you're some kind of baddy we weren't supposed to sell to. But Nick hates me too, you see, because he knows I killed a guy. As for why he's out for you, Mr. Epstein, I have no idea—I just know he is. But I withheld all of this from you, thinking it wasn't all that important, and we sold the property to you anyway. Tough break that your buildings are burning down as we speak.

I wish there's a hole I could disappear into. Maybe Nick and Rance are long-feuding rivals, and if only Rance is made aware that Nick's out to get him, he could take measures to end it. But this train of thought seems fruitless. I know almost nothing, least of all how Nick's vendetta somehow ties back to Ayden. And if Nick already wants revenge for that, what will he do if I tip off Epstein? None of this makes enough sense to act upon.

"I just can't believe this," Epstein says to my silence. "Someone did this. Someone must have." Noticing one of the Austin policemen near us, he turns. "Officer! Officer. Hey, that's my property. Do you have any idea how the fire started?"

The police officer is walking toward the building, and as Epstein jogs after him, I hear the cop say something about "we haven't determined the cause." The fire department is still working to put it out, after all.

Well, considering the buildings have been unused for decades, and there's no electrical service, what cause could there possibly be besides arson? Lightning? There isn't a cloud in the sky. A neighboring building may have caught fire, and then this one ignited. I doubt it, but I can't rule it out. I wish I could get a better view. I sigh. My arms shake as I grip the handlebars with palms too sweaty to hold them. It's time to go home.

A final, fleeting desire to chase after Epstein and tell him about Nick tugs at me in agitating desperation. Then my heart starts pounding. The lightheadedness takes hold of me and threatens to knock me out while I straddle my bike.

Think. Survive. That's what I know, and that's what I'll do. I'm going to keep my mouth shut. This is for the authorities, not for me. I'll email Detective Spade, and he can warn Rance officially. And properly.

~

I ARRIVE HOME AFTER DARK. Margarita sits in the living room, sipping a glass of wine and watching a sitcom. She and I have day jobs, while Rebecca and Ann mostly work nights. Though I can't see the TV, I can tell what's playing because of the laugh track.

"Hey, Aria. Did you just get back from Trent's?" Really, she's asking if I'm seeing him again.

"No, I haven't seen him in weeks now, except for running into him at a restaurant. I was riding my bike downtown after work." I make for the stairs to go up to my room.

Margarita straightens on the couch and takes her feet off the coffee table. "Oh." She raises her eyebrows hopefully, then sniffs, wrinkling her nose. "You smell like smoke."

"Yeah, there was a fire on Lamar." I don't offer that it was the property we just closed on this morning.

"Oh, wow. I hope no one was hurt. Was it a bad one?" She sets her glass down.

"It seemed pretty bad, but the fire department was getting it under control. I don't think anyone was hurt. The buildings were empty." My pulse quickens. Even saying that makes me feel like I've said too much or that I'm lying. But I'd rather keep it to myself.

She nods absentmindedly as the show vies for her attention. "Well, I'm glad no one was hurt. That's the main thing. Oh, I almost forgot—it's trash night. This is your week." Margarita leans back, putting her bare feet up again.

"Thanks for reminding me. I'll take it out as soon as I put my stuff upstairs," I say.

Having four people in the house, we rotate taking the trash to the curb each week on Thursday. After depositing my purse and laptop on the bed, I pat two different pockets to ensure my pepper spray and knife are still inside. They're there. I get my flashlight and go around the back of the house, where we keep the large, rolling trash bin. Grabbing the handle, I push the base with my foot to set it on its wheels. I hold the flashlight in my other hand, shining the beam down the driveway on my way to the curb. I even shine the light at the street and into the yards on the other side, just to be cautious. Nothing unusual. I roll the trash can to the verge along the sidewalk and leave it there.

However, something about the mailbox catches my attention. I'm standing right next to it, and although the flashlight beam points at the ground, I can see something—a white square against the black metal. I know it's probably a flier, but my breath catches in my throat anyway. The fire set me on edge. Stepping closer to the mailbox, I find a folded piece of paper stuck between the little red flag and the exterior. I inhale and reach out to grab it.

No. I withdraw my fingers, thinking better of it. What if this is a message from Nick Pearlman? What if he found out where I live and delivered a nastygram? He might have left fingerprints, and I'll have physical evidence of him threatening me. Providing, of course, he was stupid enough to have written it barehanded.

After going back inside, I take some pink plastic gloves from under the kitchen sink. I tuck them in my pocket and return to the mailbox. I slip them on and carefully tug the letter out from behind the red flag. Without unfolding it, I jog up the driveway and let myself in the front door.

"Good night, Margarita," I call.

"Night," she says, holding up her free hand while she sips her drink.

I get to my room and quietly close the door behind me. I click on the nightstand light. Sitting on the bed, I hold the slip of paper in my trembling, gloved hands—hands that look more prepared to clean the bathroom than receive evidence. I unfold the paper carefully.

My breathing quickens. I wasn't expecting this, and I blink as I scan the words. The letter is in Trent's handwriting. I would know it anywhere. The thin, watery letters. And the slight, left-hand slant, even though he isn't left-handed.

Aria,

I want to let you know that I've decided to move on. You're a great girl, and I care about you a lot. But I have to pursue my career, and I can't give you the safe life you need. I hope you can forgive me and come to find your own happiness.

Trent

My face burns. The familiar ache smolders instantly, but there's no point in crying over it. My body goes slack, and I release the slip of paper. It flutters beyond sight below the edge of the bed. Since I'm already sitting on the mattress, I let myself fall and land on the comforter with my shoulder. I squeeze my eyes closed tightly, clenching my jaw as a wave of pain hits me.

Why is Trent telling me this now? He seemed friendly at the restaurant like he wanted to talk. And I've been giving him space, just like he wanted. But now he leaves me this. His words solidify my aloneness. It's far too real, and I bury my head in my arms. I was coping until this moment, but I don't want this. Not now, not ever.

I sit up, finally pull off the gloves, and throw them on the floor. I retrieve the letter from the carpet and return to the bed, where I sit cross-legged. I force myself to reread the words now that the initial shock has worn off.

What does he mean he's decided to move on? Move on from what? The fact of us not having a relationship? There's nothing to move on from. And as far as pursuing his career, well, he was going to do that anyway. I don't understand what goes on in his mind.

I shake my head. I set the letter on the nightstand. While I undress, I realize Margarita was right. My clothes do reek like I've been standing downwind from a campfire. I toss them into the hamper, brush my teeth, and get ready for bed.

After flipping off the lights, I turn on a fan for noise. Then, with trepidation doing backflips in my chest, I turn the fan off. I lie in bed, listening to the silence before I try to sleep. Unfortunately, too many images badger me. They pound, they needle, they whirl and tumble inside the blackness of my skull like a cyclone of insanity, and it's as mentally loud as it is disturbing. Surrendering to slumber is impossible.

Trent pushed me away just like Kyle said. Well, with his fiancée murdered earlier this year and left on his porch, I guess he couldn't help it. The wound is too fresh. He's vulnerable and unhealed. Yet, he seemed to have no problem meeting with that Naomi woman. Why? She probably isn't a sleep-screamer like me. It's doubtful she was raped or tortured, or all the other things that I was. And unlike me, unspeakable things don't dwell within depraved corners of her mind. But that doesn't mean the rejection doesn't hurt or that being alone doesn't terrify me. It does.

I stare at the ceiling and take slow breaths. And then, in one of my nauseating, stress-induced flashbacks, the image of my stepmother lying on the filthy floor of the County Road 140 house engulfs my mind and senses. I see her. I'm there as though it's happening right now. Toward the end, Korey beat Carol so severely she went unconscious. I knew she was comatose and not dead because I could see her breathing from my higher vantage point against the wall. But she never woke up again. All skin and bones from starvation, she died like that, carelessly thrown on the floor like trash. Her elbow jutted out disjointedly in a silent cry of helplessness.

I didn't do anything to help her in the end. She had done so much for me, and I didn't reach out to at least roll her onto her side in a more natural position. I couldn't because after Korey beat me senseless, too, he stabbed me six times and chained me to the wall. Except what the papers didn't mention, and few people know, is that he didn't exactly stab me in the usual sense. What Korey really did was bloodletting. It was a part of my purification, he told me.

Six puncture wounds, and none of them in vital organs, so although I would lose a lot of blood, I would die slowly. And if the blood loss didn't kill me, the infection would. Or the starvation. Or all three. I shudder, seeing the dirty knife ooze with my own gore. I wince to shut out the memory. If only Carol could have woken up and somehow escaped to get help. If only when she and I first came around, her mind wouldn't have been damaged by the knock-out chemical. If only someone would find us, I thought. If only. And through the pain and terror, my bottomless, desperate loneliness was strongest of all—it was a chasm I fell into again and again. I have never felt so alone in all my life. I thought I would die in there, and not a soul would know.

After sitting bolt upright in bed, I gasp and turn on the

nightstand lamp. I rub my face with my hands. I hate these waking nightmares. Shock and stress always spark them without fail.

But Trent found me in January. I'm alive. It seemed like a miracle at the time, and it still does now. I can't control whether Trent wants to be in my life or not, but I can act in the present. I can make a decision that might save someone, which is something I wasn't able to do for Carol. I don't care for Rance Epstein. The man is a few clauses short of a contract. However, after what happened to Ayden, I have enough blood on my hands for one lifetime.

Lying here, as I blink up at the ceiling with red eyes, it seems to me that doing nothing is the worst thing in the entire world. Maybe one day, the police will find my cold, dead body locked in a cellar somewhere. And maybe Nick will be the murderer. But do they have to find Rance's body too?

12

E dgy after my decision to help Rance Epstein, my fingers tremble as I unlock Median Realty on Blue-bonnet Lane. My cell rings. I jump so violently this time that I drop my purse. It hits the cement porch with the metallic rattling of keys. I swear, and after catching my breath, I crouch to dig out my mobile. My heart surges into my throat again. If it's another call from that creep, Nick, I need to make sure to record. But it isn't him. I frown, the confusion and tiredness from the bad night of sleep making my head hurt.

"Yeah?" I say. My voice comes out flat.

"Aria? Hey, it's Trent."

"I know," I say. "What's going on?"

He's quiet for a moment since he's used to me being appreciative and warm. This is new.

"Did you get my letter?" he asks.

"Yep. I got it. So, looks like there's no reason for you to call me now." I walk to my office so briskly my hip grazes the door frame. I toss my purse on the floor next to my desk. I flip on the light.

"Aria, maybe I'm missing something, but I thought that would make you happy. I thought you'd be relieved. Where did I go wrong?" he asks.

My mouth falls open. I put my hand to my head, wanting to throw the phone against the wall. Or maybe scream. "You thought that would make me happy? Sometimes I don't understand you at all. Besides, there's nothing to move on from since we weren't together."

Trent sighs. "Wow. Well, I guess I really misgauged this. Okay. I won't keep you before work. Just give me a call if you need anything, all right?"

"Give you a call if I need anything?" The ice in my voice melts a little, and hot venom seeps in to take its place. I swallow and purse my lips.

"If you want to," Trent says. "I just want you to know that if you change your mind, and if you want to call me, you know, if you ever want to, you can. I'm always here."

His words ring in my ears. I wonder why. Then I recall saying almost that very same thing to him months back when we met at Cianfrani Coffee in downtown Georgetown. His tone is even, the concern evident. He didn't strain to sound genuine. But I still don't get it.

I stop pacing and blurt, "If I change my mind?"

I really need to stop repeating everything he says, but I can't help it. Standing here with the phone glued to my ear, I feel like I'm going crazy all over again. He's the one who changed his mind, not me. But maybe that isn't fair. He never made up his mind in the first place, and I was pushing him. His fiancée hasn't been dead a year.

"Yes," Trent says. "You have an open invitation. Call any time."

I sigh. "Okay."

"Okay. Until the next time we talk, I hope things go really well," Trent says.

We hang up, and I shake my head. I don't have time for emotional gymnastics right now. The office opens in forty-five minutes, and there's stuff to do. I already phoned Kyle last night and let him know the property we sold yesterday caught fire. He didn't act nearly as alarmed as I did. My belly is still full of rocks over what I'm withholding—what I'm about to do. But there are no laws against warning someone. There are, however, laws against threats and arson, which is why I emailed Spade the latest developments last night. It probably isn't much from a legal standpoint, but the detective should know what I know.

I dial up Rance Epstein on my mobile. He picks up within two rings. I arrange to meet him for lunch, and despite his understandably dour tone, I manage to avoid giving any information over the phone.

We meet at Kerbey Lane Cafe on South Lamar at noon and take a booth near the large windows. The place is casual and bustling. Mismatched, plastic chairs in bold colors skirt the smaller tables in the middle of the room. Every seat is full. A trendy section of white wall with large holes in it to our left reveals glimpses of the waitstaff coming and going. The air smells like fish and chips.

Across the table, Epstein's face reddens, and a vein pulses on his forehead. He glares at me with a constipated frown. My heart races, and I sit on my hands to stop them from shaking. All I can think about is him suing Median Realty for what I'm about to tell him. But isn't that better than him winding up dead? For a moment, I hesitate. I stare across the table at Rance's flaming skin. My mind reels with confusion. It's as murky as my untouched mug of coffee.

"Mr. Epstein, I have to tell you something which I feel you have a right to know," I say.

Rance's forehead vein tics in acknowledgment. He doesn't answer, keeping his dark gaze riveted to mine.

I don't beat around the bush. There's no point. Instead, I explain the bizarre threats from Nick Pearlman. And that because I'm concerned, I'm imparting what I was told to hopefully give him some warning for whatever this guy is planning. I leave out that Nick also seems to have a vendetta against me for what happened to Ayden. Epstein doesn't need those details, so whatever I do say about it, if anything, will be brief.

"I've already been told about Nick Pearlman—by the police. I don't know anyone by that name. But you knew? You knew, and you didn't mention this before I signed on the property? The detective who called me didn't mention the source of his information. Un-fucking-believable." Epstein nearly comes off his seat. He snorts and glances off at some distant point as he shakes his head.

A flush of heat races across my cheeks, and I straighten. I did know that Detective Spade warned Rance but not to what extent. I don't want the withholding of my direct experiences with Nick to be what gets Mr. Epstein killed.

I say, "It didn't seem relevant at the time. I don't know this guy. And if he has something against you that shouldn't affect whether you buy real estate—he has no say over that. Do you know of anyone with whom you've had a long-standing dispute?"

"It didn't seem relevant at the time? Are you kidding

me?" He runs his right palm over his short-cropped hair and looks toward the restrooms behind us. "You have to be the—"

Before he can spit out his insult, I say, "No. This was some stranger who threatened me, both in person and over the phone. As you mentioned, I did give all the information to the police. I also have a court date set for a temporary restraining order. The truth is, I thought this had more to do with me than you."

Rance's left eyebrow twitches when I mention court. He frowns and glares at the wooden tabletop. His gaze flicks back up to me. "That doesn't make sense. I thought you said you didn't know him."

"I don't know him. I had never seen him until recently when he appeared outside our office one evening. And it doesn't make sense to me either. Somehow, he knows something about my past, and he's angry with me because of it. But it's something that doesn't have anything to do with him or you," I say. I'm not going to volunteer the specifics. "If I would have told you this sooner, would you not have bought the property?"

Epstein sniffs and takes a drink of his cola. His jaw muscle twitches. "Of course I wouldn't have."

But for some reason, I don't believe him. I recall his concern about the annex building. He scrutinized the old permits, his face drawn and his body tense when he asked if Martin had done any other renovations. Of all the square footage to look over, an insignificant addition was his primary focus. That dirty, wooden building, with no insulation and basic fixtures, the concrete soiled from critters. Why was it so important? My imagination starts running wild. With my history, it doesn't take much.

"Okay," I say. "Well, do you know of any reason someone wouldn't want you to have that property or would want to harm you?" He hasn't answered my question from earlier.

Rance almost rolls his eyes. "Of course not."

He isn't going to tell me. Also, he wants me to know I'm foolish for asking. He sits there, stiff and closed off. Instead of continuing his query or being antagonistic like he was at first, he withdraws into his uptight resentment again. I must be on the brink of learning something he doesn't want me to know. Tiptoeing around the edge of it.

If Trent were here, he might be proud of my initiative. Or he might be embarrassed for me, which I am myself. My chest tightens, and I shove the thought away. Trent doesn't care, and I need to quit lying to myself.

"Unless you have anything else for me, I need to get going," Rance says, adding, "since I have hundreds of thousands of dollars in fire damage." He glares at me over his barely eaten chicken sandwich.

"I don't think the damages will be in the hundreds of thousands," I say. I try to make my voice sound reassuring, but a trace of criticism leaks in. "Since the buildings have to be renovated anyway, you're probably only looking at a little more than what you were going to have already. But yes, the cleanup will be some work."

Secretly pleased with myself, I wipe my hands on a napkin. I haven't allowed him to intimidate me. He's lucky I'm here at all.

"Anything else?" he asks. He shoves his plate away.

"No. I told you everything I know."

Rance huffs. "Well, I don't think you told me *everything*."

I guess he thinks scowling while saying the words frightens me. But I'm scared all the time anyway, so whatever comes out of his mouth doesn't matter much. He scoots out of the booth, his foot kicking the support leg under the table.

"I think I can say the same for you." I prop an elbow on the table as I swivel to look at him. "You know, I just wanted to help. To do the right thing. I didn't have to say anything, especially since doing so puts me in danger. I don't know what Nick's problem is or what he's planning, but I thought telling you might help keep you safe. I regret that your building was targeted—if, in fact, that's what happened—but better it than you."

"Yes. Thank you." He gives me a stiff, formal nod. "Now, if you'll excuse me, I have ruined property to attend to."

I say nothing. He's still glaring at me with those cold, dark eyes, and I wonder if he expects me to apologize. Well, he's not getting that.

Rance leans down and takes the handle of his briefcase. After grabbing his ticket from the table, he turns on his heel, and without waiting for the waitress, walks to the hostess stand to pay. No sooner does he exit the restaurant than my cell rings. I dig it out and stare at the screen. It's becoming too predictable.

I answer and push "record." "This is Aria."

My gaze darts around the restaurant and out the windows that face the parking lot and a side street. I wrap my left arm around my waist.

"Choosing sides with no information is as good as cutting your own throat," Nick Pearlman says.

"Did you set that building on fire?" I ask. My hand shakes so much I lean my elbow on the table to steady myself. I wonder if I'll get lucky, and he'll admit to arson. I don't know that that's what happened. But what else?

He clicks his tongue. "Please. Why would I need to do

that? Like I said, you don't know what kind of person Rance Epstein is. But I can also tell you he didn't set fire to the building either."

"No shit," I say. "No one's stopping you from telling me whatever it is you want me to know. All you've done so far is insult me and label Rance Epstein a criminal. What's really going on here?"

"That's what I've been trying to tell you. But I can't over the phone. Just meet with me one time, and you'll leave with everything," Nick says.

"Why me? Tell the police. They're the ones who need to know. If Rance is doing something illegal, there's not much I can do about it," I say.

"There's something you could have done about it. You shouldn't have sold that property to him."

"Why?" I ask. I twirl my straw while I wait for him to spill it. He doesn't.

"Please, you only need to meet with me once. We'll do it in a public place, with lots of people around. It will be very safe for you. I have no intention of harming you, and I won't if that's what you're worried about."

"Absolutely not," I say. My phone starts to slip in my sweaty fingers. I switch hands, then wipe my palm on my slacks. Some of last night's dizziness returns.

I add, "Whatever's been going on between you and Rance needs to be sorted out by the police. Or at the very least a lawyer."

"No, this is your fight too. And you haven't paid your dues. Everything comes with a price," Nick says. "Even self-defense, as you put it."

I grab a clean napkin and wad it in my fist. A small,

nagging suspicion needles me. "What am I paying for, exactly?"

"You know damn well what you're paying for. And you've had blood on your hands far too long already. I guess an eye for an eye is the only thing people like you understand."

My free hand jerks and I knock my coffee mug over. Milky, brown liquid sloshes across the table and drips onto the floor.

An eye for an eye.

Any remaining doubt bleeds out of me and disappears. He knows I killed Ayden... and somehow, he knows about the blue eye ring. A sick chill runs down my spine all over again. I lean forward in the booth, ignoring the coffee spill and putting more weight on my elbows.

In a voice so calm it scares me, I say, "Sorry, but you're too late. Someone beat you to it, and I already got what was coming to me last winter. I have the scars to prove it."

"Tell yourself whatever lies you need to," he says. He hangs up.

I wonder what it will take to satisfy Nick's thirst for vengeance—what punishment he'll deem most befitting. Will it be one of my eyes or both?

13

W hen I get back from my lunch date from hell with Rance, Kyle's waiting for me. My young boss stands near the door of his office. He's frowning—a rare thing for him. Drawing his eyebrows down, he stares at the floor and flexes his fingers.

I stop in the entryway, waiting until he looks up. "Is everything all right?"

Kyle shakes his head. "No. Rance Epstein has threatened to sue us."

I drop my purse on the floor. I glance around and rub the back of my stiff neck. I knew there was a possibility of this happening, and yet I proceeded anyway. I was so out of sorts from Trent's letter and the flashback that kept me up half the night that warning Rance seemed like the only good I could do.

"Well, I don't think he has much of a case," I say.

"Apparently, he does. He said you informed him of the garbage this Nick Pearlman character has been spouting—

the stuff he's been threatening you with, or whatever he's been doing," Kyle says.

"Yeah, the thing is, I had to tell Rance what I know. Because his life might be in danger. But I don't see how anything I said can be used as evidence for our liability for the fire," I say. "He said Detective Spade already informed him about Nick, so regardless of what I did, Rance knew about Nick going in."

"I wish you would have checked with me before meeting with him. This makes it look like we were withholding information about the property," Kyle says.

"No," I say, crossing my arms. "And I can testify to that effect because we didn't know anything. Some stranger having a problem with Rance isn't information about the property. Not really. Besides, Nick's threats have more to do with me."

"I just don't understand, Aria. Why would you tell him this? And I don't get why this Nick guy has anything against you in the first place. Are you sure you don't know him somehow? I know you don't lie, but—" Kyle sighs, leaving the doorway and stepping into his office.

I follow. On the desk, chocolate and caramel scents waft from a small, open box a client gave him. "I truly don't know him or his motives. Nick told me he knows what I did in self-defense a year ago. But I don't understand why he's bothered by that unless he knew Ayden. That's the only connection that makes sense. Spade hasn't found anything either yet. Regardless, I had to tell Rance. I couldn't leave that on my conscience—especially if Nick winds up hurting him or trying to. It might be my fault for not saying something."

"Aria, you don't always have to do the right thing. Because the right thing isn't always the right thing. I mean, not in every case. If someone is threatening someone else, you just go to the police. Which you did. But now, you've placed yourself, me, and the business in the middle of this. I just wish you would have consulted with me first." He sighs. "Well, I guess we're going to court. I hope you're right that he doesn't have a case. I'm not so sure."

My knees are shaking, and I pull out the chair across from Kyle's desk. Kyle hasn't sat down. He still lingers near the door and fiddles with a leaf of the rubber plant.

"What should I do?" I ask. I take a seat.

"Right now, nothing. But please promise me you won't say anything else to *anyone* about this," Kyle says. He turns slightly, fixing his gaze on me.

I bite my bottom lip as I lag for a response. "I can't say I can promise that one hundred percent. What if something happens and I have to tell someone?"

"Aria, please. This is a mess. And it can get worse. Just promise me you won't say anything else to Rance. Not until we go to court and get this sorted out—permanently," Kyle says.

"Okay. I won't say anything." I'm not trying to lie, but I'm not sure I mean what I say, either. I look down at my lap and smooth the creases from my pants.

Kyle pads over and settles into his chair. "Good. Now let's see if we can get through the rest of this workday." He forces a small smile, and I know he's trying to make me feel better.

The strange thing is, I do feel better. It hasn't been a good day. It was full of tense conversations and now a threatened lawsuit. But at the end of it all, my conscience is clean. I didn't do what everyone wanted. It wasn't easy, and it earned me a lot of resentment. But I did the right thing, and because of that, I'll be able to sleep tonight no matter what else happens. I'm not sure I can say the same for Rance and Nick. I'm becoming convinced they both have far worse skeletons in their closet than I do.

WHEN I PULL up to my stone façade, two-story house in Round Rock, I notice a man with dark hair sitting on the porch, watching me. I slam on the brakes before I reach the driveway. The tires squeal. My body whips forward as I grip the steering wheel.

"Son of a—"

It takes me a second to realize the man is Trent. Shaking my head and swearing under my breath, I pull into the driveway, park, and turn off the car. Trent showing up like this after giving me that letter only proves he's more confused than I am.

I get out and close the door of my sedan harder than I intend before slowly walking up to the house. I halt a few feet away from Trent, waiting for him to speak first.

"Hey," he says. He rises and steps down to the walkway. "How are you?"

I intentionally pause for a few seconds. "I'm fine. What are you doing here?"

Trent clears his throat. "Is it all right if we talk about it inside?"

"Sure. We can speak upstairs in my room. Otherwise, there's no privacy."

"Great. Thank you." Trent smiles, and I have to admit he looks relieved. But the smile soon fades. Something

concerns him. He doesn't want me in his life—not really—
yet he called me, and now he's appeared on my porch.

When I unlock the door, I find Margarita, Rebecca, and
Ann on the couch. They're seldom home at the same time.
Rebecca's short, blonde hair contrasts Margarita's longer,
black locks, and Ann's a brunette like me. Almost in unison,
their gazes swing to Trent and hold. They've never met him,
but their undivided attention tells me they suspect this is
him—the guy who rescued me.

"Aria," Rebecca says. "You have to introduce us to your
guest." She stands and grins. Margarita and Ann pop to their
feet beside her.

Well, I'm glad some of us are excited. "Of course. Everyone, this is Trent."

"*The* Trent?" Margarita asks. She raises an eyebrow at
him, then at me.

"Yep. This is Trent, the man who found me and saved my
life." It's still true, after all.

I wait by politely while Trent and my housemates shake
hands and exchange a few words. When I move toward the
stairs, Rebecca grabs my arm.

I flinch and yank it away. "The arm grabbing has to stop.
I have ears."

"Sorry," Rebecca says, giving me space. "It's a bad habit. I
just wanted to say if you want to stay here and chat, or if you
want to use the table in the kitchen, it won't bother us a bit."

If she's concerned, I don't know why. But as I peer into
her wide eyes, I find curiosity, more than worry, reflected
there. Having just met Trent, she wants to know more. She
wants to figure him out.

"Thanks, but we'll just head upstairs. See you guys later."

I give an off-handed wave and start for the steps. I turn to find Trent lingering awkwardly.

"Nice meeting you," he says to the three women before following me.

We reach my room, and I shut the door behind us. Since I did laundry last night, the air smells like fresh sheets. Clean linens—as though that has any bearing on the present situation. Maybe it would for a normal woman in an actual romantic relationship, but not for me.

My face heats as I sit on the edge of the bed. I look up at Trent. He thinks of himself as average-looking, but beyond brown hair and brown eyes, he's not ordinary to me. My heart pounds, and I can't tell if it's because he's near me, temporarily raising me from my bottomless pit of loneliness, or because I'm hurt and confused by his communication lately. Maybe both.

I motion to the chair by my small desk. "You can sit if you want."

He pulls out the chair and slowly eases into it, his gaze darting about my modest but tidy bedroom. Four library books are stacked in a neat tower on the desk. On the dresser sits my Kindle, a six-inch-tall stuffed cat, a basket containing a few makeup items, and my black alarm clock with red digital numbers.

Trent squirms like he's uncomfortable. He leans forward with his elbows on his legs, then folds his hands and studies my face. "I'm sorry I dropped by unannounced. I've been a little worried about you."

"Worried about me? Why?" I frown. He doesn't know the latest developments in the Nick and Rance saga.

"I saw the news story about the warehouse buildings on Lamar. Wasn't that the property you were trying to sell? The one you said had been on the market forever, and you finally had a buyer for it? The reporter said the Austin Fire Department suspected arson."

I'm not sure where it comes from, but I chuckle. "Yeah, that's the same property. It's kind of the nucleus of my existence right now."

"Did you hear about the fire when it happened?" Trent asks.

"I saw it, actually. I was riding my bike after work, and I saw the smoke and the fire trucks. It looked pretty bad. There's been a lot going on lately, to be honest." I shrug off a chill. "But before we talk about that, I've got to say I'm thoroughly confused. You wrote me to say you wanted me out of your life, but then you call me, and now you're here."

Trent pulls back. His brow creases, and he swallows. "How could you possibly get that idea from what I wrote? I said that—" He pauses, looking sideways while he recalls the words. "—I had done some thinking, and if you wanted to stay with me, it was okay. Because you'd been coming over to the house a lot anyway, which was fine, and I just thought there wasn't much point in you doing so much driving. It's been so quiet without you. Too quiet." He pushes his palms against his jeans with stiff arms.

"How can you say that with a straight face? I have the letter right here, and that's not what you wrote," I say.

Trent's mouth falls open, and he glares at me like I'm speaking in tongues. "Okay. Let me see it."

I sigh, turning to the nightstand where I lay the letter. The folded piece of paper isn't there. I pull the drawer out and start rifling through it just in case I stuck it there last night. There isn't all that much inside, so it shouldn't be this difficult. A few pens, a notebook, a pair of sunglasses. Maybe it fell. I check the floor, but no luck.

"I had it right here," I say. I scan the nook beneath the drawer. I look near the bed, under it, and on the floor again.

Returning to sit on the edge of the bed, I rub my face. "I feel like I'm going crazy. I had it right here. It was a letter on a blank, white piece of paper, folded in half. I found it on the outside of the mailbox, underneath the red flag." I shake my head. "Damn."

Trent raises an eyebrow. "Are you absolutely *sure* it was a white piece of paper folded in half?"

"Yeah. I would stake my life on it. Why?"

"Because I wrote it on nice stationery from the academy and I stuck it in an envelope. Which I sealed." He continues to give me that look. "What did you say this letter said?"

I blink at him and cross my arms. "Well, I don't remember the exact words. The tone was patronizing. It said something about how you thought I was a great girl and cared about me, but you decided to move on. Something like that."

"Are you serious?" He stands up, his face blooming magenta. He takes a step forward, hesitates, then comes to sit beside me on the bed with over a foot between us.

His change in proximity makes me more confused. "Yes, of course, I'm serious. Are you saying that isn't what you wrote?"

"Yes, that's exactly what I'm saying. That isn't what I wrote at all. So, I don't know what happened. I would say it could be because my handwriting is bad—but it's not *that* bad. I just don't know. But what I said was I realized some things, and if you wanted to come stay with me, it would be all right. I mean, as friends, or whatever you're comfortable with. Whatever you want. I see how I wasn't being fair. We both had the worst year of our lives. It only makes sense that we get through it together."

For a moment, I don't move. On the one hand, I feel like I'm having hallucinations. My therapist was clear that people like me sometimes experience those, some kind of post-traumatic stress phenomenon. On the other hand, it's like I've been carrying a heavy pack all this time and finally slipped it off. The relief is comforting, like opening a window on a spring day.

"Wow," I say. "So, what does this mean in terms of how you feel about me? I want to make sure I understand."

Trent grits his teeth, something I know because his jaw twitches. He's never been one to talk about feelings often, or at least not deeply. He says, "I care about you a lot. And I like having you around. I don't ever mind the times when you get upset all that much because I understand. But as far as how I feel, because of what happened to Elizabeth, caring for you is about the best I can do right now. I don't think either one of us is in a position to rush anything."

That's logical. It's nice and sensible. But that doesn't mean I have to like it, and the nagging confusion still lingers. "But what about the letter? What does it mean? That I—I saw something written that wasn't really there?"

"I don't know, but I wouldn't worry about it. I'm here, aren't I?" Trent asks.

I sigh, allowing myself a weak smile. "You are here."

We wind up talking until almost ten o'clock. Since neither of us had dinner, we order pizza. In addition to ironing out the recent bumps in our relationship, or non-relationship as the case may be, I fill him in on the bizarre situation with Nick and Rance.

"Aria, I can't tell you how much I wish you wouldn't have got involved in that." Shoes off, Trent leans against a pillow propped on the headboard. His expression mirrors Kyle's when he informed me Rance threatened to sue. For once, the two of them had identical reactions.

"I know. I wish I didn't have to," I say. I sit crossed-legged on the bed facing him and turn my phone over and over in my hands. "I already told the police what I know, but I didn't know how much Detective Spade told Rance. It was keeping me up at night, not saying anything to him. And like I told you, I've refused to meet with Nick. He's an idiot if he thinks a woman is going to meet with him alone."

Margarita, Rebecca, and Ann are asleep, so we're able to leave the house without running into them. Outside, the night greets us with cool air, cobalt darkness, and quiet streets. The leaves of the maple tree shiver as the wind brings us scents of dewy grass. Somewhere the next block over, a dog barks a few times and stops. As I walk with Trent to the curb where his Chevy Colorado pickup is parked, the butterflies start in my stomach again. I wrap my arms around myself as he gets ready to leave.

"Trent, if I do stay with you, where will I sleep?"

Trent laughs as he goes around to the driver's side and opens the door. "Wherever you want."

re you going to stay over at Trent's?" Margarita floats out of the kitchen and locks her gaze on the rolling suitcase I pull toward the door.

I guess it's pretty obvious. "Yeah. I'm probably going to stay a few nights."

That's my story, and I toy with the possibility of sticking to it. Then again, who am I kidding? I'll probably be completely packed up and moved in within a week. But before going all-in, it just seems rational to try it with a fresh perspective. As I stand here at the threshold with the retractable handle in my hand, my loneliness is less. My fear is less. I'm not shaking as much. My palms aren't soaking wet like they usually are. It's nice to get a break.

Margarita edges closer to me. Though it's only the two of us, she lowers her voice. "Are you sure that's a good idea? I don't mean to pry. I just want to make sure you don't get hurt."

I laugh. "It's not your job to make sure I don't get hurt. Besides, it's probably too late for that. Thanks for the thought, though. I'll be fine. It'll be nice not to sleep alone every night. I've never been a fan."

Margarita blinks a few times. "Aria, I know it's none of my concern, but does he expect you to—I mean, you're not—"

"Are we screwing? Of course not. His fiancée was murdered, and I was hospitalized eight months ago for what my ex-boyfriend did to me. Give us a little credit where credit is due." I smile, but she gets the point.

She tucks her loose hair behind her ear. "I'm sorry, I couldn't help wondering. I don't want him taking advantage of you."

"No worries, you're not the first to wonder," I say, but I shouldn't have to explain it to anyone—or get their approval. "I'll probably see you in a few days."

I turn the knob and open the door. Margarita watches me leave, the frown never altogether leaving her face. I guess I'll never know why. Just as she'll never understand the complexity of my life after Ayden's death and what Korey did to me in the County Road 140 house, I'll never understand whatever it is my housemates seem to want for me.

AFTER WORK, I drop by the shooting range on my way to Trent's. Besides being a good place to practice, the place also carries a large inventory of firearms. Today is as good a time as any to buy my own. This way, I'll no longer have to rent one when I go, and if push comes to shove with Nick, I'll have the ultimate protection.

I buy a Sig Sauer P238. The same model I've been practicing with, the small, pewter gray pistol fits my hand well, especially with the extended magazine. That means it'll hold seven rounds in the mag and one in the chamber. While I'm here, I also snag a gun cleaning kit and an inside-the-waist-band holster. As I emerge from the store, gripping the handle of the pistol's plastic case, my heart races. Can I really pull the trigger in a life-or-death situation? I hope I never have to find out. I stow my new weapon in my luggage with the rest of my things.

On the way to Trent's, I can't shake the feeling that someone's following me. A black car weaves in and out of traffic. It's there. It's gone again. Then it reappears. The driver's keeping me in sight. I know Nick drives a black Mercedes, but I can't tell the make of the sedan from this distance.

By the time I pull onto the gravel driveway off County Road 152 in Georgetown, I've lost the car on the way, or the guy gave up the pursuit. Good. Of course, I can't forget that I might be paranoid from Nick's threats and Rance's lawsuit. The car may have simply been a random car. Still, I can't help but remember thinking the same about what turned out to be Korey's SUV on my own street.

It's warm out, still in the upper eighties, and a brilliant orange and rose sunset lights the western horizon. After shutting off my Camry and locking it, I scan the recently mowed yard. Trent always leaves a few prickly pear cacti at various intervals along the scrubby ground. They do give the place character. The cedar post and steel mesh fence bordering the yard doesn't detract from the ruralness out here but rather lends a sense of security. It was built earlier this year and still looks brand new. I can't smell the cedar anymore, but the chocolate daisies in the adjacent mesquite prairie more than make up for it.

With my key in hand, since I never gave it back, I go up the few porch steps to the small, white house. I try the dead-bolt cylinder, and it turns. When I open the door, Trent is on the living room floor, pulling on his sneakers.

He smiles. "You're right on time. I was just about to walk over and pick up my last paycheck from Tim at Corbin Ranch. Do you want to go with me?"

The ranch where Trent used to work is a stone's throw from here. In fact, Trent's rental house and much of the nearby fields belong to Tim Corbin, the owner. Over the past several weeks, Trent has been wrapping up his employment with Tim since he's now full-time at the police academy. The cadets don't stay overnight in barracks. They end the day at 4:00 p.m. and start each morning at 7:00, so Trent having any kind of day job is no longer feasible.

"Sure," I say. "I grabbed a bite after work, so aside from changing shoes, I'm all set."

I roll my suitcase inside, slip off my heels, and tug out my sneakers. I don't bother changing out of my work clothes. I'll walk in my slacks and short-sleeved blouse and change when I get back. Trent slips his Ruger pistol in the holster inside his jeans. I like that he carries it everywhere, and maybe soon that will be me. For today, I have my little switchblade knife and pepper spray.

We head out into the warm evening, the gravel crunching under our shoes on the driveway. Beside County Road 152, wiry shrubs and cacti grow plentifully, and a few purple wildflowers nod in the faint breeze. We cross to the other side of the street and walk on the shoulder. A barbed-wire fence runs along each side of us. To our right stretches a section of Tim Corbin's ranch which comprises the sheep pasture. Up ahead, the sectional feeder and weathered, gray barn appear just as we ascend the slight grade. To our left lies a cattle field with long, dry grasses and weeds by the fence.

Trent trudges along on my right, closest to the street. He takes my hand and smiles at me. I smile back.

"Do you mind?" he asks.

I chuckle. "No, I guess I'm just surprised."

"We've held hands before," he says.

"Yeah. We have," I say. I grin back and don't add that yes, I've held his hand before, but never after getting a letter saying he wants me out of his life. Unless I really did imagine it. The sad part is, I almost want that to be true. If it were, then maybe I hallucinated Ayden's ring. Maybe I'm not a monster. I can dream.

"Besides the nightmare with that Epstein guy, how's work been going?" Trent asks.

"It's been fine. Business as usual," I say. I veer to step around a glass bottle.

"Well, good," he says. His gaze flicks at me sideways a couple of times. He's trying to read me, or he's withholding something he wants to say.

I'm not in a small-talk mood, so I go straight for what weighs on my mind. "Your friend Naomi from the police academy—were you dating her before? I mean, I don't care if you were. I was just wondering." There's another whopper. I wonder if I could put "lying" as a skill on my next résumé.

Trent stops and drops my hand. His face goes all serious. "No, we've never dated. We're just friends. I'd never ask you to come live with me if I was seeing another woman."

I nod. "Well, that makes sense."

He stares at me.

"Are you offended that I asked?" I tilt my head. My hand feels cold without his warm skin against it.

"No," he says. "I guess I just thought you knew me better than that."

He is offended. I hurt his feelings, but he'll never admit that. "No, I just thought you might have dated before. Not now, of course. I didn't think you'd date her if I were living with you."

"But you thought maybe we broke up two days ago, and then I asked you to move in? Like you were a rebound or my second choice?" he asks.

Geez. He's sure given it more thought than I have. I sigh. "No, not exactly. The thing is, I didn't *think* anything, at least not to that extent. I was curious about your relationship with Naomi, so I asked."

His jaw muscles flex, and he glances at the road. When he starts walking, he doesn't take my hand again. "There's no relationship. Just friendship."

"I understand," I say. "I'm sorry if I upset you." And I leave off that friendship is a type of relationship, just not a romantic one.

"It's fine. You didn't," Trent says. Our noisy steps punctuate the silence. "So, have you thought any more about getting a gun?"

"I have. As a matter of fact, I bought one today. I'm still not as good a shot as I'd like to be, but I'm working on it," I say.

Trent's face brightens. He looks at me now. "Oh, you bought one? What kind did you get?"

"I got a Sig Sauer P238. You wouldn't believe how easy it is to use—the slide is like butter," I say.

"Wow, that's great. Those are top-of-the-line guns. You

know what we should do next week? Go shooting together. If you're having trouble with your accuracy, I could probably help. I can't believe how much better I've become since starting at the academy," Trent says.

"Sounds like fun. I go to Shoot Point Blank a few times a week—well, within the last week." I laugh because I speak as though we've been apart for months. It feels like it.

"I'm so glad you're doing that." He smiles, a soft admiration in his eyes. Maybe the way to Trent's heart is through his holster. Will he melt when I show him my Sig?

As we head into the turn past the small ranch pond, a dark-colored vehicle looms toward us on the narrow, two-lane street. I think about being followed earlier—the feeling of it or the unproven actuality. I can't discern much yet. But as the vehicle draws closer, it appears to be the same one—a black luxury car.

My heart starts pounding, and dizziness shakes me. It's not only that I associate that type of car with Nick, but it's how oddly out of place it is for rural Georgetown. Sure, some people out here drive nice cars, like anywhere else. But since I've been visiting Trent at his little shotgun home, I can't recall seeing even one. In this pastoral section of Williamson County, it's mostly pickup trucks, modest sedans, or sport utility vehicles that pass.

Giving Trent no explanation, I stop short. My pulse rabbits frantically as I take him by the arm and pull. "Come on. I don't like the look of that car."

He complies instantly. I lead him to the barbed-wire fence, where I slide through a gap and wave for him to follow. Since we've crossed the street, this puts me on a stranger's property. It's not Tim's, but I don't know what else to do.

Trent understands the need to act with urgency when someone knows something you don't, so he doesn't ask. He glances at the approaching car. As he slips through the barbed wire, he snags his shirt.

"Hurry," I say.

I look back and recognize the vehicle as a black Mercedes like Nick's. It slows down. The windows are tinted so dark I can't see anyone inside. The car continues reducing its speed.

"Shit, I'm stuck." Trent fumbles with his shirt. He's so badly caught he's almost pulling out of it backward.

I grab Trent's sleeve and rip it free. As I break into a jog, the car's passenger's side window starts sliding down, just a hair. I swear something pokes out through the opening. Something small. Something black. Can I honestly say it's a barrel of a gun? No. There isn't time to look again or think about it. We have to move and hope it's not already too late.

Trent curses. He sees what I see. We break into a run, pushing our legs as hard as they can go. At first, Trent surges ahead of me, but I catch up in a couple of seconds.

Bang!

15

T he gunshot echoes harshly through the still countryside. The strange, metallic resonance vibrates inside my skull and chest cavity. My ears ring, and I stumble, but I catch myself before smashing into a prickly pear face-first. I pump my legs and keep running. Of everything I've experienced, this is the first time some-one's shot at me.

Trent glances in my direction. He probably wonders if I've been hit. For a second, I do too, and I wonder the same about him. But there's no pain, so I assume I'm okay. And Trent didn't cry out, and he's still racing alongside me. We're lucky so far.

I swerve side-to-side erratically as I dart through the field. Tall grass, thorn weeds, cactus, and young mesquite trees stretch over the prairie before us, and the farther back we go, the safer we become. The less likely the shooter can hit us. I try to put the trees between me and the car as much as I can. But sometimes, I'm exposed on the empty field— that's all there is. I glance at Trent every few seconds. His gaze flicks back at me, but we don't speak. We run until we can't see the road anymore. An old barn and a watering hole for livestock spring to view straight ahead.

A dark thought hits me. "Isn't this close to where someone shot at you before?"

"Kind of, but that was on Tim's property, on the other side," Trent says. "Come on."

We maintain our sprint and head for the rear of the old barn. I don't hear any more gunshots, and we're now too far away to see if the car is still there. I pant, my breath getting raspy from the breakneck run, but I don't slow down until I stop behind the wooden, gray wall of the outbuilding. My lungs ache. Huffing, I crouch down to ease my burning legs. My body shakes so hard it affects my balance, and I teeter. I lean against the barn.

"Did you see anyone?" I ask.

"No. I saw what you saw. Anything else you want to tell me?" Trent smiles, and I wonder how he could possibly find anything about this situation amusing.

I take a deep breath as sweat trickles down my face. "I already told you everything I know. But that car looked like Nick Pearlman's Mercedes. I saw it the day he showed up outside the office."

Trent nods. He pulls his cell phone from his back pocket and calls the police. While he speaks to the dispatcher, I analyze him. Standing fairly still, he only moves his foot now and then or twists to look behind us or out into the prairie on either side. He's placed his free hand on his hip. He explains our situation slowly in a calm, clear voice, as though calling in shootings is something he does every day.

Of course, he loves this sort of thing, which was why he started at the police academy to work as a deputy sheriff for

Williamson County. He *wants* to call in shootings every day. Well, that's peachy. I wipe my forehead, my core smoldering at his secret exhilaration. That guy could have killed us.

Trent hangs up. He gazes across the field of dried, brown grass.

"Did they advise you on what we should do now?" I lean against the barn to steady myself. The salty odor of sweat touches my nose, and my eyes burn. My hairline is soaked.

"She said to stay put if we're safe here, but I don't like the idea of being on this guy's property. I think Tim knows him, but I don't. We don't need to get shot at again, this time for trespassing," Trent says.

"I couldn't agree more," I say. I blink to clear my vision.

"Come on, we'll walk back, but we'll go this way." He nods in the direction of his house.

We amble through the tall grass and bur marigolds. With my senses heightened from running for my life, I notice the yellow wildflower's light vanilla scent more than usual. And it's curious that despite how the terrain is rocky, uneven, and peppered with cacti, we ran with no trouble. Nothing like a brush with death to give your feet wings, I guess. Soon, the barbed-wire fence looms into view. The narrow road lies behind it, and on the other side, I can make out part of Tim's ranch. It holds a graying, dilapidated building and a dark pond with a decaying dock. About a dozen sheep of different colors huddle around the sectional feeder.

I scan the road but don't see any sign of the black Mercedes. Every time a vehicle passes, I nearly faint. My pulse increases and a wave of lightheadedness threatens to crush me. A red truck drives by. Then a blue car. A larger, white delivery truck with "Fish" written on its side in blue letters rattles alongside us and then disappears up the road, heading toward the small town of Weir, Texas. The luxury car never reappears.

By the time we cross over County Road 152 and step onto the gravel driveway leading to Trent's house, something flashes in the corner of my eye. A black and white Williamson County Sheriff's vehicle is turning in. Its red and blue lights revolve, but the siren isn't engaged. The officer pulls up close behind Trent's silver Chevy Colorado pickup.

The deputy sheriff who introduces himself is a man named Bennet. Trent and I brief him on what occurred. With the Mercedes long gone and both of us unharmed, if shaken, Deputy Bennet takes down the information and soon leaves.

Now the sun sinks below the horizon. In the fading light, a dark cobalt and violet haze lingers in place of the sunset. I reach the porch before Trent and unlock the door, quickly locking it again after we're both inside. It's still in the lower eighties outside, but the air conditioning sends an unnatural chill down my back. I sit on the couch and wrap my arms around my middle. Shuddering as I draw a breath, I fill my lungs deeply like I'm just now remembering to breathe.

Trent's frown drives a dark valley between his eyebrows. He hesitates by the doorway, brooding, but then springs to life. He dives onto the sofa next to me. "Aria, I have a strange question for you."

"All right." I rub the stress from my face. We aren't hurt, after all, and I need to calm down.

"You mentioned that Nick was threatening you about the Lamar property, saying you should have somehow broken the contract with Epstein and sold to him instead. But you went ahead and sold to Epstein, and then later that same day, the place gets torched. You mentioned Nick drives a black Mercedes, and today someone shot at us from one. But there was something else you told me. Your buyer seemed concerned with an annex of those warehouses—that he kept asking about permits for work done in that section, almost like he was looking for something specific. But he never said what. How would you feel about me having a look at that burned building?" he asks.

My hands still shake too much, and I slide them under my legs. "Are you joking?"

"No," Trent says. "I think it's worth a look. The reporter on KXAV even said the fire was being investigated as arson. But there's something we're missing. We won't know what it is until we find it, and the only way to find it is to look. Don't worry—I don't expect you to come with me, and I'm not going to do anything besides have a look around."

My breath tremors as I exhale. "Trent, I don't think you realize what you're saying. The police taped off the area. It might still be off-limits. Like you said, it's already being investigating for arson. We don't need to go tampering with that. And I'm sure Nick is hoping I'll do something stupid, and no offense, but that's what you're proposing. That we step right in it and get caught. I can't prove he shot at us today, but I'd be thick to believe otherwise. He has it out for me, for Rance Epstein, and soon he will for you too, if you're not careful."

Trent nods. "Okay. You're right. But first of all, we're not going to tamper with it. And secondly, *we* don't have to do anything. I can go by myself. I don't mind. I have a gun, and I'm not going to be doing anything I shouldn't be, just look-ing. I'm only asking you because you probably know a way in. Maybe one of your keys to a back door still works. I'd prefer that to climbing in one of those broken windows." He glares at me, poised on the edge of his seat at the thrill of this idea.

I sigh, pull my hands out from under my legs, and run them through my hair. We don't retain keys to a property once it's sold, but I don't feel like explaining right now. I cover my face to stall before looking up again. "It's almost like you've learned nothing from everything that's happened. It's like you find new ways to put yourself in danger, and then you do it. Why not just leave it alone? Leave it for the police—I mean, the police on duty now, who aren't still in training."

"I could ask you the same question. Why didn't you just leave it alone—this thing with Nick and Rance? Who gives a shit if they kill each other? Let them. It's their life, not yours," Trent says.

"It's not right to sit by and do nothing while someone who's probably innocent gets his property torched and maybe gets killed. That's *way* too much 'leaving alone' for me." My chest twinges, and I glower at him.

"Aria, you don't always have to try and save everyone. Not everything is your fault," Trent says. He slides his arm around my waist.

So that's what he thinks. If he knew everything about me, he might reconsider. My ears burn, and I don't feel like examining whether he's right or not. I tuck my trembling hands back under my knees. "No, it's not that. I don't want blood on my hands if Nick kills Rance. He might do it anyway, but to stand by and not let Rance know Nick was after him would be gross."

"Fair," Trent says. "But why are they both so concerned with this property? What are they hiding? What's the big secret? If we can answer that question, we'll find out what all this is about."

"Yeah, but that doesn't explain why Nick has some weird vendetta against me for what happened with Ayden. He knows. And I don't know how he could possibly know. There was no media coverage. We told no one. The police said I acted in self-defense, and Ayden's family didn't file charges. Now I've got a stranger after me, saying I'm supposed to pay for what I did. But it doesn't add up."

"Exactly my point. It doesn't add up. That's why I want to go and have a look. If I find nothing, great. If I do find something, I'll just report it. It's true I don't have permission, but as long as I don't touch anything, I don't see it being a problem. Come on, Aria, humor me." Trent pulls me closer, giving me a little squeeze.

Another chill runs through me. He knows he's supposed to have a warrant. "Well, you shouldn't have to go by yourself. I want to tag along, and you need to bring your gun. Not that I need to tell you that."

I give him a brief smile. The only reason I'll accompany him is that the thought of something happening to Trent seems worse than allowing it to happen to myself. But it's not funny at all. It isn't amusing that the guy who saved my life wants to be a cop and likes seeking out danger for a thrill. He might have given other reasons, and although those reasons are also true, I know the rush he gets fulfills some need for him. I don't know what it is. But it's there. And that need seems to be there for him all the time.

"Now you're talking," he says. He grins at me, studying my reaction. "How does tomorrow after dinner sound to you? You know, so we'll have light. Oh... you thought I was going to head over there right now?"

I guess the way I'm digging my trembling hands into the couch cushion tipped him off. "I did think that. Tomorrow after dinner sounds terrible. It's a date."

I PULL up to the curb on Collier Street in Austin after eating an early dinner. I told Trent it would be best to park here, a street adjacent to Lamar Boulevard, so our vehicles won't be noticed. I got permission from Kyle to leave not long after four o'clock. I said I needed to attend to a few things, but I didn't say what. Although it's going on 5:30 p.m. now, it's still blazing hot, with a fiery sun dipping below the buildings downtown.

As I wait with my fingers curled around the steering wheel, I watch Trent's silver pickup truck pull over on the side opposite me. He gets out in a blue flannel shirt, jeans, and work boots. He pulls a brown, leather tool belt from the cabin and straps it on—police cadet turned construction worker. Trent strides my direction across the asphalt, and I swing out of my sedan.

"That's a good look for you," I say. "You'll blend right in."

"I'm counting on it," he says. He gives me a crooked grin. The excitement emanates from him. Oozing from his pores, it hovers around his body in an almost tangible glittering, fuzzy cloud. He's in his element, and we haven't even started yet.

Trent asks, "Did you bring the key?"

"No, Median no longer has one. I looked to see if there was a spare we may have forgotten to give to Rance, but there wasn't any. So, we might wind up climbing in a window after all."

"Okay. Here, slip these on real quick." He hands me a pair of latex gloves. I tug them on as he pulls on his own.

We step onto the dusty parking lot of the warehouse building, the chalky gravel turning our shoes white wherever it touches them. The yellow police tape flutters in the tepid breeze, and I duck underneath it. Trent follows. We study the outside of the main building as we make our way to the front. Windows grin darkly with teeth of broken glass. The black carbon residue reaches above them to the roof like shadows left by the flames. At least the structure isn't falling in on itself, and when we arrive where the front door used to be, I see there's no door. The firemen must have broken it down to get in. Well, that solves the problem of not having a key. A black, yawning entryway greets us with the foul breath of a thousand ashtrays.

16

My stomach wriggles like a fish as I aim the flashlight beam into the burned Lamar warehouse building and step inside. The place is black from ceiling to floor, with charred, crumbling beams and bits of indiscernible debris piled everywhere. Interestingly, the high-pressure water hoses caused the greater part of the mess. Since the building was mostly empty before the fire, there's room to walk.

Being familiar with the property, I lead the way, and Trent follows. Although I still faintly hear the traffic on Lamar, as we shuffle inside, our footfalls take on an intrusive thump within the ruined surroundings.

"The fire probably didn't start here," Trent says.

"What makes you say that?" I ask.

"If it had, it would be a lot worse. When we find the source, there will probably be a big hole or something similar."

My only experience with fire was what happened with Ayden, and since I don't remember it, maybe that doesn't count. The police said a spilled can of gasoline ignited, and that's what lit up our unfortunate shed like a Christmas tree. It was black from top to bottom, the fire raging long enough to burn through the wall and part of the floor. Because of that fact, which I observed the day after, I agree with Trent's reasoning. The side area near the shelves, where the police said the fire started, took the most damage.

"Where's the part Rance was so concerned with?" Trent asks.

"It's toward the back. We need to go through this building, through a small adjoining hallway, and into the next building. The annex is back there." I point.

"Interesting," Trent says. He coughs into the crook of his arm.

"It is," I say. "Especially since it's the least interesting part of this whole uninteresting place." I'm kind of relieved that Trent also finds Rance's behavior strange, per my description. Kyle couldn't see it.

When we arrived, I was so preoccupied with what to do if we couldn't get in that I forgot I brought masks. I pull them from my back pocket. "Here, you'll need this."

I hand one to Trent, holding my flashlight between my knees while I slip on my own. "These aren't the right kind. I got them from our cleaning caddy at home. But they're better than nothing."

Trent takes it. He heaves out a relieved sigh. "They're perfect."

Having my mouth and nose covered helps more than I thought. I'm now taking regular breaths instead of shallow ones to minimize the offensive stench. I shine the flashlight beam along the walls. We can see the old, exposed insulation—what's left of it—and the old wiring. But a lot of what we illuminate isn't decipherable as anything but a charred, sooty mess. The burnt blackness surrounding us hangs palpably like air composed of thick ink we can reach out and touch. I begin dragging myself along with effort as I wade through the dense atmosphere. While gripping the flashlight tightly in my right hand, my shaking fingers make the beam dance around erratically.

I stop and aim the light at a gnarled patch of wall. Speaking through the dust mask, I raise my voice. "You see this old wiring? In looking for a cause, besides arson, I would normally say this is something for us to keep in mind, except there's no electrical service right now."

"What's wrong with the wiring?" Trent asks.

"None of it's to code. I know from the inspection report. This was one of the many things that needed to be fixed. But since there's no power, knowing this doesn't help us much." I continue, lighting the way in front of us. "The hallway is up here."

We walk to the wall, where I find the edges of the hall doorway. I stop, my breathing and heart rate so fast I don't know if I can keep going. Whereas the part of the building we stand in currently is a dark and confusing mess, at least it's large and open for the most part. The doorway drops away from the wall like a slit into some rotting dungeon or another dimension. The smallness of the space unsettles me.

"You want me to go first? I can. I don't mind," Trent says. He places his hand on the small of my back.

I envy his normalcy. He doesn't get hit with a panic attack every time he does something adventurous. Taking a deep breath, I strain the smoky reek through my mask. I can almost taste the carbon on my tongue. Bitter. My gaze darts around for a moment, and I bend over to put my free hand above my knee and lean my weight on it.

"Yeah, why don't you go ahead," I say. "I'll be right behind you."

Trent shines his own flashlight beam into the ominous hallway. I follow, but I don't forget about the space behind us. As bits of dreck grind under my sneakers, I glance in all directions, swinging the light over every surface and trash pile. I'll be damned if someone's going to sneak up and catch us off-guard. It isn't going to happen.

Fine soot covers the hallway from ceiling to floor, but it's free of debris. We only have to walk about thirty feet before entering the more open annex area—the wooden building. This first room is about five hundred square feet with bare, uninsulated walls punctuated by charred studs. The wet floor gleams. A pool of black water has accumulated near the center.

Trent turns to me. "Is this it?"

"Yeah. This is the first room of the add-on portion," I say. "What should we be looking for?"

Trent swings the light around, searching the corners, along the wall, and across the smoke-blackened floor. "Something which won't be obvious to us. Something hidden. Anything that looks a little bit odd, we should investigate it. It doesn't look like the fire started here either."

"I agree." I crouch down to look at the concrete. There's nothing unusual about it besides how coated it is and that the foundation has shifted and is no longer level.

We wander into the next room, but it's empty like the others we've seen. There are no obvious hiding places and nothing that looks worthy of further inspection. My lungs ache, and sweat mists my face. The mask sticks to my skin, and I wish I could take it off. But the stink is noticeable with it on—without it, the smell was overwhelming.

Trent asks, "Is this all there is to the part Rance wanted more specs on?"

"There's one more room off the side of the first one we were in," I say.

My stomach dips, but at the same time, I get a nervous flash of hopefulness. I remember the lockers and large closet in that one. I recall it was that room specifically that Martin mentioned at closing. It was where workers changed out of filthy clothes to go home. But no one would hide something in such predictable places as closets or lockers—not big somethings, anyway.

After working our way to the room, we find that it's burned mostly to the studs like the others. I don't need my flashlight to find the corner. It's wide open and gaping, a raw wound bleeding sunlight from the wall and ceiling. Bare, copper wire hangs down and catches threads of daylight that burst in. Near the hole in the floor is a large, sooty, black pile of goo. It's as though something plastic melted and turned into a molten mountain of sludge.

"Looks like we may have found our source," I say.

"Agreed," Trent says. He sniffs.

I wipe my gloves on my old jeans and produce my mobile phone from my back pocket. With the flash on, I take photos. I even snap a few without the flash just in case it obscured something in the previous ones. The sunlight may reveal clues the flash washed out.

My pulse quickens, and I back up toward the lockers. "Am I imagining it, or do I smell motor oil?"

"You're not imagining it. I smell it too," Trent says.

I can't pinpoint where the petroleum odor is coming

from. I go for the closet first, only because it's something I can easily examine. It has two wide double doors, which are both unlocked. As I grip the handles and tug, they creak open on rusty hinges. My heart pounds as I shine the light into the space. It's a walk-in, about six feet wide and going nearly ten feet back, with shelves on one side. Besides being mostly black like everything else, it's empty, just as it looked before the building inspection.

Trent brushes my shoulder with his chin as he looks past. Shining his own flashlight around, he peers at the shelves and into the corners. "Are there any other compartments in here? Like small doors? I've sometimes seen that in old buildings like this."

"Not inside here. But you're free to look. I could have missed something," I say. We scour the inside of the closet, but it's as empty as it looks.

The lockers are affixed to the wall outside the right-angle turn of the corner where the closet opens. They're just farther back, near the wall opposite us that is perpendicular to the closet door. I chew the inside of my cheek as I study them. There used to be a row of plastic benches too, but now all that's left are metal stumps. One by one, I lift the locker latches, finding nothing inside. Most of them open easily, but three of them are locked.

"I don't suppose you have a pair of bolt cutters in that nifty tool bag?" I ask.

"I do," Trent says. "But I didn't bring a bomb-disposal suit, so if we find any explosives, don't ask."

"I'm glad you're not holding out on me," I say.

Trent sets the pair of mini bolt cutters on my palm. With my gloved hands, I proceed to cut the locks, patiently working at each shackle until I break through the steel. One at a time, the broken locks clatter to the concrete floor. The sound rings in my ears. Afterward, I stand quietly for a moment, listening.

Birdsong reaches us through the hole in the ceiling, and I can still catch hints of traffic from Lamar. Wind plays through flapping bits of insulation. There are no other sounds. I wipe my forehead with my shirt sleeve, taking a deep breath and telling myself it's doubtful anyone heard us poking around in here. Good. Still, I'm not letting my guard down.

I open the first locker. Though the interior is almost as black as everything else, I can identify most of its contents. It contains an old Sony Walkman, a magazine, and an empty Coke bottle. Locker number two holds folded clothes. Locker number three contains what looks like a bottle of prescription medication, a thermos, earplugs, and a rumpled t-shirt.

Trent crouches down and gives the contents of each locker a cursory inspection as well but doesn't touch anything. Then he stands and reaches toward the top of the locker section. When he pulls, it rattles slightly, like it isn't firmly attached to the wall. He darts his gaze across the torn, blackened room, and I wonder if he's looking for something to pry with. Neither of us thought to bring a crowbar. Now I wish we had, although it probably wouldn't have been wise to be seen carrying one in.

"Are you thinking of pulling that away from the wall?" I ask.

"Feel it," he says. "It's not very well attached. You try pushing up from the bottom, and I'll push up top. Let's see if we can get it free."

I nod. Maybe we can even reattach it, though I doubt it. A

slapping sound behind me makes me jump, and I whirl. It's just a piece of metal shingle flapping in the wind through the ceiling hole. I sigh, placing the flashlight on one of the metal legs that used to hold a bench and angle it at the lockers. I squat down and slide my fingers underneath the bottom of the locker nearest me.

So much for not touching anything. I brace myself. "Ready."

We heave upward in unison, and I strain my arms and shoulders. I groan as the old wound near my armpit sends a wave of pain through my chest. With a sharp, metallic pop, the lockers come away from the wall. I don't know how many we've dislodged, but the row sways and teeters in my hands. Losing my balance, I attempt to stand up. My hands slip, and my corner of the locker section hits the concrete floor. It almost stabs me in the foot. I stagger back, trying not to fall and impale myself on the metal bench legs. My flailing fingers knock the flashlight off its perch. Its light shunts off toward the black blob of goo.

Now bearing the entire weight of the row of lockers, Trent curses, and his legs buckle. He lets go, and the sound of metal striking the concrete floor shreds our ears. It may as well have been a wrecking ball. Trent releases his light from his teeth, and it drops from sight. As the lockers lean and begin to fall toward him, Trent shoves them upright before they slam into the bench legs.

I curse under my breath as I hold the searing muscle near my armpit. My vision seems spotty. I blink a few times to try and clear it. The patch of sun leaking through the hole in the ceiling gives us some illumination, but there's a lot of darkness in here.

"Aria, are you all right?" Trent asks. The lockers now rest vertically on the floor, and he slowly backs away from them.

My breathing comes loud and rapid. My heartbeat is audible too, at least to me, and it shakes me as I stand here. "I'm okay. I didn't expect that section to come free so easily or to be that heavy. I think I pulled a muscle."

"Shit. I didn't think about that injury under your arm. I shouldn't have asked you to do that. Are you sure you're okay?" He frowns, looking me over, but there's nothing visible besides my inclined bearing.

"Yeah, I'm fine." Sweat trickles down my forehead, and a wet stain drenches the front of my shirt. I shiver. A small wave of nausea churns in my belly, but it'll pass.

I bend down and grab my flashlight while Trent retrieves his. I shine the beam at the site where the lockers were attached. It's a bare, plywood wall, with only a few smears of black near the edges. It's the cleanest thing in the room, but there's nothing remarkable about it.

Swallowing down the acrid bile from the discomfort of straining, I pass around the lockers and stand next to Trent. The smoke has left a clear impression of the lockers' former position. We run our fingers along the edges of the imprint, feeling for anything out of place. My once white gloves leave black smudges everywhere they touch. I place my hand a little higher than my head, lightly brushing a slight indentation.

"Here," I say. "What's this?"

17

Trent halts with his chest against the carbon-stained wall. He places his fingers next to mine and slides them over. "I feel it."

"Anything on your end?" I ask.

"Nothing this obvious, just a couple of places where it feels uneven. But settling or wood warping can cause that too."

Toward the bottom, the fire damage is worse, and there's a six-inch hole where it burned through the wall near a stud.

I say, "And look here. Wow, this is odd. It's almost like this section behind the lockers has a corner—like this was a separate piece. Maybe they installed a piece of plywood for reinforcement because of the weight?"

Even in the dim lighting, I perceive Trent's eyes brightening as he crouches beside me. I point, and he reaches down and feels the slight, protruding corner at the bottom left. We wouldn't have found this if not for the fire which partially burned away the wood around it.

Trent shakes his head. "Maybe. I don't know. It's weird."
We stare at each other before rising.

"Can we pry it off?" I ask.

Now we're entering point-of-no-return territory. We can put the lockers back, but restoring the wall to its previous condition will be impossible. However, the protrusion is just too strange to leave alone. Or are we making it out to be more than it is? We came here expecting to find something, and we don't want to leave empty-handed. I bite my lip, my mind spinning with consequences.

"We can try. Let's find something metal," Trent says.

For the next twenty minutes, we comb the annex area and the rest of the warehouse for something we can use to jimmy the wall. In an old, burned building with wires and boards visible everywhere, you would think that scraps of metal would be lying around ripe for the picking like apples in autumn. But they aren't.

We wind up tucking our filthy gloves in our pockets and walking back to our vehicles. So that it won't seem strange carrying a tire iron down the street, we get in Trent's truck, and he drives it about two hundred feet to Lamar. He parks in the lot of the Asian restaurant adjacent to the warehouses. I take the tire iron, and Trent brings his spare donut. This way, if anyone sees us, it won't look like we're up to mayhem. We walk around the back of the restaurant, and as there's no fence, we're able to access the annex building directly and enter through the hole in the corner.

With my injured muscle, I can't tackle our next job head-on. I hold the flashlight so Trent can see. It's the only thing I can do, and I hate it. But I don't want to damage my shoulder muscle further and have to take prescription pain relievers again—it used to be that bad since it never healed properly.

Trent starts prying at the weird edge we found. As he works the bar into the space and pulls, he moves the board outward enough to reveal a nail sticking out behind it. After about twenty minutes, sweat runs down the back of Trent's neck, but he loosened all the plywood section except for the very top. We've been here for over an hour, and the daylight leaking through the roof opening starts to wane.

"Here it comes," he says. With a final push of the tire iron, nails creak as they slide away from the wood. The section hits the floor on end and bangs into the lockers. It rests against them at an angle.

My breath comes out as a choked gasp as I stare. We both stand with our flashlights aimed and gawk at the empty space formerly covered by the wall section. If it was some type of reinforcement piece, we should see bare studs behind it. We're not.

I step closer with the blood pounding in my ears. I lean over the lockers to shine the light inside. The area isn't tall enough to be a hallway. It's more like a large crawl space, going back in a shallow tunnel. However, it doesn't go very far back. Our lights stop at a vertical wall maybe six feet in. The oddness of the space silences us.

"What the hell?" I say in barely a whisper.

Trent peers into the beckoning strangeness. As though hearing one another's thoughts, we each grab a side of the row of lockers we removed earlier and lift together. I mostly use my left arm, not risking more pain to my right side. Picking the lockers up off the ground only a few inches, we scoot sideways and put enough distance between the lockers and the wall to fit our bodies more comfortably. We slide the large plywood piece over as well. Then we stand in front of the crawl space, scouring the inside for the next revelation.

I guess the weirdest thing is that there's nothing here. It could have been a utility tunnel of some sort, but there are no utilities here. The floor and walls of the crawl space appear to be nothing more than unpainted plywood, just like the piece Trent pried off. Sticking my head slightly inside the opening, I strain to sniff through the mask, but because of our surroundings, I only get a faint whiff of wood before drawing in more smoke smell.

"I guess I don't have to ask if this was on the blueprints," Trent says.

"Definitely not."

My hands are so sweaty inside my gloves I'm surprised they haven't slipped off. My heart slams against my chest cavity like it's going for a prison break. I'm used to being afraid all the time. My lingering fear is unwelcome but familiar, and I've learned to live with it. But staring into this unusual post-construction shaft, my mind drags me back to the dirty, dark room in the old house on County Road 140.

I was Korey's plaything, a desecrated piece of meat left to waste away and rot. Soaked in my own blood, I thought I would die against the wall, with my stepmother's corpse as the only witness.

I pinch my inner arm. It forces me into the present moment. I came up with this stupid routine to keep from slipping into one of my flashback meltdowns. Right now is a terrible time for one.

Trent's voice finds me, but it's muffled. Distant. Like he's talking underwater. "Do you want to come in with me?"

I glance at him but can't speak. What is it that he's asking? The crawl space. He wants to know if I want to explore it with him.

Trent's eyes are bright and alive, but when they alight on me, he frowns. "Are you okay?"

"I'm fine." I swallow, my mouth dry and cottony. "I'll stay out here and keep watch."

Trent grabs the edge and pushes himself up and in. His legs and feet disappear within the tunnel. He knocks on the wood of the bizarre passage with his fist.

Thud, thud. Thud, thud. He tests the walls, the ceiling, and the floor. *Thud, thud, thud.*

I look away, purposely keeping my eyes out of there. I attempt to put my attention on my surroundings to get my mind straight. But glancing at a gloomy cell made of boards covered in scaly char that skirt an inky water puddle isn't stabilizing.

Trent's feet shuffle as his work boots scrape against the wood. More knocking. And then a few short, quick knocks as though what he hears tells him something. The last few sound higher pitched.

Trent's dampened voice calls from far away. "I think it's hollow under here."

"I'll hand you the bar," I say.

I walk my trembling body the few steps to bring me to the tire iron, and I grab it. Trent sticks his hand out, and I place the bar across his palm. But instead of using it inside the crawl space, he shimmies in my direction, dropping his feet to the concrete in the main room. I step back. I can't help but think he's going to have a hard time prying anything inside from out here.

Trent pauses. "You okay?"

"Yeah, I'm fine. Why do you ask?" I feign a smile, not that it's visible through my mask.

"You look a little pale. How are you feeling? And don't say fine," Trent says.

"I'm not bad. I just don't want to go in there. It gives me the creeps," I say.

"Don't worry, there's no reason at all for you to go in there," he says.

I nod.

He's about to turn back to his task, but he stops again. He puts a hand on my bicep. "Aria? Are you getting a flashback?"

I start to nod, then shake my head. "No. I can stave it off if I look around. I'm fine."

Trent stares at me for a few seconds before replying. "Okay. But if you start feeling bad, you tell me, and we'll leave. Okay?"

"Okay," I say. I don't add that it would be silly to leave now that we've come this far, barring police intervention or Nick showing up with firearms. But at least if that happens, I won't be alone. And I'm a good runner.

"Okay," Trent says. "Just *please* let me know if you start feeling bad. I'm going to see if I can get this off, okay?"

"Sure. I will." I give him a thumbs up. It's half-sarcastic because chances are I won't say a word. A wave of lightheadedness hitting me, it occurs to me that Trent's going to try and remove the crawl space floor.

His gaze still burns into me, so I add in a steadier voice, "That's a good idea."

"Good," he says. I can tell he smiles because of the creases beside his eyes. He gets back to work.

Continuing to pinch my arm, I move my fingers to the tender skin on the inside of my wrist and dig my nails in. Not psycho at all. And I *don't* scream in my sleep or take souvenirs from dead people, I swear. However, the pain makes it possible to continue standing here. Trent pries and pounds at the plywood. He groans through gritted teeth as he tries to work the bar into any available crack. It's no wonder he's having trouble. Anyone who would have gone through the hassle of constructing such a thing wouldn't have made it easy to disassemble.

Finally, as wood creaks and splinters, a layer of "floor" pops off. Trent broke it in half, and I can plainly see another layer beneath it. He takes the bar and removes the first layer completely, tossing the pieces of wood out into the main room.

After climbing back inside the tunnel, he removes the screws along the perimeter. Then he pushes himself back out and stands on the annex floor, peering inside the crawl space one last time before the moment of truth.

Trent's fingers shake as he tucks his screwdriver back into his tool belt. He inhales and wipes the sweat from his brow with the back of his arm. For a moment, the building lies silent. The crawl space now beckons us like Pandora's Box. It's waiting to be opened—and it wants to be. Trent wedges his fingers under the board and strains. He pulls, leaning back and putting his feet against the wall as he tries to get this second layer to come free.

"Are you sure you found all the screws? I know you were thorough, but it's dark in here," I say.

"I'm pretty sure I got them all. I think it's just heavy." He steps back and jams the tire iron farther under the board. His eager, expectant expression is too much.

I put the end of my slim flashlight in my teeth and do my best to wriggle my fingers under the thick board.

Trent stops pulling. "Aria, no! Your arm."

"I'll be careful. We'll just go slowly. And I'll mostly use my left arm," I say.

After I get a grip, I find it's a lot thicker than I first thought. It isn't just a half-inch piece of plywood. It's a half-inch piece of plywood nailed on top of a bunch of two-by-fours which were fastened together to make one solid and heavy slab.

This makes it like pulling a log from mud. It's easier when we get it about halfway, and we use the board's weight against it, directing it toward the floor. We don't let it fall because that'll mean we'll need to pick it up again. Instead, we slide it sideways and lean it against the wall.

With my pulse whooshing in my ears, I stand back and rub my pulled muscle. It's not too bad. Trent shines the light inside the newly unveiled space. A gasp escapes me, and I jerk involuntarily—not once, but twice, with a secondary reaction to my first. I clamp my hand over my mouth and stifle a cry. My mind tries to process this new vision, but the effort hurts somehow. So painfully real. Reality plays tug of war with my psyche, and it's winning. I want the image to cease. I want this beholding to stop, to cover my eyes and then uncover them to see something else there instead. Of course, I couldn't tear my gaze away if my life depended on it.

nd yet, the sight within the crawl space isn't gruesome. It isn't terrifying. It isn't like what Trent saw when he found me eight months ago. It's just... strange. There, in the glow of one hundred thousand lumens, lies a complete human skeleton. The clean, white bones no longer attach to one another yet are arranged mostly in the proper order. The hollow sockets of the skull stare up at me with everything unspoken. Its jaw has fallen away. It tilts across the vertebrae now.

The makeshift coffin is lined with a burgundy, satin fabric, the cloth marred with dark spots from the humidity here and there. Around the human remains are dried flowers, their previous colors of red or pink or purple now faded to dusty brown. A few small envelopes in pastels of lavender and pale green also rest with the deceased. I inhale to find wood and a faint, odd scent of some preservative.

My chest tightens, and I blink back the discomfort in my aching eyes. I try to get a good breath, but my lungs feel constricted. I should be horrified and shocked at what I'm seeing—and I am. But more than that, I just feel sad. A poignantly sweet, disturbing sorrow swells within me at the notion that someone hid the remains of a person who was obviously a loved one. Yet, he didn't love her enough to bury her in public. He hid her away in an old warehouse building like a macabre sideshow, like something from the Museum of the Weird.

I know nothing about skeletal remains identification, but I'd bet my life this is a woman. It has to be. With those flowers and quaint envelopes probably containing cards strewn all about her. Yes, she may have been loved and hated, the same way Korey loved and hated me. But he wouldn't have taken the time to entomb me nicely in a hidden vault with dried flowers. He would have let my carcass putrefy in that back room of the house. The maggots my only company, the light dying all around me as he snuffed out my flame.

Bile begins rising in my throat, and I swallow it. I taste the acid first, and then a metallic dryness. My tongue grows thick, and I put the back of my hand over my mouth to stop myself from heaving. I sidestep away from the lockers. After making a fist, I place it against the wall to steady myself. While I keep the back of my other hand over my mouth, I listen to the sound of my panic-stricken, frantic breathing. I squeeze my eyes closed and clench my jaw.

I reel. I can barely focus on Trent's voice. He's on the phone with the police. "Yes, that's right. Fifteen-fifteen South Lamar Boulevard. We're in a wooden building toward the back. It's the one with a hole burned through the wall and ceiling..."

I step farther away from the lockers and the crawl space. My stomach churns. My heart pounds like a war drum, and I wave my flashlight around wildly as I try to remember where the exit is. The wan sunlight streams from the space in the ceiling—a gash more reflective of an explosion than a spreading fire—and my mind shows me the dirty windows of the old house where Korey held me prisoner. The knife blade gleams in his hand. I moan and fall to my knees. I drop the flashlight and vomit, spilling my half-digested dinner on the blackened concrete.

My ears ring. They did that when Korey beat me. He struck me in the head, in the face. Across the nose once. I scoot away from my puke and sit with my back against a bare stud. I press my hands to my forehead as I try to get a hold of reality.

It's not happening now. It's over. It's not happening.

But the flashes of memory beat and pound. I can't stop them. My body goes limp and useless beneath me as I pass out.

I AWAKE to the stench of all-encompassing smoke. An odor so thick and deep I could get lost in it and drown. I flutter open my eyes, darting my gaze around in the semi-darkness. Around me, I catch the sounds of men talking and the buzz of radios clicking on and off. Intermittent static fills the gaps between sentences.

My head aches, and I realize I'm sitting with my back against something hard. My jeans, shirt, and latex gloves on my hands are covered in black soot. The walls, floors, exposed joists, and studs—or what's left of them—are charred, and some are partially burned away.

I remember. Trent wanted to explore the warehouse buildings. He wanted to see this area because, like me, he found Rance's concern a little off. An image of the skeleton among satin and dried flowers grips my mind. It hurts. I don't know why, but it does. The strange ache in my chest is something akin to a combination of jealousy and mortification. My thoughts and feelings are so fucked sometimes, even to me. I would throw up again if not for the fact that my stomach is empty now.

"Ms. Owen, are you all right?" a man asks.

I draw a breath and look up, focusing my eyes on a muscular, dark-skinned police officer. Yeah, he's a detective now. I recognize him as Jeffrey Spade, my contact for my case with Nick Pearlman.

"Yes, I'm fine," I say. My weak voice is barely audible over radio static and the bustling feet of officers. "I—I got dizzy after our discovery. I guess I passed out."

Detective Spade squats down next to me. He offers a smile. "Okay. We just got here, but Mr. Lemend told us this isn't uncommon for you. Is that true? I just want to make sure that if you need medical attention, we get it for you."

"No, what Trent told you is correct. I do pass out sometimes. Not a lot, but just seeing that—I guess I wasn't expecting to find..." The dizziness returns, and I push my back and head against the board to steady myself. The floor teeters beneath me like a carnival ride. I press my fingers to its griminess.

"All right, no problem. I'm just glad you're all right. We'll get all the information from Mr. Lemend, so you don't need to concern yourself with that. I'll have Ms. Sedgeworth walk you out to the car. The air in here is terrible."

I nod, noticing my mask was removed, and start to push

myself up slowly. My knees shake, and I grab Detective Spade's massive palm. With his other hand behind my back, he smoothly pulls me up as though I'm a small child. I know I'm standing now, but I can barely feel my feet on the floor.

A young woman materializes at Spade's left. She smiles at me as she steps closer. She's wearing a baseball cap, a white button-down shirt, and jeans. I can't place the recognition with my head spinning, but I feel like I've seen her before. If she's a police officer, she's not in uniform.

"Ms. Owen," the woman says, the lilt in her tone indicating I seem familiar to her too. "It's nice to see you again, though I'm sorry it's under these circumstances. Come on. I'll take you outside where you can catch your breath."

She places a hand reassuringly on my upper back, indicating the exit with the other. I start walking.

"Have we met?" I blink and try to ignore the throbbing in my temples. Dehydration is what's probably giving me this headache. My blood sugar's probably out the bottom too.

Ms. Sedgeworth chuckles. "Yeah, but I probably look different with this hat on." She reaches up and touches the bill, grinning. "I'm Naomi, Trent's friend. We met at the restaurant."

I put a hand to my head. A wave of jealousy hits me all over again, but at least this jealousy is somewhat normal. "Oh. Have you graduated from the police academy already? I thought you and Trent were enrolled together."

We weave between two men who block our way to the next room.

"Oh no, you're right. Like Trent, I basically just started. Trent mentioned this morning that he might swing by this place and have a look. When I saw half the Austin PD outside, I got worried. I don't know if you saw him, but the tall guy, Officer Sedgeworth, is my dad. Most of his coworkers know I'm in the academy, so I got lucky and was allowed in here. I'm really glad you and Trent are okay." Her blue eyes study me.

"Oh," I say, trying to smile. "You've got connections."

I didn't notice the tall guy she mentioned, but I'll take her word for it. So, Trent told her he would be here, and her dad is a cop. For some reason, these facts tick me off, but they do explain her presence.

I do my best to make it look like I'm not having difficulty walking in a straight line. What must she think of me after whatever Trent probably told her, and now this? Aria Owen, the mess. Aria Owen, the traumatized girl who nearly died in January, now found unconscious on the floor of a burned building after a flashback. I swallow and pretend to check the ground for debris so that I won't trip on anything.

Naomi stays close by my side as we enter the main warehouse building where I first came in with Trent. She motions for me to go first, and I exit through the front door where the evening greets me with a dusty violet sky. Two police cruisers are parked at the curb, along with a black, unmarked car. I can't remember where I parked my Camry, but I'm hoping it'll come to me in a moment.

"Thank you for walking me out," I say. This time, relaxing my face, I manage to put on a better grin. I meet Naomi's gaze briefly before digging into my jeans pocket for my car keys.

"My pleasure," she says. "But please don't try to drive yet. Why don't you sit here by the curb, and I'll get you some water? I want to make sure you're feeling okay before you get behind the wheel." She points to a clean spot on the concrete between the two police cars.

I want to barrel home. I want to disappear like a bat under the Congress Avenue Bridge, but she's right. I'm having trouble focusing, and my feet aren't entirely connecting with the ground.

"That sounds good. Thanks," I say.

I lower myself down and take a seat, then stripping off my blackened latex gloves. I shove them in my back pocket. Naomi places a bottle of cold water in my hands, and I accept it numbly and drink. I glance up and down Lamar, watching the comings and goings of the officers. Now I notice a white crime scene van a few vehicles down. And then, like a bad hallucination, my gaze finds a man. He's not a cop. He doesn't fit. He shouldn't be here.

Nick Pearlman. He's standing in a dark suit, watching me from the other side of the street. Since I know his silhouette, the twilight doesn't hide him much.

"Naomi?" I call.

I turn for her, but she's gone. I scan my nearby surroundings for one of the policemen, but it seems they've all disappeared too. Tugging my cell phone from my other back pocket, I dial Spade's mobile number. I listen to it ring. I keep my eyes on Pearlman. As I hold the phone to my ear, Nick starts to walk over. I leap to my feet and back away as I get my balance.

"Are you going to listen to me now? Do you think it might be worth hearing what I have to say?" he asks.

I don't answer, my pins-and-needles fingers barely keeping my cell phone in place.

Pick up. Pick up. Please pick up.

Spade isn't answering. I search for Naomi, but she hasn't returned.

"Stay the hell away from me," I say.

I back up a few steps toward the nearest squad car. How can there be so many cops here but not one of them outside? I saw several less than a minute ago. Can I run? I doubt it. With my stomach cartwheeling, I take another look at the black police cruiser. I grip the passenger's side door handle and tug. It's unlocked. I slip inside and slam the door. Then I press the button to lock myself in. The heat of the black interior stifles me, but it's safer than being out there. If the bastard wants me that bad, let him break into a cruiser.

Nick Pearlman slowly strides to the police car and stands there. The windows are tinted, so I don't know if he can see me. Maybe it doesn't matter. He lingers a foot away in that dark business suit in the waning heat of August evening. His body motionless. His head fixed. He continues to stare, his eyes burning into me like he wants to tear my throat out. I jerk my gaze away and face the windshield. I breathe in scents of leather and Gatorade while I continue pressing the phone to my ear. The call goes to voicemail.

"Hi, Detective Spade," I say as I scoot as far to the left edge of the seat as I can. "This is Aria Owen. I'm outside in one of the police cars right now. Nick Pearlman came out of nowhere, and he's standing by the cruiser staring at me. Can you come out? Please. Please help."

19

Pushing "end," I disconnect the call to Detective Spade. My message sounded mental. Completely insane. When I turn back to the window, Pearlman is gone. Ms. Sedgeworth is coming up to the cruiser with her ponytail swinging. I unlock the door and stumble out, my legs buckling before I straighten. Naomi stops dead. Her mouth falls open.

"I'm sorry," I say. "There was someone here who's been threatening me, and I didn't feel safe, so I just got in the car."

"That really isn't allowed. Why didn't you come get me?"

"I tried. I wanted to. No one was out here. He was right —" I scan all around. "He must still be here. He was standing there seconds ago while I was on the phone. He was just here. His name is Nick Pearlman. He's wearing a dark suit." I glance everywhere but still don't see him, and I shake my head. I feel crazy.

"Okay, no problem," Sedgeworth says, her words softer now. She frowns as her gaze sweeps our surroundings. "Did you see which way he went?"

"No, I was in the car. I couldn't tell," I say. Nick may as well be my personal apparition.

"If you want to sit down a while longer, I can get all the information from you and take it to your contact," says Naomi.

"No, it's all right. I left a message on Detective Spade's voicemail. He's been helping me with the case so far. I don't want to be left out here alone. I either need to go back inside with you and the police, or I need to be allowed to drive home."

"If you feel okay to drive, then you're free to go. I'm not holding you here by any means. I just wanted to make sure you were okay." She blinks and regards me with kind eyes, her head tilted slightly. "Where are you parked?"

Finally remembering, I reply, "I'm over that way, on Collier Street. You can't see my car from here, but it's close by."

"Okay. I'll walk you over there," Naomi says.

I'm so relieved I nod too many times and let out a long, shaky sigh. I stay close by her side as we make our way to my Camry. I look for Nick everywhere, but there's no sign of him. It's like he showed up at the precise moment necessary to make his point before melting into the background. Clever. Convenient. How was his timing so perfect? I wonder if Sedgeworth thinks he was my hallucination. I almost wonder myself.

Another wave of relief floods through me as I step up to the driver's side of the car. I unlock it with my remote.

"Be safe, and if you need anything, just give us a call," Naomi says. She holds up a hand and starts to move off.

"Thanks." I return a small wave of my own.

As I lock myself in my sedan and start the engine, I think about Trent inside the building. He's probably having the time of his life, explaining to the police exactly how we discovered the remains. What will this mean for Rance? Will he be a suspect? Will Spade try even harder to identify Nick?

As I drive north on I-35, back to Trent's house in George-town, my cell phone rings. It's Kyle. I groan before pushing the button on my steering wheel. This answers the call and sends the audio through the stereo speakers.

"Hi, Kyle," I say. I try to make myself sound calm, as though I'm taking a leisurely drive back to Williamson County and not leaving a crime scene covered in carbon residue.

Without saying hello back, Kyle says, "It's on the news, Aria." He exhales heavily, restraining the anger in his voice. "It's really on the news. At this moment. Your suspicions were right, but what were you thinking? I thought you agreed not to mess with Rance and the property anymore. I'm so furious right now I can't think straight. I don't mean to be, but damn it."

I hear static and wonder if he's pacing around outside.

Kyle adds, "And I know Trent must have been involved for you to go that far. Damn it, Aria, you don't always have to listen to him."

My chest twinges and I snap, "I don't always. I just didn't want him to go alone." Crap. Now I basically blamed him.

"This is bad. Really bad," says Kyle.

"I understand. And I'm sorry I broke our agreement, but —" The thoughts come to me slowly through my headache and brain fog. "Those remains belong to someone. Now there's a chance to find out the truth about who and why."

"Yes, but what you guys did was wrong. Plain and simple," Kyle says.

"I know. But just like you told me that doing the right thing isn't always the right thing, sometimes it is. And once in a while, doing the wrong thing is the right thing."

AT TRENT'S house in Georgetown, I shower and scrub myself. The adrenaline rush quickly bleeds out of me, pouring down the drain with the black soot. Now I'm only exhausted. Even after washing my hair twice with strawberry mint shampoo, I swear I can still smell the smoke. It seeped into the keratin itself.

Detective Spade calls me back and lets me know he received my message, and he's glad I'm safe. I can't tell if he believes me or not, but I'm not about to ask. Afterward, I down a badly needed glass of water that rinses the bitterness from my tongue. Then I remove the throw pillows so I can lie on the couch. The well-worn cushions are a little lumpy and upholstered in rough tweed fabric. Using my arm as a pillow, I close my eyes until somewhere around nine o'clock when the doorknob rattles and Trent walks in.

"Aria, I'm so sorry."

I prop myself on an elbow and wearily try to bring his image into focus. I can't figure out what he's apologizing for.

"I tried to come check on you again," he says as he pushes the door shut and locks it, "but I couldn't get away from them—the investigators. They were questioning me, and I was about to go back to you, but then I saw Detective Spade and Naomi. When you left with her, I knew you were all right. But I'm sorry. I wouldn't have just left you there like that."

I knew from the upright position in which I awoke that he didn't just leave me. "It's okay. That's what I figured happened."

He sighs like maybe he's relieved. Then he slips off the tool belt and sets it on the small section of tiled floor.

I add, "Kyle said the story was already on the news earlier."

Staying where he is, Trent begins taking off his shoes. "I believe it. When those reporters see something that looks good, they swoop like vultures."

"You mean when they see something that looks dead," I say. This gets a laugh out of him. I slowly sit up completely. I'm not nearly as shaken as I was, but I'm drained.

Trent holds up an arm and sniffs himself. "Geez, I reek. So, how are you feeling? Do you need me to get you anything?"

"I'm okay now. I just had a flashback and threw up."

"And passed out," he adds, his gaze wandering over my face. Remaining on the tile, Trent strips down to his boxers and wads his clothes up in a ball. Otherwise, he'll wind up leaving a black trail. He tries to smile, but I can tell by the lines on his forehead that something bothers him.

I ask, "So, did you get in trouble for what we did? You're not an officer yet, but even if you were, you didn't have a warrant to search the property." I stretch my arms and back.

Trent's frown deepens. He clenches his jaw. "Well, regarding that, there's something else I'm going to beg your forgiveness for. I guess..."

He pauses, looking down at the wadded clothing in his

hand while he lags in telling me. "I told a lie. And I'm sorry, I didn't mean to. I guess when we started out today, I didn't expect our investigation to be so productive. I mostly *hoped* we'd find something. And I knew how much trouble I'd get in if I said it was my idea. I'd probably be expelled from the academy. So, I told them that as the real estate assistant who participated in the sale of the property, you were concerned that your client might be in danger. And you wanted to have a look for your own peace of mind. And that I told you I would accompany you for your safety. I'm sorry. I shouldn't have done that. I was rattled, and I wasn't thinking. I know I have this terrible habit where I don't think things through, and I just rush in—"

He shakes his head, shifting his gaze from the floor to the coffee table and back to his soiled clothes. "I'm sorry, Aria. It was really stupid."

Leaning back and folding my hands in my lap, I wonder if I should be angry with him. It's true that he told a lie. It wasn't my idea, and I didn't want to go. I'm already in deep shit with Kyle, although he mentioned he suspected Trent was involved in our little detective stunt. But regardless of whether Trent told a lie, I'm still accountable for going. And if he hadn't lied, it wouldn't change that.

I take a deep breath. "Well, I don't like the idea that you blamed it on me. But I'm exhausted. Far too exhausted to be angry. But honestly, I did want to investigate in a way. I mean, not actually in real life. Like if there were a way I could have remotely done it, as though I were playing a video game, I would have preferred that to going there in the flesh and having the experience. I don't know."

My lips press into a wry smile. "And it's hard to be mad at a guy confessing in his underwear."

Trent gives a little chuckle before taking his clothes to the kitchen. I hear him stuffing them into a plastic bag. He returns to the living room and stands across from me with his arms crossed. "Thanks. Thank you for being so... More understanding than you should be."

"Sure. I just hope I won't be fired for this," I say. I pick up the brown and dark yellow throw pillows from the floor and arrange them.

He looks at me hard. "You're not getting fired. I'll twist Kyle's arm myself if I have to."

It's not his job to do that since I went to the Lamar property of my own volition, but I don't feel like disagreeing. "I'm turning in for the night. You going to stay up a while after your shower, or are you coming to bed?"

"If I'm able to wind down, I want to get some sleep. I'll see you in a bit," he says. He pads barefoot to the bathroom.

I have a light snack of chicken soup before getting in bed. On my back with my knees up, I listen to the water pummeling the bathtub floor as Trent showers. Then I pull the blankets up to my chin and lie still so I can concentrate on my strong heartbeat and breathing. Since my trauma with Korey, I've found a way to fall asleep. What I do is evoke a memory from my childhood.

I visualize a day spent with my mom. We lived in Dallas, and one day we visited my maternal grandmother, who had an especially beautiful backyard. My mother and I sat at the patio table beside the Texas lilac tree. We were alone for a little while because Gram was napping after lunch. Across from us, black-eyed Susans, purple asters, and red roses burst with brilliant colors along the fence, and the honeyed scents of so many blossoms felt otherworldly. I was just a little girl then, but my mom gave me a small glass of sweet tea—she allowed it sometimes if I was good. I sipped it happily. I swung my short little legs up and down in the space under my chair. Just when I thought it couldn't get any better, when I was basking in my floral paradise and unbridled caffeine exhilaration, Mom surprised me with a bottle full of bubbles.

I don't know why I've chosen that particular memory to calm myself whenever I freak out. I think it's because now, as an adult, I know that my mother planned everything about that magical memory. She carefully crafted it all—the trip to Gram's backyard garden, the sweet tea, the bubbles, the retreat to the quiet patio where we could enjoy our time together. That day, I was young and happy. I didn't feel alone and afraid. As I slip into the memory more deeply, my body slowly relaxes. I drift to sleep.

Perhaps I dream. Perhaps the light is too bright, or the yellow flowers glow almost neon, overpowering me in the strong sun. I turn my head, trying to shut my eyes. Something continues blinding me.

I gasp and sit up in the darkened room. Light stabs through the curtained window, very sharp and out of place for this rural property at night. I can still hear the running water in the shower. I must have only been asleep for a few minutes. After leaning to reach, I lift a corner of the curtain and peek outside. A car is stopped in the road, turned so that the headlights point straight at the house. I pull back and wait. Maybe it's just someone turning around. But after a short while, the car hasn't left.

I slide out of bed, take my pistol from the nightstand, and pad to the bathroom door. I knock. "Trent, there's a car in the road with its headlights aimed right at the house."

"How long has it been there?" he asks through the door.

"A few minutes. It's odd how it's in the middle of the road, turned like that. I thought you might want to come take a look." My words are calm somehow. The image of Nick Pearlman standing outside the baking-hot police cruiser springs to mind.

"Okay, I'm coming right out." The faucet knobs squeak. The water heavily drips a few times and stops. A few seconds later, Trent appears with a towel wrapped around his waist. He flings open the bathroom door, and it bangs against the adjoining wall. Water runs down his face, and he leaves wet footprints as he jogs into the bedroom. I follow.

"They must have gone," Trent says.

I check. The car has disappeared, and the two-lane road is dark. Trent returns to the bathroom to finish drying off while I sit on the edge of the bed with my Sig in my hand. It's cool to the touch and has that new gun smell. There's no way I can fall back asleep now, at least not until Trent joins me. And even then, I'm not so sure. We uncovered human remains earlier in the day, and only yesterday, we were shot at right here on County Road 152.

When Trent slides under the blankets beside me, I try to sleep again. I have a fleeting thought about Margarita. There's no way she believes we aren't having sex, but even if we are, it's none of her damn business. Trent lies with his back to me. He's pretty careful not to touch me much whenever we sleep next to each other. That's probably another thing Margarita wouldn't believe. I hardly believe it myself.

Lying on my back, I bend my knees and close my eyes. Again, focusing my mind on the memory of my mom, I try to slip into the images and conjure drowsiness. But it isn't meant to be.

Thud.

I sit bolt upright from my shallow sleep, my breath catching in my throat. Did something hit the side of the house? There are no trees close by, so it couldn't have been a branch falling. Trent rises beside me at almost the same moment. He grabs his 9mm by the table lamp.

"Aria, here." Trent's low voice is thick with sleep. I'm glad one of us got some. He thrusts the grip of my own pistol at me—there's only one nightstand, and it's on his side.

I take the proffered weapon. Trent snatches his cell, slides off the bed, and drops to the floor. He dials 911. I follow, rolling myself in his direction and dropping down to the carpet beside him. My heart hammers and my hands have already started to sweat. After giving what information he can, Trent hangs up and sets his phone beside him.

Thud.

Something else hits the side of the house, dangerously close to the window. I twitch, keeping my fingers wrapped firmly around the grip of the pistol.

Thud.

I glare at Trent in the semi-darkness. Nick's cold, pasty face springs to mind, but it's hard to believe he would throw things at Trent's house. It seems so... sad. Pointless. Unless it's explosives. I straighten and grab Trent's shirt sleeve.

"Let's get away from the wall," I say.

Trent nods, and we scoot to the opposite side of the room.

Minutes tick by, and nothing happens besides more "thuds." I wonder if the person is trying to hit the glass or if he's just trying to hit the exterior of the house to scare us. Maybe some kids are pulling a prank. But that's a laugh. It's never kids with me. It's never something minor—never an accident or a childish game.

Another thud against the wall, this one louder. Closer? I can't stand not seeing and not knowing who or what is making the noise. I crawl back over and lean up toward the mattress, where I reach out trembling fingers to draw back the curtain.

20

As I curl my fingers around the curtain to draw it back, Trent materializes behind me and squeezes my bicep. "Whoever's out there wants us to check. That's the whole point. They want us to look out the window, go out there, and get shot, grabbed, or God knows what else. That's how Patrick Durham nearly killed me with a flashlight by getting me out in the open. And it's not happening again. Not to me and certainly not to you. I'll kill the person myself before I let that happen."

I crouch beneath the sill again. Sometimes it surprises me that Trent seems almost as protective of me as I am of him. "I don't disagree. I'm sure as hell not going out there, but I can't stand doing nothing. What can we do?"

Thud.

This time, the impact rings with an extra bite, like the wooden siding cracks. Is he throwing rocks? Or maybe something metal?

Trent snorts. "Not much—yet. Wait for the police to get here. If I had a nickel for every time I wished I'd done that."

"Better late than never," I say.

Thud.

Staying near the closet, Trent starts tugging on his jeans. I pull out my own from the dresser and wriggle into them. I yank a t-shirt over my sleepwear. Trent's cell phone lights up and starts ringing. With bleary eyes, I watch him answer.

"Deputy Reyes, yes. We're still in the house," Trent says. He listens. "No, since we don't know what the person's throwing, I haven't looked out the window again. But Aria said there was a car in the road earlier with the headlights shined at the house."

After getting dressed, I get a whiff of a clean, metallic scent as I tuck my pistol in my back pocket. I position myself near the corner of the wall opposite the striking projectiles.

"We haven't left the bedroom," Trent says to Reyes.

Thud. Thud.

"Okay, thanks. We'll see you soon," says Trent.

I lean against the wall, my legs trembling. My rabbiting pulse betrays my adrenaline rush, but my heavy eyelids tell another story. I'm so tired. I just want it to end.

Thud.

Of course, today is nothing compared to the exhaustion I felt when the paramedics pulled me out of that house on County Road 140. It's a level of tiredness I don't think many people have experienced. So, every time a projectile whacks against the siding and gives me an involuntary muscle spasm, I keep that in mind.

The thudding continues at erratic intervals. I try to envision what he's throwing. I think of rocks, or maybe metal ball bearings.

Thud. Thud.

It's got to be something heavy enough to damage the

siding, like in the cracking sound I heard earlier. But until I go out there and have a look, there's no way of knowing. A police siren wails outside, and tires grind to a halt on the gravel drive. With one hand on the wall, I remain still as I strain my ears to pick up anything significant. The thudding sound has stopped. Trent slides into place at my left and remains motionless there, frozen like I am in perplexed listening. Nothing new meets my ears. Maybe our antagonist ran off.

My gaze flicks to the clock on the nightstand with its glowing red numbers—12:17 a.m. At 1:01, Trent glances at me. I pick up his unspoken statement—that our surroundings are still silent, and we haven't heard a siren again or an officer's voice.

Trent says, "Stay here, okay? I'm going to see what's happening."

I nod.

His work boots thump softly across the carpet as he leaves the bedroom. Shortly after, the front door swings open. I catch a brief exchange between Trent and another man but can't make out what they're saying. Then finally, I discern the officer saying clearly, "They're gone."

The familiar voice of Reyes stabilizes me, and I exhale. I leave my sentry place at the wall and join Trent and the deputy sheriff in the living room. The two of them stand in the middle of the space with the overhead light on. It glares down upon Trent's pale face and the dark circles under his eyes. Reyes is tall and tan and looks the way I remember him, a mid-fifties guy with a face creased from experience.

"Did you happen to see what they were throwing?" Trent asks, slouching a little. He wipes his forehead with the back of his hand.

Reyes gives a little chuckle. "Yeah, just a bunch of rocks. There's a good pile of them back there. Because of your history, I'm going to investigate this further. But it might have just been kids. I imagine there's not much to do out here in rural Georgetown at night. Maybe a few boys got bored."

I place myself near the two of them, ruminating over how we went from getting shot at to finding human remains, and now we have rocks. What kind of criminal would waste his time on that? I ask, "Did you see a car? Or anyone running off?"

"Unfortunately, no," Reyes says. "I looked all through the yard here, up and down the street and in the adjoining fields. They probably left just before I showed up."

"But the rocks were hitting the house right up to the point when I heard your siren," I say. "How could they have hidden so quickly?"

"They probably planned their escape route before I got here. That's the kind of thing juveniles pull. Don't worry, Ms. Owen. Like I said, I'll continue checking and make sure he or they aren't lurking around here somewhere. Safety-wise, I don't think you have much cause for concern. Just keep your eyes open, as usual. And if anything else happens, you or Trent can give me a call." Reyes gives me a closed-mouth smile. He holds a clipboard in his hand and quickly notes a few things.

"She's had someone threatening her," Trent says. "A guy named Nick Pearlman. She's been giving all the information to Detective Jeffrey Spade in Austin. We thought this might be related."

I notice Trent doesn't add how we found human remains in the South Austin building that Pearlman showed an interest in purchasing. This is probably due to the whole going onto private property without a warrant thing and Trent not technically being a cop yet. I still can't figure out if that comes to two strikes or just one. But Reyes will find out eventually. I wonder if it will affect Trent's employment eligibility with the Williamson County Sheriff's Office. Trent's shifty eyes tell me he's wondering the same thing.

Reyes frowns. He glances between Trent and me, lowering the clipboard. "Threatening you? Is this in any way related to what happened to you earlier this year?"

"Not directly, but I think Nick may have known Korey's brother, Ayden. His death was accidental, but he died about a year ago," I say.

Reyes raises an eyebrow.

"I accidentally killed Ayden in self-defense when he attacked me on my stepmom's property," I say. Right on cue, a vignette of the bloody blue eye ring consumes my mind. My face heats, and a light sweat prickles my skin. Or is that liquid guilt?

"I see," Reyes says. "Would you mind giving me a brief rundown of what occurred?"

I tell him. I include that I've never recovered full recollection of the incident but that there are, of course, police and forensics reports for reference. There are also records of the statements I made to Officer Davis that day before the amnesia kicked in and what I told the detective at the Round Rock Police Department the day after, post memory loss. Reyes might already know these things, but I say them anyway.

Once the deputy is satisfied with that information, I summarize the situation with Nick and the Lamar property, including what Trent and I found. Now Reyes hardly bats an eye. Scribbling furiously, he notes whatever he deems significant and interjects a question now and then. But I keep my answers terse. I wonder if Reyes will still think juveniles are to blame after this.

"All right, Ms. Owen. Mr. Lemend," Reyes says, giving us each a nod in turn. "Unless you have any further questions for me, I'll be on my way."

We have questions, but none he can answer. After a few final words of caution, the deputy sheriff shakes our hands and departs.

I lock the door behind him and collapse onto a wooden kitchen chair. With my elbows on the table, I let my body relax. The sweat on my back begins to dry as I think about what Reyes told us. I glance at Trent. "Kids."

Trent huffs. "Yeah. We'll see about that when we look at the footage from the security cameras."

"We'll see," I say. At the same time, it's hard to believe well-dressed, haughty Nick Pearlman stood out there and threw rocks to antagonize me further. And Rance might have broken a nail, so that makes him unlikely suspect number two. The unnamed person was petty enough to waste his time and agile enough to disappear right under the deputy's nose. Whether Nick, Rance, or someone else, I know it wasn't kids.

With our pistols beside us on the kitchen table, we review the security camera footage on Trent's laptop. It doesn't show much because whoever threw the rocks stood out of range. We can't see anyone or even a part of their body, only the projectiles sailing into the wall. The throwing angle gives us the idea the person must have stood near the street, not far from the field beside the house.

"Do you want to get a hotel for the night?" Trent asks. He rubs his face and folds the pc closed.

"Anywhere is better than here."

WE TAKE separate vehicles and meet up at Candlewood Suites in Georgetown. When I open the door to our room with the key card, the faint scents of chlorine bleach, white tea, and fig perfume are oddly reassuring. The bright oak furniture adds a warmth to the surrounding colors of taupe and light gray. Inviting and safe. I weakly toss my suitcase on the bed.

Trent digs through his own bag and piles his clothes on the white comforter. Then he paces, searching around for something. "Did you see me bring a small case in?"

"No. Why?" I ask.

"I thought I brought the gun bag with the extra ammo," he says.

I wonder how the hotel staff would feel about us coming in here packing not only two pistols but extra magazines and rounds should we somehow run out between now and dawn. Because of a change in Texas law, we no longer need concealed carry licenses to bring our guns, but still. I scan the floor and bed but don't see anything besides our two suitcases.

"No. It must still be in your truck. I don't mind going out to get it." I'm too worked up to sleep anyway. I'll be lucky if I get two hours in before I have to go to work tomorrow.

My arms, legs, and back are stiff and sore from all the exertion at the warehouse, so I recline in the toffee-colored stuffed chair. I stretch. I rub the pulled muscle near my shoulder—I should never have strained to take the lid off the homemade coffin, but I wanted to help. I shut out the memory. There's no point in getting sick again.

"I don't want you going out there alone," Trent says. "I can go, or we can go together."

His cell phone rings. Trent swears under his breath before picking up his mobile and answering. Without saying a name to clue me in on the caller, he takes the phone into the bathroom and shuts the door. He's never done that before. I frown as I stare after him.

"It's not her fault," Trent says. The door muffles his voice, but not enough to keep me from hearing.

Is Kyle asking Trent about trespassing on the recently sold property turned crime scene? That's doubtful. It's nearly three o'clock in the morning. I chew my cheek and contemplate. A greedy craving seizes me, like when I listened in at Chupacabra. I creep across the short, tan carpet and put my ear by the door.

"It's not her fault," he repeats. "She's not going to lose her job. Not for something that was my idea."

Interesting. Maybe it's Kyle, after all. That's not impossible, just unlikely. Resolving to ask Trent about it later, I decide to make myself useful in the interim and retrieve the case. After that, I'm going to bed whether Trent is still on the phone or not. We're not in rural Williamson County now, and our surroundings are perfectly safe. The hotel parking lot is well lit, and I kept an eye on the rearview the whole way here. I saw no black Mercedes or any other vehicles following us this time. The switchblade is in my back pocket, and I stick my cell phone in the other one. My pepper spray is in the front. I tuck my pistol in the holster under my jeans.

I grab the keys off the bed and make my way to the elevators. The hallways are empty. I pad along the short, red and taupe patterned carpet, nearly walking face-first into a potted fern next to the elevator door because I took an extended glance at the turn in the hallway. Downstairs, I take note of the receptionist at the desk. A mid-forties lady with dark blonde hair, her name tag says "Nicole." She looks up and smiles at me as I pass her on my way to the front doors.

As I step out into the parking lot, I take in my surroundings. The hotel faces the Interstate 35 access road—nice and visible, just the way I like it. Intermittent whirs from fast-moving highway drivers reach my ears even at this hour. To the left of the hotel grounds is an empty field, and to the right is a short, wooded area that conceals this property from another business. I'm the only one out here. Aside from vehicles in the parking lot before me, the coast is clear. The light of many streetlamps glints across the shiny auto exteriors on the black asphalt.

I jog straight to Trent's truck. When I pull out the keys and see the remote, I curse quietly. In my exhausted state, I accidentally grabbed my own set of keys, not Trent's. I sigh and smack them against my leg. But when I turn to go back to the hotel, my eyes find something odd. I freeze and hold my breath.

21

About fifty feet from me stands a man. With his back to the entrance of the building, he faces me directly. The man is dressed head to toe in black in a ski mask and long coat. Nick? This ridiculous criminal attire is so obvious that for a moment, I wonder if this is someone's idea of a joke. Then the man starts toward me.

I gasp and back up but run into Trent's Colorado. My body hits it so hard the truck rocks back and forth on its tires. The alarm goes off, and I scream. My hand jerks wildly, and I nearly drop the keys. I shove them in my pocket. As I practiced, I tug my pistol from its holster and aim.

"Stop, or I'll shoot!" I yell.

The man complies. He stops, and I keep my Sig trained on him.

Images of "what ifs," of putting a bullet through Nick Pearlman's skull in the hotel parking lot, almost make me lose my nerve. Who in their right mind would believe I killed two men on two different occasions in self-defense? My heart hammers so hard and fast that a wave of lighthead-

edness threatens to melt me. This can't be happening—
shouldn't be happening, but it is. Now I either have to face it
or suffer the consequences.

For a moment, a thin idea courts me. Trent will hear the
alarm. He'll recognize it and come out. The hotel receptionist has also surely heard it by now. She'll see what's
happening and call the cops.

The man gets moving again. He saunters toward me
slowly at first, his feet barely making a sound. Then he
breaks into an easy jog. I see-saw back and forth near the
Colorado, the .38 caliber held firmly at the end of my rigid
arms.

"I said stop!"

He doesn't this time. If I fire from here, I risk hitting
someone inside the hotel. The glass doors and lobby area
are right behind him, and he knows it. But if I take off
running, I'll bring myself away from the hotel, away from
people, which is exactly what this asshole wants. He gives
me no choice. With my stiff hand, I rack the Sig's slide and
chamber a round. I aim for the pavement by the man's feet
and pull the trigger.

Bang!

Flecks of asphalt pop on impact. The man jumps—no,
levitates. He lands on unsteady feet and dances backward
before he turns and darts toward the field.

My unprotected ears ring from the gunshot. For a
moment, my fuzzy hearing mutes the deafening boom and
the blaring truck alarm as I dig my mobile out of my back
pocket and call Trent. I can't tell when—or if—Trent picks
up. Maybe the call goes to voicemail.

"Come outside," I yell. "Now!"

I start toward the doors of the hotel but stop short. The

man is closer now. He didn't run into the field and disappear but instead went around the outer row of cars and made his way back. He's calling my bluff.

I wave at the glass hotel doors. The receptionist's navy-blue polo shirt floats above the desk as she stands at attention, craning her neck with the phone to her ear. She pins her gaze on me. Even from here, I can see her panic, her frantic movements as she talks into the receiver. The Colorado's alarm keeps screeching, pounding my eardrums as I plan my next move.

Trent, please come out. Please hear the alarm and come out, I silently beg. But I don't have time to wait for him.

I struggle to keep my legs under me. The racing of my heart dizzies my senses, and I'm afraid I'll pass out again. Shooting is risky. Running is riskier. Staying here will end badly. But no matter how fiercely the terror courses through me, I have to choose. The man is probably thirty feet from me now. Too close. I aim at the space to the man's left, but my arms shake so much it's harder to steady my weapon. I'll probably wind up hitting him. How will I prove to a jury that I wasn't trying to kill an unidentified man who didn't injure me and didn't draw a weapon himself—at least not yet? And at the same time, why the hell do I have a gun if I can't use it to protect myself?

I growl between clenched teeth. Trying to stem my panic attack, I wipe my sweaty palms on my jeans in turn and get a better grip on the Sig. The man approaches silently, only twenty feet away now as I take better aim. I fire a shot to his left.

Bang!

The bullet widely misses him as intended. He ducks out of sight behind a forest green sedan. With the crisp smell of gunpowder in my nostrils, I force out the breath I was holding. I shove the pistol in its holster. Willing my quivering legs to comply, I propel myself away from the truck and surge into a run. I beeline straight for the hotel doors. The receptionist will let me in, or she won't. As I sprint from Trent's pickup, the man runs along behind the row of cars. He keeps up with me, his black silhouette flashing through the empty spaces between vehicles as he matches my pace.

If I can get inside first, we can lock the doors and steer clear of the entrance until the cops come. But if what's-her-name won't let me in, I'm screwed. I'll have to shoot Nick and will probably go to jail. As I near the building, he veers toward me and blocks my way. He's very close now. Almost close enough to touch me. He knows I don't want to blow his brains out.

The receptionist bursts outside and jogs to the edge of the porte cochère, a little distance behind the man. I don't know if she can tell he's wearing a ski mask from her perspective, but she notices my reaction as I dart back and forth in an attempt to make a break for the building.

"You need to leave right now! I've called the police! Leave right now!" The woman glares at the creep's back. Then her appalled gaze alights on the pistol in my hand. She turns and runs back into the building. Oh—she thought that *he* was shooting at me.

Where the hell is Trent? That truck alarm could raise the dead. It still wails, its siren vibrating my lungs and chest and amplifying my fear. The man ignores the receptionist. He poises himself as he makes ready to grab me right in front of the building where the raised security cameras record everything we do.

He's too close now, but it's now or never. I have to act. I

weave and dodge before aiming straight for his chest. My finger touches the trigger. He lunges at me. With a skilled pivot and twist, he knocks the gun from my hand by sliding alongside me and hitting upward against my arms—right at the moment I fire. The barrel jerks vertical, and the bullet sails straight up. The recoil flips the pistol somewhere behind my head.

His nasty surprise stifles my scream. I lash out in adrenaline overload as the man tries to get his hands around me. His black-gloved hands reach and claw, barely missing me each time. If he gets a hold of me, it's over. I know that from Korey. So, I turn and run. But even as my sneakers drum the pavement, I wrench the can of pepper spray from my front pocket.

The man takes another swipe, and I swerve just beyond his grasp. His fingers brush my arm but don't get a grip. If it's Nick under that mask, he must be in great shape. He comes at me with agile, measured motions, like he's used to it. I just hope I'm faster. I have to blast him as soon as possible—the next chance I get. The knife is my last resort since him taking it from me would be worse than not having it at all.

Just as he forces me to turn and head away from the hotel—the worst direction I could go—a few male voices call from the building.

"Hey! Hey! Leave her alone!"

My heart surges with hope, but I can't see-saw anymore. If they're going to help, they better do it quick. Though Trent's truck alarm blares continuously in the night, he hasn't appeared. What the hell is he doing? What phone call could be so important? But in the back of my panic-stricken mind, I know it's been barely over two minutes since I first set eyes on the man. And that's what no one seems to understand about crime—the act is often over before anyone notices or can do anything. Even the ridiculous stuff. Stuff like this.

I dart across the parking lot, my feet slapping out a frantic rhythm on the asphalt. The pavement ends. I sprint into the small, wooded tract on the other side. I wonder if the guys who came out in response to the commotion will chase after us. I clutch my can of pepper spray with a death grip as I crash through the underbrush. Small twigs snap and break under my feet. The wind fans my cheeks as I push myself into a breakneck run, and trace scents of gasoline and burnt cooking oil reach me from somewhere unseen. The man closes from behind, his feet pounding the earth after me. My thoughts go blank. Blood rushes through my veins and into my pumping legs. I risk a glance back. As hard as I push myself, he's getting closer.

A few low-hanging branches loom, and I shove them out of my way. I trip. I stumble on a short, hidden tree stump and almost fall. My palms sting as I catch myself on the wiry terrain. I push myself back up and keep running as fast and as far as the land allows. The man closes on my heels. His footsteps slow, and I know he's also moving the branches, so he can pass without getting whipped in the face.

With a couple more strides, I dash out of the wooded area and into another parking lot. This one's behind a closed gas station. I dart past, wanting to bring myself within view of the feeder road. It's currently vacant, but maybe a driver on the interstate will see me. It's worth a try. As my feet thunder over the pavement of the empty parking lot, I turn to see the man almost on me. My speed isn't helping much after all. I don't understand how Nick can be so fast. Continuing to sprint over the asphalt, I make it to the other side of the lot and surge into the adjacent field. After this, only a subdivision lies ahead.

My legs burn, and my lungs strain with a heated ache. I have to push myself harder. I must. The injuries from my abduction still pain me sometimes, and an old stab wound near my groin flares up and sears like fire. If I can get to one of the houses, maybe I can knock on someone's door. Maybe a kind soul will help.

A hand grabs my shoulder. A crushing weight bears down on my back, and I stagger forward. My knees buckle, and I stumble and fall. I let go of the pepper spray. I have to —I'm barely able to shield my face from slamming into the ground in time. The man has caught me.

Disarmed of my weapon, I lash out in a frenzied panic. I need the knife now, but I can't get to it. I scream, wriggling forward and clawing at the earth with my fingers to try and pull myself away from him. That failing, I struggle and thrust my hands in his face, at the same time sliding my knees up and pushing against his chest. His leather glove scrapes my cheek as he slaps me hard across the face.

I scream again, but no one comes.

22

H elp!" I yell at the top of my lungs. "Fire! Fire!"
I can't understand why no one has followed us or where Trent is, but there's no time to think about that. As I struggle against the man on top of me, I realize he isn't all that heavy. He's lighter than Korey was. I remember because Korey's weight could hold me in place. But although light, the man is still strong, and his vise-like fingers compete with mine as he tries to get hold of my neck with both hands. He grasps for it, finally clutching my throat and squeezing.

But he made an error. I'm able to draw my knees up higher. I put both feet against his stomach and push back with all my might. I strain, my eyes bulging as he throttles me, and with a grunt, I heave him off me. I don't know how I do it, but I do. He releases my neck and puts out a hand to catch himself from flying backward.

As I grind my palms and elbows into the grass and try to get up, he grabs me again, this time by the hair. My scalp stings as he forces my head to the ground. The disorientation makes me reel, and I paw at the earth with unsteady fingers. A surreal perspective takes over. It's a moment of "outsideness." A sort of detachment, a way of stepping back so I can determine what to do.

When I try to get up, and the man shoves my head against the ground again, for one shattering instant, I visualize my knife. I pull back and thrust my feet against the ground. With just enough room to move, I reach into my pocket and grab the switchblade. I stab straight for the neck.

Like a striking snake, the man's hand whips out and grabs my wrist. I send my other hand straight for his ear. I'll rip the thing clean off. By the blood that flows in my veins, I will. But he twists his head out of the way. My knife-hand trembles as he squeezes my wrist so hard, I think he'll break it. I twist my arm to free it, but he plucks the blade from my grip. He tosses it aside in the tall grass. Then to punish me for trying to stab him, he slaps me across the face again. He grabs my wrist and grates my hand against a thorny thistle.

"Stop! Just—" I can't catch my breath. "Stop. I'm sorry, Nick. I'm sorry. I was just trying to help."

I didn't mean to say it. It just came out. I lie on the ground shivering with the side of my head burning. My right arm aches in a feeble trembling. For an instant, I squeeze my eyes closed, anticipating he's going to shove my face in the spiky plant as well. Instead, he releases me. As my chest heaves with ragged breathing, I peer up at him. He's not only stopped his attack but is drawing away. Just slightly. Is he surprised?

But whatever triggered this pause, it passes. As I sit up, the grassy field around me spinning, he drops his full weight on me and locks his fingers around my neck again—but not before I put my own hands there. My fingers block his, and he can't get a good grip. I, however, can't get my feet against his stomach this time, and the knife is out of reach. I have one last thing on me—car keys. I can use them, but like the switchblade, I must get to them first. I push back against Nick, and my pulled shoulder muscle screams. A small cry escapes me.

I shove with everything I have. I exert so much force the veins protrude in my forehead, and my eyes ache from his death squeeze. But I fail in pushing him off me this time. Instead, I twist my body. This throws him to the ground, but he continues to try to strangle me with his inadequate hold. I can still breathe—not well, but I can. I won't let him make me pass out. Because if that happens, I'm done for. He'll put me in his car and take me wherever he wants to take me. He'll do with me what he wants, and I'll never be seen again. But before I die, my last moments will be the most miserable of my life.

He keeps pushing in his superior position, and my breathing decreases. I'm still drawing air, but my lungs begin to burn. The pressure builds, and my eyes ache. A tear slides down my face and into my hair, but I barely make a sound. My vision goes a bit spotty. I won't be able to hold him off much longer. My strength slips away from me like sand through my fingers. Soon he'll cut off my air completely. It's come to this. After all this time, after everything I've managed to live through, it's finally come to this.

I've heard when you're about to die, your whole life flashes before your eyes. For me, it isn't my whole life. It's my loved ones. First, I see Carol. Memories of her that flick by so rapidly, it's probably no more than one or two seconds. And then, I see my mom. She's young the day we took that trip to grandma's so long ago when we sat beneath the Texas lilac on the warm, sunny day. She smiles at me with her blonde hair hanging loosely at her shoulders. And last, I see Trent's face. I see him knelt beside me on the kitchen floor, a comforting hand on my back during one of my episodes. A few more snapshots of him burst and disappear. Nick will take these memories, and then my life.

As the last of my energy fades and my tense, trembling arms start to go limp, something clicks. I don't know what it is or where it comes from. A small voice tells me I'm not done yet. I'm not going to die today.

Pulling back as hard as I can to inhale more air, I wildly kick my feet and attempt to strike Nick even though the angle doesn't allow it. I pry my right hand from its defensive place at my neck and then draw it back. I make a fist and punch him in the nose. It's not a good hit. It's a weak, puny thing that falls silently against the soft ski mask. But oddly, it startles him. He slightly loosens the death grip around my fingers and throat. Keeping my hand in a tight fist, I punch him in the face again and again. I direct all my energy at hitting him as hard as I can because now he has two hands on my neck to my one. This is my only chance. I pop another blow straight to his nose—this time a good one—and cartilage cracks. He releases my neck from his constricting fingers and reels back.

Free from Nick's death grip, my mouth flies open, and I gasp for air. I gulp it in, taking loud, heaving breaths. I shake and tremble with each intake as I push myself to a sitting position. He never fully constricted my windpipe, but my throat still feels sore when I swallow, like I'm coming down with a cold. My lungs ache too. But I didn't pass out. I'm going to live.

Now it's time to run. But instead of scrambling to my feet

and getting the hell out of here like I should—like a normal person—I jump on Nick and start unloading on him.

Technically, I could say I've never been in a fight before. But that would be markedly untrue. I've fought for my life twice. With Ayden, I won. With Korey, I didn't. It's only because Trent found me that I lived. So really, it would be correct to say I've never been on the *offensive* in a fight—like I am right at this moment.

My face contorts in a twisted grimace that rivals the demons of hell. I pound Nick's face with my fist, and he grunts like a wounded animal. My knuckles split open when they crack against his teeth. I don't care. He manages to get to his feet between blows. So, I whack him so hard he falls backward and lands on his ass in the dirt. Then I bitch-slap him across the face, just like he did when he first got his hands on me.

All my earlier qualms about "killing someone else" flee to oblivion. I guess he choked them out of me. I think of going for his neck. I seriously consider it. Do I have enough strength to do it? Could I strangle this man to death? This man who's strong and agile but also thin and no longer young. I don't know that I can. But it sounds nice. I want him to feel the pain he caused me. I want him to feel the pain every other man before him caused me, too. But just as I'm about to go for his throat, he clambers to his feet again. His shoes slide in the weedy grass a few times, and then he takes off running.

I start to go after him. In my crazed, revenge-driven frenzy, I know I have it in me to chase him. I have just enough endurance left. And when I catch him, I'll kill him. So help me, God, I will. But after staggering a few steps in his direction, my chest still heaving, I pull to a halt. I'm panting and out of breath. My knuckles are raw, sore, and bloody. My lungs are an inferno, and my throat aches. I let him run. I watch him disappear into the woods behind the field. Within a heartbeat, the shadowy stand of trees conceals him. Branches snap and crack in his wake, and I just let him go. But it doesn't matter. I won.

No one followed my screams. No one came to my aid. I reach for my cell phone, but it's gone. It must have fallen out of my pocket either during the run or in the struggle. My knife lies somewhere in the tangled grass. I scan the ground nearby, where the blade glints softly in the dim glow from the streetlamp. Ten feet away. That's the ironic distance I cover before reaching down to grasp the black handle. I pocket it as I look for my mobile. It's here, too, a couple of paces away. I can't find the pepper spray. My pistol should still be in the parking lot unless someone picked it up. It's brand new, and it wasn't a cheap gun.

I could try to call Trent again, but I don't. I'm too... something. Unsettled? More like delirious. I trudge back toward the hotel, stumbling over rocks and weeds as I walk. That fight took almost everything I had.

Trent calls my name. There he is, at the edge of the parking lot on the other side of the field I plod through. I glance at the ground and snort.

He bursts into a run and reaches me within moments. His face hovers sheet-white over his dark coat. "Aria! Oh my God, what the hell happened? Your nose is bleeding."

I chuckle but don't stop walking. My nose is bleeding? I didn't even notice that. I guess I was too busy focusing on protecting my throat—and not dying. But since he mentioned it, I catch the scent of blood. I taste it too.

"Nick attacked me in the parking lot. He was wearing a

ski mask, right out in public like some freak. He knocked the gun from my hand, and I couldn't get to the hotel, so I ran. He tackled me to the ground and tried to strangle me. I fought him. He ran off into the woods," I say. I don't feel like explaining that before I lost my weapon, I intentionally didn't shoot him.

My voice comes out slightly hoarse. But I'm not sobbing. I'm not breaking down into a weeping mess, slipping into Trent's arms and wanting him to hold me. While my heart rate slows, I give him the details of the assault.

As we walk back to the hotel, Trent asks me questions and puts his hand on my shoulder. He stares in a sort of disconcerted horror, at times almost afraid to touch me since he doesn't know what hurts or where.

"I'm okay," I say, sneaking a grin. "You should see the other guy."

Trent blinks like I've lost my mind. "You don't sound okay, Aria. God, I'm so sorry. I wish you wouldn't have left like that. I heard the alarm on the truck, and I tried to come down, but a bunch of stuff happened and—" He breaks off. He sighs heavily and keeps his head down.

I frown, wondering if I heard him wrong. "A bunch of stuff happened? Like what?"

"I didn't know you went outside. I thought maybe you went to the lobby for snacks, but not outside alone," he says.

"No, I understand that part. You said a bunch of stuff happened. What?" I ask.

As we set foot in the hotel parking lot, the police pull up. Trent waves at them. The blonde receptionist, a man in a white shirt and blue tie, and the two early-twenty-something guys who were too timid to follow Nick and me all start heading in our direction.

The white-shirt man is the hotel manager, I find out. With him and the receptionist standing by in apologetic shock, I tell the police what occurred and mention how Detective Spade in Austin already opened a case for me. I know I have no proof the man who attacked me was Nick Pearlman, and I tell them so. I explain that I fired a few shots to deter the attack but that because I erred on the side of caution, he called my bluff and eventually knocked the gun from my hand. I also tell them the man's reaction when I mentioned his name.

The policeman offers to call an ambulance, but I insist that it's not necessary. My injuries are minor and don't warrant a trip to the hospital. When I'm free to go, Trent and I retrieve my pistol. It's lying in the middle of the parking lot near the tire of a white Ford diesel pickup truck.

"You should have just shot him," Trent says. "That's the whole reason you bought a gun."

My face heats. I tuck my now scuffed Sig under my jeans. "Well, if you still feel that way after taking someone's life, let me know."

That silences him.

DAWN BREAKS over the horizon as we drive back to Trent's house. Not wanting to give Kyle any grim details, I leave a hoarse message apologizing that I'll need to miss work today. I change into my pajamas. Then I slip into bed—the softest, most delicious bed ever created—and try to rest. Trent gets ready for another day at the police academy. He may have said goodbye. He may have even kissed me on the cheek as I lay under the blankets. Or did I imagine it? I'm so disoriented I'm not sure.

With the house locked and the security system armed, I sleep for most of the day. Nothing happens, or if it does, I'm so knocked out I don't notice. After I finally drag myself from my cocoon to eat dinner, I shower away the grassy sweat grime that clings to me. Then I crash again. A gentle pressure on my arm wakes me.

"Aria?"

Opening sleepy eyes that blink at the speaker, I see that Trent has pulled a chair near the bed. He leans over and faces me. It reminds me of what I once did for him eight months ago while he was in the hospital. Our odd conversation from yesterday bubbles to the cloudy surface of my thoughts. My sore throat has improved. Mostly what hurts now are my bruises and strained muscles. Man, I got off easy.

"How are you feeling?" Trent asks.

"Better," I say. "Especially from the sleep."

"Good." He gives me a sad smile and studies me. "Do you need anything?"

I shake my head. My eyes focus on his navy-blue Dallas Cowboys t-shirt that he's had forever. It's faded but somehow looks great on him.

Trent nods before reaching over and taking my hand. He smells like wood, citrus, and geranium—his deodorant since he's never been a fan of cologne. "All right. But let me know if you do." He softens his voice and asks, "Aria, if you're up to talking about it, is there anything else you need to tell me about Nick? Anything that maybe you haven't told me already?"

The question itself isn't that strange. It's the way he asks it so carefully and tilts his head while he looks me over. Kind of like a father asking a child to give up her secret, naughty deed.

"What do you mean?" My voice is still scratchy, my mouth stale and dry.

Trent swallows. "Has there been anything else going on with Nick—I mean, not—not now, but was there maybe something in the past?" It's unusual for him to stammer like that.

"What do you mean?" I repeat. I inhale deeply, push myself up on an elbow, and pull my hand away from his.

"The last thing I want to do is violate your confidence. But I think you need to be completely honest with the police. It will help them understand Nick's motives and nail him for this." Trent folds his arms and puts a hand to his mouth in contemplation.

If there's a hint here, I'm not taking it. "What are you talking about?"

Trent shifts again. His fingers brush my cheek as he tucks a lock of hair behind my ear. "Aria, I normally wouldn't bring something like this up. But I want you to know you don't have to be ashamed of it. A lot of women in your situation have found comfort in affairs, even if they were short-lived."

I stare at him, thinking I heard wrong—I *must* have heard wrong. Because it sounds like he's insinuating I had an affair with Nick Pearlman, the same man who not only just tried to kill me but is nearly forty years my senior. Of course, my brain isn't one hundred percent right now. My aches and pains could decrease my comprehension level too. But Trent faces me without blinking. Because I'm so confused and my dizziness isn't completely gone, my mind starts conjuring up nonsensical answers of what else he might have meant.

Coming up with nothing, I finally blurt, "An affair with who?"

Trent leans back with his palms on his quads. "With Nick. I know it might be difficult and awkward, but I think it would be a good idea to tell Detective Spade about that."

First, I frown. Then my mouth drops open as I glower at him. I want to scream, but I can't. My disbelief envelopes me like a chasm. I dive into it back first, falling down, down, down.

"Trent, I never had an affair with Nick. I don't know him. One evening, he showed up at work when I dropped by to get my laptop, just like I told you. He's been threatening me ever since," I say. "And we don't even know if 'Nick' is his real name."

Trent sighs. "Well, I know I can't make you talk about it, and it's not my place to. Just think about it, okay?"

Saying nothing in reply, I let my eyes go out of focus. I flop down on my back again. My blank gaze points toward the open closet at the row of clothes on hangers. With the lights off, the simple bedroom around me melts into a cold, shadowy blur. Did something happen with Nick that I can't remember? My therapist once agreed that people like me sometimes have lapses in their recall. An understatement, really, since after a year, Ayden's death is still a blank.

"Aria," Trent says. "Please don't worry. You don't have to feel embarrassed around me."

I raise my hands to my head and hold them to my temples. Sighing, I slowly lower them again and let them fall limp at my sides. "I didn't have an affair with Nick. I'm terrified of most men—with reason. I couldn't have an affair with someone I don't know. I'm not even having a real affair with *you*. Where did you get this idea? Did someone say this about me?"

Trent exhales forcefully. He scratches his cheek before speaking. "I don't think it's appropriate to say."

"Not appropriate? Are you kidding me?" I ask.

I want to press him more, but I'm too confused and light-headed. Maybe tomorrow I'll be closer to normal if there is a normal for me. Then I remember Trent's statements from last night, and I wonder if they're in some way connected to this absurd, new idea.

After shoving the sheet away, I sit bolt upright. "What happened in the hotel when I was attacked? What prevented you from coming out?"

Trent runs his hand over his forehead. "Okay. I took a phone call from a friend, but then, the Chief of Police picked up and threatened to expel me from the academy if I didn't explain my involvement at the warehouse on Lamar. I was on the phone with him when my truck alarm went off. I ran outside as fast as I could, but you were already gone. I went after you. I really did, Aria. But I know I didn't get to you in time."

"Did you get my phone call? I called you from right outside your truck," I say.

"No—I mean, yeah, later I did, but I didn't hear the phone ring. I was on a three-way call, and it went to voicemail."

I frown. Narrowing my eyes at him, I say, "I thought you tried to come out as soon as you heard the alarm."

"Yes, I did. I told the Chief of Police I was sorry, but I had to go because my truck alarm was going off. I put the phone in my pocket and ran out. But Aria, why did you go outside alone? You knew that wasn't a good idea," Trent says.

I can hear what he doesn't say, which is that my going outside alone was damn stupid. But why should I be scared in the illuminated parking lot of a nice hotel? Being on the defensive all the time gets old. So does being afraid. And hiding.

"I took my gun. There was plenty of lighting, and the receptionist saw me go out. Wait—the Chief of Police called you at three in the morning?" I ask.

"Yeah. Well, no, technically, the phone was handed to him, I think." He sniffs and squirms in his seat.

I gaze down at the blue and white blankets while I think. I recall a fuzzy memory of Trent talking on the phone with someone before I left the hotel room. What was he saying —"It's not her fault?" I assumed he was talking about me.

"Who were you talking to last night? I thought it was Kyle," I say.

Trent shakes his head. "No, it was someone from the academy. It was about our training."

I pull my head back. "Okay. So, who was it?"

Trent sighs. He pinches the upper bridge of his nose.

"Why won't you tell me?" As I wait for his reply, a plunging dread races to the pit of my stomach. "Oh. Were you talking to a woman? And you think I'll freak out?"

A slim blonde comes to mind, and within seconds, I'm very awake and crystal clear. Anxious jealousy races through my veins as I glare at Trent with new scrutiny.

"Was it Naomi?" I ask.

Silence.

23

I see. So, you were talking to Naomi, and that was more important than coming out to see if I was okay?" I ask.

Trent stiffens and puts his hands out for emphasis. "No. I mean, yes—yes, she called me, but no, that wasn't more important. Damn it, Aria, that's not how it happened." His cheeks catch fire, and he almost comes off the seat. "Damn it! Why the hell did you go outside alone? That was so stupid!"

For a second, I say nothing and glare at him with my eyes burning. Then my punched-in-the-gut feeling takes on another aspect. "What's really going on? What aren't you telling me?"

"Nothing," Trent says. He huffs. "At least nothing bad that I know of."

"There's something you're not telling me. Something big," I say.

"Aria, I'm not withholding anything bad from you. I promise," Trent says. His brown eyes are stricken with bruised purple circles underneath. He put in a full day at school on zero hours of sleep.

Not answering, I look away and suck in my bottom lip. Trent left a note for me on the mailbox. He and I have two different versions of what it said. He blamed me for our unauthorized investigation of the Lamar property even though it was his idea. He asked me if I was having an affair with Nick Pearlman, and now I find out he was talking with his cute friend at three in the morning while I was getting attacked. I've been so grateful to Trent it's usually hard to see his faults. But either Trent is a wolf in sheep's clothing, or I'm really as nuts as I feared.

"Trent, I appreciate everything you've done to help me, but I think I need to go home for a while to rest—and collect my thoughts," I say. I swing my legs over the side of the bed.

Trent's face goes wooden, and it takes him a full five seconds to speak. "Oh. Well, sure. If that's what you want—if you think you'll be more comfortable there. But you know you're always welcome here."

Of course, it's not what I want. I don't want to go. I don't want to be alone. I want everything just to make sense. I want Trent to be the person I thought he was instead of the person he seems right now.

"I wish you would tell me where you got the idea I had an affair with Nick. Who told you that?" I ask. The dizziness comes back. Arguing is exhausting.

"I can't say. I'm sorry," Trent says. I hear the wounded note in his voice, but I can't figure out what he's hurt about.

I slide my feet to the floor and stand up, trying to recall where I set my suitcase. "Why? Why can't you tell me?"

"Because," he says as he rises from the chair. He pauses

like he's not sure what his explanation's going to be. "It's not for me to say. And I know it's not really any of my business. I just happened to find out. But knowing what I know now, I want to help."

My ears flush, and though I haven't been straining my voice, anger alone makes my throat hurt more. "Well, if you can't tell me who told you, and it's not for you to say, then maybe you shouldn't have said anything at all. Especially since it's not true."

"Aria, please. I just wanted to make sure we did the right thing—that you told the police everything, including your history with Nick."

As I scowl at him, it finally hits me. No matter what I say, it won't make a difference. He has this odd idea in his head because of a bigger thing—the bigger thing he's not telling me about. And I know he won't 'fess up about that either.

"I already did that. I told the police everything I know, so my conscience is clean. I'm going to pack up and get going." Now I remember putting my suitcase in the closet. I grab it, set it on the bed, and unzip it. Since the Sig Sauer's case and the cleaning kit are still inside, that new gun smell wafts out. So much happened that besides handing it to me in the dark, Trent didn't get to look at my pistol. We didn't even talk about it. A sadness settles over me.

Trent's voice is soft, almost brittle when he speaks. "All right. Of course, you can go if you like. But you should know I don't want you to."

Tight-lipped, I turn and give a single nod. I have no response. Within twenty minutes I've packed my suitcase full and sit inside my Camry. I turn the key in the ignition.

And just like that, I'm alone again.

SINCE I'M ONLY BRUISED and sore for the most part, I only miss one day of work. However, I'm forced to wear a turtleneck to conceal the redness on my neck. I tell Kyle that despite the summer heat, I've been getting chilly from the air conditioning in the office. Concealer does a decent job of covering the mark on my cheek. And at home in Round Rock, to explain my hoarse voice, I tell my housemates I have a cold. Naturally, Margarita is interested in why I'm back from Trent's already when it looked like I was moving in. I tread carefully. One wrong answer, and she'll think he beat me. I field her questions the best I can while unloading a small bag of groceries in the kitchen.

"It was just something we were trying out," I say. "We didn't intend it to be a permanent thing. More of an experiment." I shrug before leaning down to open the bottom vegetable drawer. I stick a package of romaine lettuce inside.

"Aria, you need to be more careful with him. A couple of weeks ago, I was in your room thinking you might have left the corkscrew up there. Anyway, while I was looking for it, I saw a letter he wrote to you—I wasn't snooping. Well, not at first. I just happened to see it on your nightstand. Then I guess I got nosy." She sits at the table, manicure implements before her, and shakes a bottle of devil red nail polish.

As I stand up, my stomach sinks and the same confusion I grappled with at Trent's revisits me. Unpacking the next paper bag from HEB, I set a case of yogurt on the table. "So, you saw it? Can you remember what it said? I tried to find the paper again, but I couldn't."

Her forehead wrinkles and she aims shifty, dark brown eyes at me. "I don't remember it word for word. I just remember a 'you're a nice girl, but we don't have a future together' type of thing."

An orange rolls off the table. My hands drop to my sides. "I knew it! When I asked him about it, he said he didn't write that. He told me he wrote a letter asking me to move in with him. Did it also include anything like that?" I squat to retrieve the fruit.

Margarita pushes out her bottom lip. "No, it definitely didn't say that. The guy is a jerk. I know you like him because you feel like he saved you. And I know I'm always butting into your life and trying to give you advice. At least I feel like I am. But he didn't really save you. He just kind of found you. It was more like his boss who rescued you. Don't forget, Trent's boss asked him to check up on the house. So, Trent discovering you was an accident. You view him as a hero, Aria, but I really don't see that he deserves that status."

I lean on the table to steady myself as the gravity of her words sinks in. I sigh. Staring at the floor, I kick at a tuft of black fur left by Rebecca's cat. "Maybe you're right. I don't suppose you set the letter somewhere else after reading it? I'd like to have another look at it. Just because he told me something different than what I remembered."

Margarita shakes her head. "No, Aria. You remembered correctly. And I didn't move it. I'm pretty sure I put it back on the nightstand."

"I haven't been able to find it again. You're sure you didn't throw it away?" I ask. I remove the canned vegetables from the bag one by one, and they thump against the wooden tabletop.

"No, but I wanted to. It made me angry, and I don't like

you being treated that way. You don't deserve it," Margarita says. The smell of nail polish reaches me as she drags the brush across her left thumbnail.

I restrain a look. She doesn't have the right to mess with my things, even if it was a hurtful letter from my cop-in-training non-boyfriend. But maybe she really didn't misplace it. "All right. Well, maybe it will turn up."

After finishing with the groceries, I pop a green grape into my mouth and head back to my room for a final look. There's one place I haven't checked. I squat beside the night-stand and peer behind it.

There's a single piece of paper suspended between the small dresser and the wall. Well, well. My pulse increases as I draw it out and hold it under the lamp. Yes, this is it—the letter from Trent. My gaze races across the watery, left-slanted script, hoping the words will prove Margarita and me wrong.

Aria,

I want to let you know that I've decided to move on. You're a great girl, and I care about you a lot. But I have to pursue my career, and I can't give you the safe life you need. I hope you can forgive me and come to find your own happiness.

Trent

It's exactly as I remember. I shake my head and shove the note in the drawer.

THE NEXT MORNING as I drive to work, I try to piece together everything that doesn't make sense. It seems to me I'm living out a sick adaptation of a choose-your-own-adventure story. Like, I can pick the good version of Trent, and he'll willingly play that part. Or, I can select the bad version, and I could cast him as the villain with no trouble. And apparently, so can everyone else. But even after finding the letter, I still don't know what I don't know. That's the problem. I'm missing the big something. It remains hidden from me.

This week there's some kind of film festival going on. The organization must have chosen a nearby venue because cars are parked in every conceivable spot near the office. As I drive past Median Realty's dark gray building, our lot is full. I turn the corner but find no available spaces. Finally, I get a spot, but I have to park nearly four blocks away. I lock up the Camry and set the alarm. Since I bought more pepper spray after my fight with Nick, I grip it in my right hand. Under the waist of my slacks rests my pistol in its hidden holster. And the next time I use it, I doubt I'll play nice. Already feeling sticky in my turtleneck, I head out on foot toward Blue-bonnet Lane.

I'm not the only pedestrian on this fine morning. The air is a little more humid than usual for Austin, with a pleasant temperature somewhere around seventy-two degrees. The blazing heat hasn't struck yet. A young couple walks about twenty feet in front of me. Across the street on the sidewalk, a group of eventgoers laugh and talk as they make their way to the venue. People are on the move behind me as well, but they're some way back.

I follow the sidewalk of the South Austin neighborhood in my high heels. Caramel-stained wooden privacy fences make clean backdrops to the shrubbery at the curb, shielding some of the houses from view. A black and tan, modern-style McMansion was recently built in one yard without such a fence, leaving only about ten feet of lawn in front. After tugging my gaze from the house's obtrusive boxiness, the group of about eight people on the other side of the street crosses over and gets in front of me. They're still a good distance ahead, but I walk faster than they do, even in these shoes. I have to get to work after all, and they're just going out for a good time. Pretty soon, I'm almost on them. I try to go around to the right, which puts me closer to the street. Someone spilled a smoothie by the curb, and it dribbles over the asphalt in a sticky, red ribbon with chunks of strawberries. The sweet smell lets me know the drink was freshly dropped. I walk in the road to avoid getting it on my shoes and wait behind a parked car as more people pass.

Another troop of attendees comes into view on the opposite sidewalk. Between them and me, a few cars drive by slowly. I remain where I am and wait for an opening. A blue pickup truck rolls along past me. Next comes a dark green convertible, an older model. It looks like a Mazda Miata. After that is a silver Honda Accord. It pulls up to me and stops.

What the hell? My heart pounds at the idea of any vehicle stopping like that, and I start to back up. The driver's side window descends, and a middle-aged woman with brown hair calls out to me.

"Miss? I'm sorry, but could you help me with directions real quick? I'm not from around here, and my GPS has me turned around," she says.

I frown. I can't see the vehicle's plate from here, and I didn't bother to look when the car approached.

Without caring if I hurt her feelings or not, I take a few steps forward and crane my neck to get a look at the license plate. It depicts a blue lake with an orange sun rising behind it—Michigan. She wasn't kidding when she said she's not from around here. I return to the curb so that I can face her again. But I don't approach the car.

I say, "I can try. What are you trying to find?"

"Thanks." The woman smiles, and I glimpse the smartphone in her hand. She scrolls with her thumb. "I'm looking for—"

Sounds of whirling bicycle pedals and a gyrating chain grate my ears.

"Look out!" the cyclist yells, but he's already colliding with me.

He shoves me out of the way with his hand—probably so the tires won't hit my legs. I pitch forward and stumble toward the woman in the car. My hand releases the pepper spray, and it rolls out of sight to my left. At the same moment, the back door of the sedan swings open. A man steps out. It's Nick Pearlman as clearly as the day is long. No ski mask this time. No long trench coat. He's wearing a navy-blue dress shirt, black slacks, and dark sunglasses.

As I catch myself on the asphalt with my hands, Nick surges toward me. He wraps an arm around my middle and clamps his hand over my mouth. I thrash wildly at his face, pull forward, and try to dig my heels into his legs. I kick at his shins. I get a few jabs in—especially when I stab the top of his foot with my high heel, and he yells. But he crushes my body against his so hard I can't break free. My stifled screams die against Nick's palm as he scoops me up and tosses me into the back seat. He slams the door and locks us in. Three seconds. That's how long the abduction took from the time I fell.

Confusion overtakes my senses with nearly as much force as fear. Nick seems so much stronger than the night he attacked me in the field. He's the same man, the same height and build, yet it's like fighting against a completely different person. The scent of his thyme and leather aftershave lingers, and I want to spit away the salty taste where he touched my mouth.

"Drive," Nick commands the woman behind the wheel.

The car lurches forward, and I reach for my pistol. It starts a wrestling match—one that Nick wins. Disarmed, I scoot away from him on the back seat and try the door lock on the other side. It won't budge. I scream and pound on the window. Maybe I can break it. The dizziness and terror consume me, and my head throbs. Like the day inside the burned Lamar building, I'm about to pass out. The small car interior presses from all sides like a trap and crushes my will. I need to stay strong. I need to focus like when we fought in the field. I won that time, and maybe I can win again. But Nick's strength has doubled since then, and I don't understand.

The woman turns onto a quieter street. "You didn't tell me you were going to hurt her."

"I'm not hurting her," says Nick. "I just want to show her something."

"Well, it better not be your penis or the wrong end of a gun, or this deal is off," the woman says. Her gaze finds me in the rearview. "Are you okay, honey?"

"Hell no, I'm not okay! Let me out. Pull over and let me

out." I beat against the window, trying to get the attention of a group of teenagers on the sidewalk.

"Help! Call the police! Get the plate number and call 991!" I yell at the glass.

The kids smile and wave at me like it's a joke.

24

Honey, please don't break the glass," the woman says. "This is my car. I'm just doing a favor. No one's going to get hurt. If he does anything stupid, I'll let you out. I promise. Just sit tight."

He's going to kill me. This I know. Once someone gets you in their car, it's over. I might have got in some good licks and escaped in the field, but it's easier in the open. But now I realize that although I dropped my pepper spray and he took my Sig, I have my knife. I can use it on him, as long as he doesn't take it from me. Like the gun, he probably expects me to have it, so I need to prepare. My stomach whirls. I swallow.

My panic attack kicking in full force, I start hyperventilating. I alternate between clutching the car door for its solidity and pounding on the window she told me not to break. Beside me, Nick sits with one hand slightly extended, palm in my direction, as though warding off my stray slaps as I scream for help. He leans away from me toward the other door. He angles a sidelong glance in my direction.

He says, "She's right. You're fine. Now hand me your purse."

Nick mentioning my purse makes me think of my knife again. It's inside the pocket of my slacks. I slip my purse from its crosswise position over my left shoulder and push it along the seat toward Nick. He grabs it and tosses it on the floor at his feet. My phone and ID are in there, but not my little switchblade.

"Now give me any other weapons you have," he says. My eyes must flash guilt because he adds, "Do it, or I'll force you."

I'll never surrender my weapon. I guess he'll have to force me. I whip out the switchblade and lunge at him. His rear comes off the seat like a bug on a hot pan, and he dodges just before I stab him in the carotid artery. The knife buries itself in the upholstery with a neat *zip*.

"Oh, for Pete's sake! You're going to pay for that," the woman says, whether to me or Nick, I don't know.

And I don't care. I yank the knife out and stab straight for Nick's face. With the snap of a rattlesnake, he catches my wrist in his bony fingers. I growl. My arm trembles as we push against each other. He adds his other hand to the force and pushes me backward. I haven't let go yet. I won't. I grit my teeth and strain every muscle. With my free hand, I make a fist and punch him square in the nose.

"Goddammit! You—" His face blooms red, and he removes a hand from my wrist to grab the one that struck him.

My back and arms sear with pain, but still, I push. My quivering muscles finally give out, and Nick thrusts me against the edge of the seat, where I slide off. My head cracks into something—the door handle, maybe.

"You *said* you weren't going to hurt her!" the woman says.

Nick wrests the knife from my grip. I try to catch myself before falling completely into the narrow floor space, but my hand slips off the back of the passenger's seat. I push myself up and scoot against the door. I pant like a rabid animal. Nick closes the knife. As he shoves it in his trouser pocket, I slam the heel of my hand into his nose.

He wails. He spouts profanity and covers the wound, rocking back and forth a few times.

"You deserved that, I think," the driver lady says.

"Shut up!" says Nick.

"Let me out of this fucking car, or I'll hit you again," I say.

"No, this is your fault. You wouldn't listen. I told you—I'll let you go. I just need to show you something first," he says.

I make for his right ear. I'll tear it clean off if it's the last thing I do. But as I lash out to grab it, Nick shoves hard against my breastbone. The force hurls me against the door. My head hits the window.

"Stop it, both of you! Just stop!" the woman says. She slams on the breaks.

"Shut up!" says Nick. "Keep driving."

The back of my skull throbs, and disorientation shakes me. I grab the passenger's seat to steady myself. Then I notice the window—it's cracked. Now I can break it the rest of the way. I might even be able to jump out before the driver takes us on the highway. My arm shakes uncontrollably as I make a fist. I'll pound every shard of glass from that window if I have to.

"No," says Nick. His voice is weary.

Blood trickles from the left nostril of his fire-engine red nose as he withdraws a semi-automatic pistol from beneath his waistline. It's not mine. It looks like a Glock. He racks the slide, clicking it in place with a portentous *snick*. He aims the black barrel at me.

"You brought a gun? What the hell were you thinking?" the driver says. "I didn't sign up for this. If you hurt that poor girl, it's not going to be my ass on the line. You need to think about what you're doing. Because we're not both going to jail. You better not be planning to kill her."

"Shut up, Goddammit," Nick says. "You're doing what I paid you to do. Force is the only thing some people listen to."

With my eyes aching, I give up my window idea. I lean against the corner of the back seat with my hands in my lap. Nick calmly keeps the gun trained on me. He doesn't look angry, even though I probably broke his nose. He looks annoyed.

Korey was really calm at times, too, just like this. He had his crazy, emotional fits when he screamed, smashed things, or threw stuff. Sometimes the thing he threw was my body. Not up in the air, but he would shove me so hard I'd fly against the wall or floor. But he also had moments when he was so sedately insane. Those were some of the worst. Those were the ones that got me drained of blood and strung up against the wall in the house on County Road 140.

But before he sank the knife into my flesh, he put me in a white dress. The white dress—I finally remember. It would have been my wedding dress, he told me. I betrayed him in life, but I would marry him in death.

"You're a filthy whore, Aria," he said. "Even though you don't deserve forgiveness, through your pain and death, you will be absolved of your sins against me. And your blood will consummate the marriage you should have given me in life."

But being in this car now has nothing to do with Korey. It's about killing Ayden, an incident in my past that seems sadly minor in comparison. Yet I'll die all the same. People always have their reasons, don't they? But my mind isn't showing me the occluded memory of Ayden's death. It's reeling with the untimely flashback of my torture. I can still smell the filth of that back room, feel the almost tangible yellowish-brown darkness against my skin while I wasted away from starvation. I continuously plotted how to feed myself and my stepmom. Xero's dog food. I shoved my face in the Purina bag and dropped sticky kibbles into Carol's mouth. And then I was so tired. The weariness eventually dragged me under like an anchor pulling me to the depths of the sea.

My head snaps up, and my heart begins pounding. I started to black out without even realizing it. A wave of dizziness hits me, my hands sweat, and my entire body trembles. The car is slowing down. I lean forward slightly, glancing between Nick and the driver. The sound of my frantic breathing envelopes the car's interior. How long was I half-conscious? I look out the windshield and find we're coming up to a wide, paved space, like a small airport. Ahead, a dark green helicopter looms on the asphalt, its rotor blades unmoving.

Nick turns to me. His annoyance is gone, and now his eyes are cold and unreadable. "We're going to change vehicles."

Why bother telling me that? My hands and feet are unbound, and I'm not blindfolded or gagged. Doesn't he know I can run? That I can still scream? "Why?"

Nick flutters his eyelids, the same as he did outside the office when I irritated him. "Because it's too far to drive."

Asshole. With my hands clamped between my knees, I sit rigidly and stare straight ahead. The woman at the wheel takes us along a driveway of sorts. There's a large, gray, metal building to the right. Presumably a hangar. On its side is a large number "2" written in black. The metallic emerald helicopter bears a few thin, gold stripes with a rounded front that draws into a pointed nose. Its cockpit is enclosed with black-tinted windows. Beneath the rotors are written the letters N507TV. I try to commit that to memory, although I doubt I'll retain it in my present state. The chopper is parked on a white "H" within a circle.

Beyond the helicopter pad stretches an empty field. The terrain is typical of Central Texas—low-lying, wiry shrubs, agave, prickly pear cacti, scattered grass, and stones. Beyond the expanse of meadow is a wild forest. Besides telephone poles, I don't see any buildings or any other signs of civilization. This little airport or whatever it is seems to lie in the middle of nowhere.

The woman pulls into a small parking lot about a hundred feet from the helicopter pad. She parks the Accord and turns off the car. "I'm glad you're doing better, honey. Don't worry, this will all be over soon, and then you can go home."

"I'm not paying you to talk to her," Nick says.

He doesn't look at her or me but keeps his eyes on the chopper. The morning sun hits the high gloss paint, making it glimmer green, yellow, and blue. My stomach dives at the sight of it, and I think I might be sick. But my mind lingers on what the woman just said. *Then you can go home.*

"Well, talking to her is the least I can do," she says. She undoes her seat belt, and when the buckle slaps the car's vinyl interior, I jump.

She adds, "The poor girl is scared out of her mind."

A tiny thought blossoms in the back of my consciousness. Maybe I'm not going to die. Although, that's fanciful of me. Too generous. Maybe she only said that to try and keep me calm. Maybe that's part of how she's working with him—to be the nice, stabilizing influence of the operation. What an idiot Nick is not at least to bind my feet. When that door comes open, I'm bolting. As long as he doesn't grab my head like before, I can try and outrun him. I'll go straight for those woods, and I can walk for days if I need to. I'm not afraid of the wilderness because there are no people there.

"You're not going to run. Understand?" Nick asks. He scoots beside me and puts the barrel of the Glock to my forehead.

The woman stands just outside, waiting for Nick and me to exit the car. The window slightly muffles her voice as she says, "Oh for heaven's sake."

Nick presses the pistol against my skin enough to move my head. "Tell me you're not going to run."

I can't make myself say the words, but I nod. My arms go rigid, and my hands turn to ice. I clutch my legs to give myself something to cling to. Everything else has fled my control.

"Get out of the car and walk toward the helicopter. Slowly, like you're walking down the aisle at your goddamn wedding," Nick says.

A wave of terror shoots from my heart to my abdomen at his eerie choice of words. Like he's watching images of my flashback play on a movie screen. This time I manage to mumble, "Okay."

I hear a click, and the door lock springs up, which makes me jump again. With my hand shaking, I force my fingers to pull the handle and open the car door. I swing my right leg out and then my left. I can't feel my feet. I know they're there at the end of my legs, but they're numb, almost like wooden blocks. I put one leg in front of the other. I'm the marionette, and he's the master. He pulls the strings, and I obey.

It's very hard to hit a moving target. But I assume that's considering the target isn't two feet away from the shooter. If I run, I'll be dead before I get to the other side of the "H."

25

My insides compress, and I'm back in that room with Korey hovering over me, my blood pooling around me on the urine-stained hardwood before he strung me up. And at the same time, I'm here. A stranger's kidnapping me at gunpoint and forcing me into a helicopter. My frail hope of running away or of living past this afternoon evaporates.

Nick says, "Buckle your seat belt." Holding the gun in his right hand, he slides something out of his pocket with his left. "After that, blindfold yourself." He tosses a black strip of fabric onto my lap. "If you allow yourself any gap, I'll know, so do it right."

I don't answer, snapping the seat belt in place before picking up the fabric as instructed. My fingers quiver as I wrap it around my head and tie it in back. The sloppy knot catches strands of my hair. It pulls them sharply against my scalp. Folding my arms across my chest, I lean back in the seat. I brace my feet as far in front of me as they can go while keeping my knees bent. Even when I open my eyes, the blindfold material is so dark I can see nothing. I strain to hear and perceive what Nick is doing, but all I catch is the metal click of his own seat belt locking and the whoosh of helicopter blades turning. Faint scents of aviation gasoline and warm plastic reach me.

The tempo of whirring increases, as does the steady, rhythmic hum. The sound continues for what feels like a long time and becomes loud. We sit here forever. No new information meets my ears. Finally, with barely a bump, we're airborne, lifting smoothly off the asphalt. I press my arms inward, tighter against myself. We're going up. My stomach drops, and soon my ears clog with cotton. The sounds around me grow muffled as though I'm underwater. Yawning would make that go away, but I resist the urge. However, the fabric itches the bridge of my nose, and I start to reach up a sweaty hand to scratch it.

"Keep your hands away from your face." Nick's voice cuts through the noise.

My breath hitches. I tuck my hand back against my side. I sit here, listening to the whirring blades, and somewhere behind that, the sound of my panicked breathing. I feel the subtle motion of the helicopter beneath and around me. So different from a plane. It sails along fluidly, like a ship upon a sea as smooth as glass. Keeping my arms clamped against my chest, I hardly move with my mouth pressed firmly in anger. I won't give Nick the satisfaction of seeing me squirm —of seeing tears roll down my cheeks. There are none, and my face is dry.

I don't know how long we fly or in what direction we travel. If I have to guess, we might have been airborne for close to an hour before we start our descent. The pressure change clogs my ears anew, and I swallow, trying to get my full hearing back. As we drop in altitude, my gut sinks, and I clench my hands into fists. The ache builds behind my eyes again. I fight it. I grit my teeth and squint behind my black blindfold. There's no way for me to gauge where we'll land and what will happen to me once we get there. But I'm not going to cry. Not yet, anyway.

The helicopter gets into landing position, hovering slowly as the pilot—the same woman who drove us whose name I still haven't heard—lowers us down. I reach my hands under my legs and grab onto the seat. Lower and lower, the helicopter descends until finally, it touches down with a soft thump. I twitch again but keep my grip on the plastic chair.

"Leave your blindfold on," Nick says. "I'll lead you inside the location, and you can take it off once I tell you to."

I say nothing in response but fumble for my seat belt latch. My shaking fingers finally get hold of it, and after about thirty seconds of grappling with the unfamiliar lock, I get it unfastened.

Finally forcing myself to yawn with my mouth closed so my ears will pop, I jerk when Nick places his hand on my arm. He barely touches me this time instead of grabbing me and shoving me wherever he chooses.

He says, "Stand up."

I do. He guides me to the door, which I hear the woman open. At least, I presume that's the noise because I feel the wind on my face and hear birds. The warm, outside air touches my skin.

"Stay there, and once I get out, I'll lower you down," Nick says.

I try to keep my arms at my sides but mostly only succeed in keeping them suspended awkwardly somewhere around my abdomen. My gut contracts constantly as I think of what will happen if I tumble out onto the asphalt. I assume there will be concrete and not grass. But even if there's grass, it will still hurt if I fall flat on my face. I shudder and wait.

After a few seconds, Nick tells me, "Kneel down."

Dread plunges through me. I do so slowly, placing one hand out in front to make sure I'm not going to pitch through the open door. Soon after, I feel hands sliding under my armpits, the way one does to lift a child. I gasp and shut my mouth quickly. Nick pulls me forward and lifts me toward him. This makes the poorly healed muscle near my shoulder sear like a bad rope burn, and I grit my teeth and cry out. Then I get a whiff of his thyme and leather-scented aftershave, and I cringe. As he lowers me down and sets me on the ground, my body presses against the front of his. I stiffen, pulling back involuntarily. But I'm not resisting, so I guess that's why he doesn't strike me. Korey would have.

The woman clinks keys together nearby. She says to Nick, "I'll walk ahead of the two of you and get the door."

The trepidation in her voice is plain. I guess she's referring to the house door if it is, in fact, a house we're going to. I have no way of knowing.

After wrapping his fingers around my upper arm, Nick guides me along beside him. He walks more slowly than I expected. He doesn't drag or push me. He allows me time to take cautious steps, knowing I can't see anything or where I place my feet. I don't know what to make of this.

After about a hundred paces, he halts and says, "There are stairs here—five of them."

I nod. I take each step carefully, pushing my toe forward each time to make sure there's enough surface under my foot. After the fifth one, we walk onto a landing or porch, I assume—we're still outside. Keys rattle, and a deadbolt slides open as the woman unlocks the door. Heavy wood creaks on its hinges.

Nick steers me forward into an atmosphere that holds a light scent like vanilla candles. My high heels dig into what might be a rug. Next, my shoes click across something like a hardwood floor. He directs me to the right.

He says, "Another flight of stairs. This time there are twenty."

The woman's feet patter up a stairway in front of us. From the sound, it also seems to be hardwood. While Nick keeps his hand on my arm, I do the same as outside and carefully navigate each step. We reach the top, and Nick turns me to the left. Now it seems I'm walking across a carpet. He leads me to the right, and a door closes behind me. I exhale loudly and shiver. I hear the woman, or perhaps Nick himself, locking us in.

"You can take the blindfold off now," he says.

My clumsy fingers dig into the knot and try to undo it without ripping hair from my head. I pull the blindfold away from my eyes and reveal a brightly lit room. The woman stands a few feet from us, scowling and worrying the keys in her fingers. I blink and glance around the space to take in its design and contents. It's an office or something like one.

The room is small and plain, with no decoration. It smells like glue and wood. There are no windows that I can see. To the left of the door is a wall with a row of gray, metal filing cabinets. Upon the last one sits a wire basket which contains a few papers. In front of me stands a desk piled with manila folders and more papers, a canister of pens, another container filled with markers, and various office supplies. Above the desk is a corkboard affixed with newspaper clippings and photos. On the right-hand wall hangs a giant map of the state of Texas, surrounded by several smaller maps. From here, I can't discern if the smaller ones depict parts of the same state or elsewhere. Three chairs are placed in front of the desk.

Holding the blindfold limply in my right hand, I hold it out and offer it to Nick. He takes it and stuffs it in the pocket of his trousers. I notice he's no longer holding the gun. Maybe he holstered it sometime after I blindfolded myself.

"Have a seat," he says.

He extends a hand, gesturing to the middle chair. The woman takes the chair to the far left, air whooshing from under her jeans as she plops her ample backside down. She sits sideways and looks up expectantly. Her gaze darts back and forth between Nick and me. I wonder if she expects me to fight back again. I wonder it myself.

I walk over and take a seat in the middle chair, facing forward. I don't look at the woman or try to ask her for help. If she were going to help, not just protest Nick killing me, she would have done it a long time ago. She's here, so she's, therefore, just as much a part of this as Nick.

Nick takes the chair to my right. I fold my hands in my lap and turn my head halfway in his direction. His body faces more toward me than the desk. He smooths imaginary wrinkles on his blue dress shirt as he studies my stricken face. I guarantee his looks worse. His broken nose is now more purple than red, and he has two black eyes. When he sees he has my attention, he begins to speak.

"That building catching fire was almost the best thing that's happened to me in thirty years. Almost. The best thing that happened was you and your boyfriend ripping the wall out." He stares at me as though this is supposed to mean something to me. He continues. "I'm going to tell you everything. Show you everything. When I'm done, I'll give you a packet. You're going to take it to the police, and Rance Epstein will be arrested for murder."

Nick regards me, his face expressionless as I glare at him. Is he saying he's not the one who set the fire? I almost reply but think better of it. I inhale and nod frigidly. Sure. I'll listen to what he has to say. It's not like I have a choice. And I'll deliver a bunch of papers too. You bet I will. But behind my anger and sarcasm, the little flicker of hope ignites again. Is he really going to let me live? Did he truly fly me here to give me information and not for some darker purpose of revenge?

Nick leans back slightly, seeming satisfied with my icy acknowledgment. He blinks at me, but not with his arrogant eye-flutter thing. His brows relax, and he breathes deeply, almost like he's relieved. Then Nick begins to impart information.

This impartation starts with him saying, "The remains you found in the warehouse belong to a woman named Juliana Lange. She was murdered on September 28th, 1987."

"In March of 1988, I was tried and convicted for this crime, which I didn't commit. I was sentenced to life until my exemplary behavior, and finally, a breakthrough from my legal counsel got me out on parole a month ago. Maybe I didn't do life, but thirty years is a long time for an innocent man to go to jail, and violating my parole will put me right back in. My problem this last month was that the only way to prove my innocence was to violate my parole. One of the conditions was that I couldn't go within a hundred yards of Rance Epstein. Unfortunately, I've already done that a number of times, including visiting the warehouse on Lamar, which he now owns. All of this would have been so much easier if you hadn't screwed me over. Obtaining your cooperation by force was my last recourse."

Mentally, I hear one of the first things he said when he began threatening me. *I know what you did in the shed.* Nothing in his current monologue relates to what happened with Ayden. My mouth drops open, and my bottom lip hangs numbly. In a brittle voice, I say, "I still don't know what you're talking about. How did I screw you over?"

"I asked you to take a leap of faith and sell the property to me. To discuss it with me. But you wouldn't even give me a few minutes of your time to listen to what I had to say. Instead, you sided with the murderer and sold to him, no questions asked. The buildings went to Rance, and with them, I thought, any chance of Juliana's remains being discovered. At first, I thought you were acting out of fear, or maybe stupidity. Then I learned otherwise. You found out he was hiding something, and he paid you to keep quiet."

Without meaning to, I snort. "That doesn't make sense. Why would I have opened the wall if I was paid to keep quiet? We called the police, and the story was front-page news."

Nick almost smiles. "I wondered the same. I considered it evidence that you had a conscience. That you wondered what, in fact, you had actually agreed to. Like I said, it was the best thing that happened to me in thirty years. And here we are."

I glance at my lap. Despite the fear factor, this discussion has taken on a remarkable resemblance to my last conversation with Trent. I look up at Nick as though he's just an ordinary man and not my kidnapper. "Who told you that?"

"Excuse me?" He raises his eyebrows.

"Who told you Rance paid me off? Not Rance if you can't speak to him, so who?" I ask.

Nick hardens his brows, and his forehead furrows with deep lines. "My contact is not your concern."

"Oh, I fucking well think he is!" I want to launch myself off the chair.

Nick's hand flashes at his side, producing the handgun. He makes sure I can see it. But I can't deliver a packet for him if I'm dead. He knows it.

My chest heaving in anger, I say, "Rance didn't pay me anything. I don't know him, just like I don't know you."

Nick says nothing and keeps the pistol aimed at me. With everything he's put me through so far, I still don't have my basic questions answered. I bristle, wishing he'd get to the punch line. We aren't there yet.

I ask, "You know for a fact that Rance murdered that woman and put her body in the warehouse?"

The eye-flutter thing again. How I hate him.

"Yes, he murdered her on the date I told you. But he didn't put her body there originally. He had buried it elsewhere, dug it up later, and moved it," he says.

"And cleaned it? Because it didn't look like anyone had dug it up. It was an immaculate, white skeleton surrounded by flowers and little cards inside a homemade vault lined with satin." My stomach turns over as I recall the scene in the dingy lighting of that room in the annex building—the morbid, covetous beauty of it all.

Nick slams his palm against the desktop. "Yes, of course he cleaned it! He made his little shrine to her. Do you understand what this is? Are you getting some inkling of the kind of person who would do this?"

I know Nick sees the irony flash in my eyes as I glare back at him. He's holding me at gunpoint. I ask, "Why did he murder her?"

"I thought you'd never ask. Very simple. In 1987, Juliana left him. For me."

Now we're getting somewhere. I blink, trying to insert the last puzzle piece I can't make fit. "But... even if I was paid by Rance, which I wasn't, I still don't understand what this has to do with Ayden. Are you related to him? You told me that you knew—that you knew about the shed, about what I did. But you haven't mentioned Ayden once."

Nick frowns and tucks his chin. The chair creaks beneath him as he leans back and observes me. He takes me in carefully, his gaze devouring the abject confusion stamped across my face.

"Who's Ayden?"

26

The dizziness comes upon me again, the reeling which makes slipping out of the chair and falling unconscious to the floor a real possibility. "Ayden Nemeth. He was a man who... died in our backyard shed."

I stop myself from saying more. If he doesn't know who Ayden is, if I've been that off base about everything, then it seems even worse to tell him the details of what happened. Silent, Nick looks at me with the sour disdain I'm growing accustomed to. My cheeks heat.

I say, "You said you knew what I did in the shed."

And then Nick starts to laugh. He begins slowly at first, then his sardonic chuckle takes hold of him, and he clutches his stomach. My heart flutters in an anxious panic, and I slowly wipe my sweaty palms on my slacks.

"Unbelievable. You thought I was talking about something from your past?" He smiles grimly, shakes his head, and looks down at his lap momentarily. He snickers. "'The shed.' I was talking about the room in the annex—that whole section is a storage building. From the outside, it even looks like a large shed. And it should because that's what it is."

I swallow, wishing I could drop through the floor and disappear. "But... I don't understand. You said I've had blood on my hands for too long. That everything comes with a price and that what I did was as good as murder."

Nick snorts. "Yes. Like I already told you, I know Rance paid you to keep quiet. So, don't bother trying to keep up the lie to the contrary."

"But you said you were there. You couldn't have been there because it never happened," I say.

"All right, technically, I wasn't present. I was outside the property when you spoke to Rance on the walk-through. You were alone together. My contact was the one who overheard you and reported back to me."

I grit my teeth. Another wave of anger turns me rigid. "Wow. Because people hired to spy and do bad deeds *always* tell the truth."

"Enough!" he says. His white cheeks turn pink as he shoves the gun at my face.

I guess I'm supposed to shut up now, but I don't. "If you knew the woman's remains were inside the wall, why didn't you find a way to alert the police yourself? Especially if you already knew Rance had murdered her."

Nick sighs, tilting his head in exasperated weariness. He bends his elbow, bringing the gun closer to himself. "I have found a way—you. And I already told you the answer to that question as well. Had I done so, it would have been a violation of parole, and I would have been arrested. I'm not taking any chances. If our justice system can lock me away for thirty years for a murder I didn't commit, they wouldn't bat an eye at sending me back to prison for trespassing or getting too close to Epstein. Everything is explained in the packet I'll give you. It should take care of this, once and for all. If you're smart, you'll read through it before you turn it in."

"And how do I tell the police I came by this information?" I ask.

"You'll tell them you compiled it yourself. That you became engrossed in your discovery about your client's property and decided to do your own investigation." Nick draws a handkerchief out of his pocket and dabs at his brow. His gaze never leaves my face.

"You want me to lie to the police. What if I don't tell them that? What if I tell them you gave me the information? What if everything you're saying is a lie, and you're the one who murdered Juliana, and you're trying to frame Rance for it?" My arms tremble as I shove my hands between my knees. The nervous jittering in my belly hasn't let up once.

The subtle smile from Nick again. Then it vanishes, and he clenches his jaw. "If you don't tell the police you compiled the information yourself, I'll kill Trent Lemend. I know where he lives. I know he's enrolled in the police academy. I know where he gets his kicks on the weekends. I even know where he goes for a screw occasionally—if you were wondering."

He may as well have shot me in the gut. I exhale, my body drooping as the strength leaves it. I draw a shallow breath and wrap my arms around my waist to stave off the next panic attack. He knows. I don't know how he knows, but he does. He knows Trent is the one person who's important to me—the one person who, in the end, I would do anything for, no matter how complicated our relationship.

"Does that put things in the proper perspective?" asks Nick.

"Yes. I'll do it," I say.

"Good," Nick says.

He turns and opens a desk drawer from which odors of plywood and ink escape. He reaches in and takes out a fat, brown folder that he holds in both hands. "This is the packet. Once we fly back to Austin, you'll have a week to take it to the Austin Police Department. Read it, make copies, whatever you want. You will if you're smart. Then you can give it directly to your contact—whoever you've been reporting to about me."

"All right," I say. The words are deflated. Weak. But I'm going to live. And granting that Nick is telling the truth, so will Trent. I'm walking out of here alive, and all I have to do to stay that way is tell a lie. Worse things have happened to me.

"Any questions?" asks Nick. He puts his back against the chair again, the thick, vinyl folder resting in his lap.

"Why did you shoot at us?" I ask.

He gives me that look again, the little twitch at the corner of his mouth. Almost a smirk. He's silently laughing at me like my misfortune amuses him. "Us?"

"Yes. Trent and me. Why?"

"I never shot at you. Today is the first time I brought a gun anywhere near you," Nick says.

I huff. I open my mouth but take several seconds to speak. "But... you attacked me outside the hotel. You were wearing a ski mask. You chased me into the field and tried to kill me. That was you."

"No again. Looks like I'm not your biggest problem," he says. "I guess after you read through my information, you'll have some more research to do."

I swallow the lump in my throat before forcing myself to

ask another stupid question. "Did you throw rocks at the house?"

This time Nick chuckles. "No. Sorry."

My face burns and I feel my skin ignite crimson. He didn't shoot at us. He didn't attack me. And rocks, of course not. I still don't have the answers I want. Ayden is long dead, and Korey is behind bars for life. There's no one else. I blink back tears, ignoring the ache in my eyes as I study Nick's face.

Nick's face.

I can't believe I didn't realize it before, but I guess I was too caught up in being abducted for the second time in my life. During the fight in the field, I punched my attacker in the face again and again. His nose even cracked beneath my fist at one point. But when Nick grabbed me today, his pale countenance bore no marks at all. His broken nose is brand new.

The woman clears her throat in the chair to my left. I almost forgot she was there since I'm turned to face Nick. She says, "It's almost—"

"Don't say what time it is," Nick says, his booming voice pervading the room. He sits up rigidly. Like he's scolding a child, he adds, "She doesn't need to know that."

I hear the woman rise. She clears her throat once more and coughs a couple of times softly in embarrassment. "Do you want me to get the helicopter ready?"

"Yes," Nick says. He produces the black strip of fabric from his pocket and dangles it close to my face. "Time to go."

～

AFTER FLYING us back to the small airfield, the woman drives us like before. She doesn't speak to me again. It's now afternoon, and she pulls into Zilker Park, where I'm to be dropped off.

Nick's face is pallid around his swollen, red nose as he hands me my purse. "Your gun and knife are inside."

"All right," I say. I take my handbag and slide out of the back seat with the heavy file under my arm. The day is hot and bright now, and the sun glints off the lake. People are jogging on the trail nearby or walking their dogs. A cyclist in a pink helmet flashes by the pedestrians. An odd buzzing courses through my limbs at the idea of being free. Of being alive. Before walking away, I tear my gaze from the trail and look back at my kidnapper.

"Do what I said, and your boyfriend lives," he tells me.

I nod. Nick reaches over and pulls the car door closed. After a couple of seconds, the Honda Accord slowly rolls away. I draw a shaky breath and start walking in the direction of Median Realty in my high heels. As trivial as it seems, I know I'll have to come up with an explanation for Kyle about why I'm late—and why I look like hell. Not to mention that by the time my turtleneck-wearing self gets to the office, my face will be sunburned.

FOR ONCE, fortune favors me. I don't have to lie to my boss and make up a story about why I'm dragging into work at noon with messy hair and red skin. When I arrive, I learn via the post-it note on my desk that Kyle's been out all morning with clients, and he's left me a short to-do list. Score.

That night, I sit at my desk at home with every light on as I unwind the cord from the button of the brown vinyl folder. When I open it and slide out the thick stack of papers, I get a whiff of the office where Nick held me—glue, wood, and that vanilla scent when I first entered the house blindfolded. I wince and begin poring over the contents.

Nick Pearlman was right about one thing—the folder's contents explain everything, including the fact that that isn't his real name. He's Logan Weber, the son of a late, wealthy owner of a local retail chain. I make copies of every page in the folder, many of which are highlighted with conflicting information noted by journalists about the 1988 murder trial. It occurs to me that Logan likely wants me to keep these records as evidence that I compiled the information myself. If I make digital copies as well, that will back up the claim even more. I'd rather get a root canal than appease him. However, right now, this situation isn't about me. It's about keeping Trent safe. I'll do anything to ensure that. But what about six months from now? A year? No matter how much I analyze it, resigning myself to lifelong acceptance of the injustice Logan put me through just isn't an option. There are better ways to solve your problems than the one he chose. Someday, I vow, I'll set the record straight—when it's time. And I'll know.

One week after receiving the packet, I do as Logan instructed and deliver the information to Detective Spade at the Austin Police Department. But the irony of the whole thing is that since Trent and I discovered Juliana's dismal crypt, the packet of documentation probably isn't even needed. The case's first present-day news article echoes my thoughts—a lot has changed in thirty years.

27

New DNA evidence may exonerate man for 1987 murder.

AUSTIN — (KXAV) A thirty-year-old murder case has
been reopened due to the recovery of human remains.
Last week, Austin police were notified of a near-complete
skeleton found hidden at the recently sold, disused warehouse buildings at 1515 South Lamar Blvd. The forensics
team believes the remains to be those of Juliana Lange, an
Austin woman thought to have been murdered in
September of 1987.

The body of Juliana Lange, who was age twenty-eight at
the time of her death, was never found. The 1988 murder
trial involved two suspects: Rance Epstein, Ms. Lange's
former lover, and Logan Weber, a man who was purport-
edly then seeing Ms. Lange. Forensic DNA testing was
relatively new at the time, and the victim's body had not
been recovered for inspection. Based on testimony and

circumstantial evidence, Logan Weber was sentenced to life in prison. Rance Epstein was acquitted.

On the evening of September 28th, 1987, Austin police responded to a distress call from Logan Weber, a 31-year-old man living in the Oak Hill community. Per reports, a hysterical and barely coherent Weber told officials that his girlfriend had just been murdered. According to Weber, Rance Epstein had murdered Ms. Lange in Weber's own living room while he was at work but had then removed Ms. Lange's body before Weber returned that evening. Investigations revealed large amounts of blood in Weber's living room sufficient to result in death without medical attention. Also recovered were bloody clothing belonging to the victim, several strands of the victim's hair, and part of a right index finger. Blood was also found on the floor and back door frame of the home, indicating the victim had been dragged. Authorities found nothing at the crime scene which could be linked to Epstein. An exhaustive search of Epstein's home, belongings, and person also revealed no evidence connecting him to Ms. Lange's murder.

Logan Weber was convicted of murder based primarily on circumstantial evidence. But according to Detective Jeffrey Spade of the Austin Police Department, with the DNA that has been collected from Ms. Lange's remains, Weber's previous conviction may be reversed. Spade told KXAV that, "Mr. Weber had been released on parole over a month ago. Since this evidence came to light, we've already obtained a DNA sample from him, and it doesn't match the DNA found on Ms. Lange's remains. We've since

detained the new suspect, and the forensics lab is
performing a comparative analysis."

So, Logan may be off the hook, and Rance has already
been arrested. Since being kidnapped and held at
gunpoint, it's hard to cheer for Logan's victory
against the wrongful conviction. I want him out of my life
forever. But now that I've done my duty, I can't stand waiting
for the outcome any longer. There's no way of knowing if
Logan won't hurt Trent anyway if only to spite me for
refusing to speak to him and then breaking his nose. After
spending thirty years in jail for a crime he didn't commit,
Logan was desperate enough to obtain my cooperation
through violence. Additionally, he thinks the real murderer
paid me to hide something for him. That's too much reason
for vengeance for comfort. Before delivering the packet, I
tried calling Trent to warn him, but he didn't answer. I also
sent numerous texts explaining that because Nick may target
him, Trent should be extra cautious until he hears from me,
but he hasn't returned those messages either. This means I
haven't heard from Trent since a week ago when I packed up
and left. I call the Austin Police Academy and ask if he's been
in attendance, and I get confirmation that yes, he was
present every day this week. So, he's okay—probably just
upset with me.

On Friday evening, I decide to pay him a visit in Georgetown. When I pull into the gravel driveway, the sun is still up,
and the western horizon is a dusty gold and blue. It rained
yesterday. The temperature came down a little, bringing it
into the lower eighties. Trent's silver Chevy Colorado is

parked in the driveway. But in front of the small, shotgun house is another car—a black Mercedes.

"Oh God, no. No!" I scream at the windshield. I can't tear my gaze from the vehicle—Nick broke his promise.

My heart plunges to my feet as I mash the brakes and slam my Camry's gearshift into park. After shutting off the engine, I fling open the door and don't bother to shut it. I sprint across the gravel drive to the porch.

With effort, I stop. I need to think this through, so I try to collect my thoughts before opening the door. My pulse races, and my stomach contracts into an iron knot, but that's irrelevant. No matter how terrified I am, I have to make sure Trent is okay. I draw my pewter gray Sig Sauer from its holster and keep it aimed downward beside my leg. Today might be the day I use it. Maybe Logan hasn't killed Trent yet. Maybe he's still alive.

Wrapping my fingers around the doorknob, I can almost hear my heartbeat keeping count of how many cowardly seconds I stand outside.

One. Two...

I stand here panting, trying to compose myself enough to do what needs to be done.

Three. Four...

I put my left shoulder against the siding next to the door frame.

Five...

I brace myself.

...Six. Seven...

Twisting the knob, I find it unlocked. I shove the door open and thrust my body inside but keep the gun down. The tiny living room is empty, its air tinged with a sweet scent like tea.

"Trent! Trent! Are you here?" My hand trembles as I clutch the grip of the .38 caliber. I conceal it behind my hamstring. I'm not going to cock and aim until I know what's going on, or I could be the one going to jail for thirty years.

"Aria?" It's Trent's voice, slightly muffled from behind either the bedroom or bathroom door. Bedroom seems more likely because it's closer. In confirmation, the door swings open slowly, and Trent sticks his head out. He frowns. He cranes his neck like he's not sure it's me.

I exhale, and some of the tension releases from my back. He's here. He's alive—still alive. "Trent. Is Lo— is Nick here? Do you need me to get help?"

Trent opens the door the rest of the way and steps out. He's barefoot and wearing jeans and a white t-shirt, his brown hair messy and unbrushed. "Is who here?"

"Nick," I say.

Trent's gaze alights on the right side of my body, where it's evident I'm holding something behind my back. He rubs his chin, his gaze tracing over my face and body again. "No. He's not here."

As I blink at him, the sinking feeling in my gut tells me that somehow, I've got this all wrong. Trent looks as though he's been lying around watching TV in his room. I catch the sweet smell again. Trent isn't a tea drinker.

"I thought—I thought you might be in danger," I say. I slowly bring my Sig into view and return it to the holster under my jeans.

"You thought Nick was here?" Trent asks, the concern not leaving his face.

"I did." I sniff awkwardly. I don't know where to put my hands, what else to say, or what to do. "I—I saw the car outside. I thought since he threatened me and since we were shot at—and since he drives a black Mercedes...." I bite my bottom lip.

"It's okay," Trent says. "I'm fine. Thanks for coming to check on me."

But his tone tells me he isn't fine. He doesn't sound like he did the last time I saw him. I guess my harsh words before I left changed something. I used to come in without knocking, but maybe he's not okay with that now.

Another face appears in the bedroom doorway, and I start. My feet backstep almost involuntarily as I strain to process what I'm looking at. It's a woman standing there—a slender woman with blonde hair, with a white piece of medical tape across her nose. A woman. A broken nose. My mind starts racing in circles. Naomi Sedgeworth rests her long fingers on the door frame and peers out at me with condescending blue eyes. The light, fruity scent swells. It's ginger and tea rose—her perfume.

All my adrenaline, fear, and nerves pivot and start rushing in a different direction as I stand frozen now, glaring at her. The jealousy hits me first. It's like a slap in the face, so poignantly painful it nearly knocks me to the floor. I'm not supposed to be jealous. Trent and I aren't together—have never been. I even put some space between us for a time. Too bad these emotional things never work according to logic.

"He's fine," Naomi says. "He's well taken care of." She gives me a tight, closed-mouth smile and slides her hand to the small of Trent's back.

I begin easing myself toward the front door.

Trent pulls away from her. "Aria, it's okay. I'm sorry if this is awkward. This must look bad. Naomi and I were just talking."

"You don't owe her an apology," Naomi says. "You can't cheat on someone you're not with."

Trent keeps his eyes on me, but he doesn't rebut her statement, either. She's pretty much right, after all.

I back up a little farther. My mind goes blue screen of death. I can't summon a witty comment to save my life, so I give a half-hearted wave in their direction. It's an attempt at farewell without making a complete fool of myself, or at least no more than I have already. Without waiting for Trent or Naomi to reply, I open the door and let myself out. I rush into the dry, evening air, straight to my Camry with its driver's side door wide open and the dome light on.

My upper body shakes. My bottom lip trembles, and as I swing myself into the car and slam the door, a tear rolls down my cheek. No matter how much I grit my teeth, I can't help it. The reality of Naomi appearing from Trent's bedroom overwhelms my senses.

The black Mercedes. There it is. The sleek luxury car parked on a gravel driveway in rural Georgetown. Its shiny tire treads are dusted with chalky, white powder from rolling across the dolostone. The vehicle's new significance plugs in nicely to my current emotional state, and the mental gears start turning. As ridiculous as it seems, Naomi being the owner of a black Mercedes suddenly explains a lot. This is the "something" Trent wasn't telling me about—the big something. And maybe he missed it too.

"Looks like I'm not your biggest problem," Logan told me. He said he didn't shoot at me. That he didn't attack me in the field.

As I start the car and turn around to head for the road, the house door opens, and Naomi steps onto the porch. She locks her icy blue gaze on me, and I can't help noticing how motionless she stands as she watches. But most of all, I observe the white medical tape across her nose. The assailant in the ski mask was Logan's height and build, just a little taller than me. Was I really fighting with Naomi? Giving a sardonic snort, I recall jumping on the person and unloading everything I had, cracking my knuckles open on his—or her—teeth.

I turn the wheel roughly, and the tires grind as I pull onto County Road 152. I head for Interstate 35 North. I'll beeline for Round Rock, and when I get home, I'll email Detective Spade with a full report. Then I'll copy that report, and any earlier pertaining ones, to the Austin Police Academy.

My vision blurs as I pass the multicolored sheep in the field next to Trent's place. The animals roll by outside my car windows as blobs of fur clustered around the wire, sectional feeder. The small pond for the livestock breaks up the rocky terrain like a flat, black puddle.

Wiping my wet face with my bare fingers, I try to think. I have no proof it was Naomi who shot at us from a black luxury car. I don't even know if it was a Mercedes that time. But if it was her, she risked hitting Trent since we were walking side by side. I exhale hard and shake my head. Naomi's dad is a cop, and the academy runs background checks on their enrollees. My new theories are pretty far-fetched. Maybe downright absurd.

The narrow, country road straightens out after the turn by the pond. A short woodland, followed by another field, looms into view on my left, and on the right appears a pasture containing two brown horses and a large, red barn. When I glance in the rearview mirror, my breath catches in my throat. It's hard to believe Naomi's following me. But there's her black sedan, and I'd be crazy to ignore it. She's only about fifteen feet back, and she's gaining on me with each passing second. After a heartbeat, I can no longer see her front bumper. The Mercedes' engine revs as Naomi rams her car into the back of mine.

28

I whip forward. My forehead and nose smack the steering wheel. I grunt at the impact, and the sharp pain brings more tears to my eyes. I reflexively push down harder on the accelerator in the same moment, and my Camry surges forward. After turning the wheel sharply to the right, I keep driving half off the street. I can't get over all the way because of the drainage ditch. My gaze darts to the rearview constantly as I try to increase my speed and stay ahead of her before she hits me again.

Berry Springs Park comes up on the right, as I swear under my breath. I slow down and make a hairpin turn into its two-lane, divided entryway before the gate. I press the brakes. The car slides toward the bucolic scene ahead. Neatly mown fields of green grass stretch before me under rows of pecan trees. A few people gather in the park, but they're far away near the weathered, gray historic buildings which once belonged to pioneer settlers. From here, I can just make out a cedar fence encircling the unpainted barn.

I pull onto the grass, off the entryway pavement, so that I

won't block it. My tires skid to a halt. I grab my light jacket from the passenger's seat and dry my face with it. I lick the salt from my lips. Then I glance in the rearview again, this time craning my neck. Naomi's car is there. I also catch a glimpse of my red, puffy eyes. No matter how unpleasant it proves, I need to end this nonsense once and for all.

Naomi slips her sedan right behind mine, parking it about an inch away from my dented rear bumper. She flings her door open and stands outside before I've even unbuckled my seat belt. I keep my motions steady and get out of the car slowly. I turn to face her.

"Poor Aria," Naomi says. "Have you been crying?"

I put my hands on my hips. "What do you want?"

She slams her car door but never takes her gaze from mine. For the first time today, I notice what she's wearing besides the nose tape. Skinny jeans over her muscular legs, an army-green tank top, and shiny, black boots with thick tread. "I want you to stay away from Trent. Forever."

She doesn't have the right to tell me to stay away from Trent. However, I should probably acquiesce until I can report her. I don't want to, though. "I don't take orders from you. If you want a mutually exclusive relationship with Trent, then talk to him about it. Otherwise, you can piss off."

"No, sweetie, it's definitely you I need to talk to." She takes a few steps toward me. "I want you out of his life permanently. But you won't do it, at least not for long. Because you're such a victim. Who could possibly compete with *you*?" Her voice takes on a mockingly sympathetic tone. "Aria Owen, the victim of a horrifying crime. It's like a special talent you have. A talent for having the worst things happen to you, so people will feel sorry for you. So you'll always have someone. Maybe Trent is fooled, but not me.

You don't care about him. You just need someone. And who better than the man who discovered you as you were dying?"

Her words produce a strange twinge in my core. It's more than her criticism—it's something else, but whatever it is isn't immediately clear to me. Naomi saunters closer, the gravel crunching beneath her black boots. My mind flashes back to the night someone attacked me in the hotel parking lot. The height of the man. His thin build.

I blink at Naomi, this new truth sending shockwaves through my body. "It *was* you. You were the one—the guy in the ski mask. You chased me. You attacked me."

I shake my head, drawing connections between the events of the past weeks as I stare at this psychotic woman. Being assaulted by a "man" in a ski mask wasn't the only thing that happened.

"Very good," Naomi says. She reaches into her back pocket and draws out a knife. It's a black switchblade, not unlike the one I carry. She holds it close to her leg, out of view of the road.

Nothing that happened was about Ayden at all. Somehow, I chuckle. It escapes me wearily because, in a grim sort of way, it's kind of funny. All I need to do is pull my pistol. She called my bluff once, but if she comes at me with that knife in her hand, the law will be on my side when I fire. Ironically, though, I don't want to kill her. I don't even truly want to hurt her. My mouth twists into a wry smile, but my eyes must look sad. Because if anything is sad, it's this.

"I'm going home, Naomi. You should too. And while you're at it, find yourself a life."

She rushes at me. I spring back, shielding my face and middle with my arms. As I stumble and almost trip, Naomi grabs my wrist and pulls me close to her, holding the knife at my abdomen.

"I can't go home," she says. "Not while you're still alive. Because as long as you are, Trent will always choose you. I don't think any woman anywhere could compete with the special needs case you are. I've always hated people like you. You're nothing but a victim, and you don't deserve him."

I look into her cold, blue eyes that regard me like a piece of trash. Something inside me snaps. Somewhere between "special needs case" and "victim," I lose it. Though she has the knife aimed at my gut, I take my palm and shove her in the face as hard as I can. She thrusts the blade forward but loses her balance and starts to tumble back. As she gets her footing, I clock her across the face with my fist. She drops the knife. It flies off somewhere between our vehicles. My adrenaline starts kicking in with a vengeance. She has the advantage, being trained in physical confrontation at the academy, but it's doubtful she has my experience with pain. I can take a lot of pain.

Naomi swings at me, and I duck. I punch her in the stomach, and she doubles over but gets in a good lick to my jaw immediately after. Her fist collides with bone, and my teeth click together with a painful crack. The ground spins beneath me. I lunge at her and try to get my arms around her waist. I want to drag her down. If I can get her on the ground, I have a much better chance of winning. Instead, she grabs and lifts me off my feet before spinning me around. She slams my body on a rocky strip of land next to the asphalt. I grunt, the wind knocked out of me as a sharp pain explodes in my back.

I try to roll out of the way, but my legs won't comply. I only make it to my side. I fling my arms out and dig my fingers into the grass to drag myself. Naomi gets on top of me, squeezing with her legs to hold me in place. Her ginger and tea rose scent invades my nostrils. She aims for my face with her bony fist, but I block with my arms. Again and again, she punches me, knocking my arms into my face, but she can't get in any strong facial hits. I try lifting my feet to push her off. She's too far up my torso.

Then she aims just right and smashes my arms against my nose. I guess this is payback for breaking hers. It hurts like hell, and for a second, my vision goes spotty. I groan, flailing my arms to deflect another blow. Finally, realizing she has no padding or gloves this time, I grab her hand with both of mine. I bend her finger back hard and hold it there. At first, she jumps and gives a small cry. Her body goes stiff on top of mine. Then she screams, jerking and convulsing like a fish on a hook. But I don't let go, even as she pounds my face with her other hand.

Naomi shouts profanity. She calls me by all the bad names she thinks I am, but she rolls off. Now she desires only to get away. I sit up and shove her to the ground by her breastbone, then reversing our roles and punching the crap out of her face. I get in one particularly good lick to her taped nose, and an instant trickle of blood runs down to her lip. She wails, and the high pitch assaults my eardrums, but I know that's nothing compared to the headache she'll have tomorrow. She'll probably need a splint for that finger, too.

"Stop, stop! Get off me!" she yells.

In a final, desperate attempt, she thrashes about like a feral dog and pushes me off. I don't think she was prepared for how strong I am, even after what happened when she attacked me in the ski mask. I guess she was hoping the knife would do all the hard work this time. But as soon as she gets out of my grasp, I jump on her again. I grab her by the hair and hold her in place—this ought to feel pretty familiar.

Yanking her face close to mine, I tell her something slowly and deliberately. I want to make sure it's the last thing she hears. "I am not a fucking victim."

Gripping the base of her ponytail, I slam her head into the side of her Mercedes. It thuds like a bowling ball on a hardwood floor. It leaves a nice, melon-size indentation. Naomi's eyes roll back, and she goes limp. I let go, and her body slackens in the weedy grass next to the well-oiled tires of the luxury car. Her ponytail has mostly come loose, and her long, blonde locks spill over the ground. One slender arm lies straight out at her side.

I get to my feet and try to catch my breath. Panting as I glance around, it dawns on me now that my head and body hurt in about a dozen places. At least I shielded my face for the most part. After wiping my top lip, I pull my hand away to find blood. She did get in a few good ones to my nose and jaw. My back aches. Even my legs hurt. I reek of sweat and bodily strain. I stumble a few paces to my car and pull my cell phone from the console. I call 911 and explain what happened.

After hanging up, I return to Naomi and make sure she has a pulse. She does. She's knocked out cold, though, and I can't say I'm sad about it. I hope she'll stay that way until the authorities come. But before any blue and red flashing lights dance or sirens break the peaceful birdsong in the pecan trees along County Road 152, a silver Chevy Colorado pulls into the entrance of Berry Springs Park.

Trent flings open the door. He bursts out like he just got word of the apocalypse. "Aria! What the hell happened?"

My adrenaline races so fiercely there's no room for anything else. My emotions have all but fled, and I don't feel much for him—besides the irony of his timing. Maybe he wondered if something was wrong when Naomi left, but he sure took his time investigating. Instead of the numerous things I could say to him—all of which would be warranted —all I do is give a little snort. With blood dripping from my bottom lip and dirt streaks covering my torn shirt, I lean against my car and look across the two-lane road at the range and woodland. The trees sway gently in the evening breeze against the backdrop of a hazy, blue sky.

"You missed one hell of a catfight."

29

After the Williamson County sheriff's deputy guides an embarrassed and cuffed Naomi Sedgeworth into the back seat of his cruiser, I stay and talk with Trent for only a little while. An unfamiliar energy buzzes through me, and for once, I want nothing more than to immerse myself in the quiet of my room without a soul around. Yeah, I know. Weird.

As the navy sky fades to charcoal, I do something I haven't done in a long time. I lie in bed with the windows open and listen to the crickets sing. The draft of outdoor air blows cooler than usual, and the wind smells like rain and freshly mown grass. Lying on top of the soft comforter, I put my hands behind my head with my knees bent and just take in the pleasant tranquility. I don't need to do anything. I don't need to think about anything. My body relaxes, and for once, I feel—dare I consider it?—safe. And at that moment, the memory of Ayden's death, the incident I thought was lost forever, finally resurfaces.

One Year Ago

ON SATURDAY, I drive back from Korey's and mutter. As usual, his harsh words nip at me like biting flies that leave behind their nasty, little marks. I blast the radio to drown them out as I head back to Carol's house—my home in Round Rock since my birth mother passed away.

"Don't forget your drink," was the last thing Korey said on my way out. He extended my bottle of lemonade with that greasy smile on his face, the unspoken insinuation that I was "too emotional" dripping from his voice like corn syrup.

"Thank you," I said. My words were impassive. Without pausing, I took the lemonade by its black cap and whisked it from Korey's grasp as I passed him in the hallway. His bulldog Xero padded after me. He just missed my calf with a snap of his jaws, but I pretended not to notice. I dragged my rolling suitcase by the handle and calmly strode to the door. My face was dry. I hadn't screamed or even told him what I really thought. "Too emotional," I learned, was doing or saying anything Korey disapproved of, and that mainly consisted of whatever he couldn't directly control.

Today, Korey chewed and spat the usual fodder of our arguments. He didn't want me seeing other people, a phrase he meant quite literally. Visiting my friend Rebecca was tantamount to cheating on him. So was spending too much time with my stepmom. So was going to the library.

We haven't officially broken up. Regardless, as I pull into Carol's driveway, I know we're done. After sleeping over the last two nights, I can't take another minute. I think he knows it. I shut off the engine, drop my bottled drink into my purse, and gather my suitcase and the smaller bag with the shoulder strap. My chest flutters with rebellious energy as I take my stuff to my room. I unzip my luggage with stiff fingers and yank out my clothes. I heap them onto the bed. I can still smell sandalwood or whatever's in that sophisticated cologne Korey wears. Wrinkling my nose, I realize it's coming from the shirt I'm wearing. I take it off with a grimace of disgust and shove it in the laundry basket. Then I tug on my favorite blue blouse.

An invisible force tugs my gaze up to the picture on the wall—the picture of us. Korey's strong features and dark hair remind me of a real-life version of Aladdin from the Disney movie. I used to find him irresistible. Now his face makes me sick. I want to scour every last trace of him from my life— that's what I'll do today. And I'll stay busy. I don't want my mind running wild about what to say if he calls.

Abandoning my pile of shirts, slacks, and underthings on the comforter, I yank the photo from the wall. I dump it in the rolling trash can outside. Unfortunately, the heavy-duty hook left behind splays against the bedroom wall like a black, metal insect. It's obtrusive and ugly. Since I don't have another photo to hang, I decide the hook is coming down too, but it's the kind I can't pull out. I rummage through Carol's tool drawer in the kitchen, but the Phillips screw-driver isn't in there. It's probably in the shed. I grab my keys and the lemonade from my purse and head out to the backyard.

It's probably pushing one hundred and three degrees already. That's not unusual for August. A baked-lawn scent pervades the air as I stomp across the dry grass. My edgy gait fueled by tightly reined anger brings me to the rough particle board of our tan, ten by twenty-foot storage struc-ture. It's seen better days and leans slightly to one side. Not enough to prompt Carol or me to do anything about it, just enough to make it unattractive.

By the time I've unlocked it, my forehead and upper lip already bead with sweat. I step inside, and the thick summer wind swings the door shut behind me. That's okay—I won't be in here long. I pull the string dangling from the ceiling. A single bare bulb illuminates the inside of the shed just enough for me to see. The place is so dim. We never bothered to put anything stronger than a 40-watt there. Much like the shed itself, I guess it's an afterthought, just one more thing we haven't got around to yet.

It's probably twenty degrees hotter in here than outside, and my thirst kicks in with a vengeance. I twist off the cap from my bottle of lemonade and down the entire thing. The metal toolbox rests on the shelf nearest me, so I take it by the handle and set it on top of a dusty crate where I can rummage around for the screwdriver. Metal implements grate and clang together as I dig through them.

"Aria," a muffled voice calls from somewhere outside.

I stop my vigorous rooting and listen.

"Aria," the person repeats.

It's a man. His voice holds an odd edge, like a tremor or a nervous pitch. And behind that, a little bit of cockiness. Not an aloof, city boy kind of cockiness, more like backwoods snark. But the suffocating heat of Texas summer and the shed walls blanket the voice, and the tone, slightly. My spoken name, muted by the heavy, wooden door reinforced with cross boards, reaches me like it's straining through pea soup.

I wipe my forehead with my arm and toss away the hair that's sticking to my face. Now the sweat runs down my back and chest. My blue blouse adheres to my skin, and my jeans cling like wet wool. The tools blur. I blink to try and clear my vision, and I steady myself with a hand on the shelving unit when my legs go weak. The heat must be affecting me a lot quicker than I thought.

"Aria," the man says.

Sighing, I look up. Drowsiness comes over me, and I wish whoever it is would go away. It's probably one of the neighbors. Maybe that redneck guy I've never met who lives on the other side of greenbelt.

"Who's there?" I ask. If he has something to say, he can make himself known. Otherwise, he can get lost.

The shed door starts to swing open slowly. It groans outward on its rusty hinges, and I couldn't have locked it from the inside even if I wanted to. The bright sun floods into the weakly lit, dingy space, and I squint. I put up a hand so I don't get blinded. A man's dark silhouette breaks the glare at the end of my vision, and that first glimpse sets my belly on edge. He stands almost six feet tall, and he's pudgy in the middle with big, beefy arms. He sets down a heavy work boot beyond the door frame and begins to step inside. Once he does so, his girth blocks my exit.

"I'm Ayden," he says. "I'm Korey's brother." His voice is unmuted now. It's crisp and clear inside the dusty, one-room building.

Ayden, Korey's brother, I mentally note through worsening brain fog. I peer at him through blinking eyes as more sleepiness takes hold. Is this heat exhaustion? I've only been out here for five minutes, so I don't see how. Maybe I got dehydrated from being in the air conditioning all day, so it snuck up on me. I try to get my dilated pupils to adjust to the intense sunlight the man's letting in. I force my posture straight and set my hands on my hips. I get a good look at him.

He has sandy blond hair and simple features with a broad nose, full lips, and dark eyebrows. He looks nothing like Korey at all. His red t-shirt bears only one symbol and no lettering—a white figure of a mudflap girl. Ayden holds a cigarette in his right hand. The smell of tobacco smoke makes me wrinkle my nose and take shallow breaths. Korey did tell me he had a brother, but I've never met him until now. The nerve of this jackass to show up like this, and the nerve of Korey for giving him my address.

"What do you want?" I ask. I glare at him, this looming oaf who came onto our property without asking like he has a right.

Ayden takes a drag from his cigarette, pulling his round face back slightly as he regards me. I guess he's sizing me up. I'm five foot five with a slim build, and it would probably take two of me to equal one of him. His swinishly searching gaze sweeps me from head to toe. He blows smoke over his right shoulder, but the wind pushes most of it in my direction.

"Korey told me what you did," he says, half-smiling. He takes another step forward. His footfalls are loud against the plywood floor, and the wood creaks beneath his weight.

I frown as I try to figure out what Korey could have told him. That I left his house this morning? Why would his brother care? But something about the way Ayden stands there with one knee bent and his head cocked makes me stiffen. And that look on his face—that stupid smile. It's almost a smirk, but he manages to rein it in and wear it subtly.

The cigarette dangles between his fingers, stinking up

the shed and giving me second-hand fumes. It intensifies my dizziness and brain fog. Ayden's so relaxed—almost pleasantly so. And I guess he has no reason not to be. I'm alone. My face heats and the muggy breeze from outside makes a chill ripple across my sweaty skin. Glaring at him with my upper lip slightly raised in disgust, my pulse rate increases.

I open my mouth to ask him what Korey said when I realize that doing so would be taking the bait. Otherwise, he wouldn't have made that enigmatic statement. Did he know I was alone in here? Or did he knock at the house, and no one answered, prompting him to look out back and decide he might check the shed? The door was closed. But since it isn't locked, and there's no way to do so from the inside, he would have seen it resting open just a crack. Everything about this reeks like three-day-old fish. The hair prickles on the back of my neck. My adrenaline kicks in, but at least it curbs my confusion a little.

"You need to leeb," I say. Damn. "*Leave.* You don't have permission to be here."

Ayden snorts, bringing his full lips into a wider smile before he drops the amused demeanor and scowls at me. He fiddles with a large ring on his right hand before flicking his cigarette ash on the floor. "Korey told me what you did, you little whore. He said you were cheatin' on him, and then you left. Now," he says, pausing before he delivers the next part. "If I was you, I'd be real careful."

My stomach lurches and folds in on itself. The creep is threatening me. I swallow lemony saliva, another wave of lightheadedness making me grab the shelving. A ribbon of sweat runs down my forehead and into my eye, but I don't wipe it. I need to think. Carol is at work. We have neighbors, but it's doubtful they're home either. Even if they are, the houses in our suburban neighborhood are more spread out than some, each with a large, long backyard going back to the greenbelt.

I wonder if Ayden's lying or if Korey misinformed him. Not that it matters since both are wrong. There's a faint quiver in my words as I reply, "I never cheated on him. Korey knows that. I need you to leave, please. I'll call his and get this sorted out."

Leeb? Call *his*? I can't remember the last time I spoke so badly. My arms and legs tremble, and I wish I could sit down. I glare at Ayden hard, but I know my eyes are wide and shifty—he can see my fear. That fear embarrasses me, but even worse is that this man considers me so powerless he thinks nothing of trespassing uninvited onto our property. And I cringe at saying "please," as though that will make any difference if he has bad intentions.

"That ain't what he said," Ayden tells me. "He said you been screwin' around on him for months, and that's why you been so weird lately. Now I don't know about you, but I'd say that's pretty messed up."

He takes another step forward, the thud of his heavy boots reaffirming our weight difference. Dust motes mockingly glitter around him in the harsh afternoon sun.

My heart rabbits faster with every footfall. Every step closer means I've already waited too long to do... something. My mobile is inside—I didn't need it for a five-minute trip to the backyard. I grit my teeth. Seeming unable to wipe the sneer from my face completely, I take a deep breath and try again. "I hear what you're saying, but Korey's mistaken. I never cheated on him. There's a misunderstanding here. Now get out."

Ayden tilts his chubby head the other way now. His hair

reminds me of dirty straw. But my gaze pulls to his hands as he twists off the large ring and sets it on the shelf. "Hmph. You're scared, ain't ya? I'd be scared too if I was you. Where's your momma? Ain't she home?"

Obviously not. Otherwise, you wouldn't be here. I don't answer. Telling him I'd call Korey made no impression. I swallow again, tightening my grip on the shelf support. Does he have a point? Unable to keep the anger and fear out of my voice, I ask, "What do you want?"

Now Ayden smiles. When he draws his lips apart, he reveals a few yellow teeth among his more abundant off-whites. He laughs, a kind of stifled chuckle that makes his head bob and his belly jiggle, but he hardly utters any noise. "I'm just saying you better be *real* careful, girl. Nobody likes whores."

I'm not prepared. He twitches. That's all I get, the only warning before his body lurches toward mine. My heart pounds in stark terror of the motion, and I jump, but at the same time, I'm paralyzed like a lump of jelly. I've barely moved at all, and I have nowhere to go. I have to run, I have to get out, but he's blocking the way. I sidle back and forth, trying to anticipate and dodge as he approaches, but I don't really go anywhere.

Ayden reaches me with a few more steps of his hefty footwear. He thrusts out his hand at me, his fat fingers splaying against my breastbone. The heat of his meaty palm against my damp blouse sickens me. His acrid sweat and body odor burst through failing, cheap deodorant. My stomach gurgles with nausea.

I jerk away from his touch and try to back up, but my calves only bang into a pile of boxes against the wall. I can't take more than a few steps. As I sidestep toward the corner, my feet hit a stack of plastic buckets, and I knock them over. They hit the dusty plywood floor with a hollow sound, and they roll until they crack into the shelving unit. Ayden shoves his body in front of mine, pushing hard against my chest and slamming me into the wall next to the boxes. I grunt and lose my breath. Then I scream.

30

F ire! Somebody help! Fire!" Yes, "fire" is what I scream, and I scream it over and over again because I've always heard you're supposed to yell "fire" instead of "rape."

Ayden claps his sweaty palm over my mouth. I inhale his dirty-hand smell—metallic, like a car engine. The man who claims to be my boyfriend's brother squelches my pleas to a muffled gag. He pushes his pudgy middle against me. He squeezes me between his gut and the wall, and I can barely breathe.

There are things in here. Things I could use. The toolbox is now just on the other side of him. Besides that, there's a crowbar not far from the door. There are some metal rods leaning against the wall. There are cans of paint on the shelves, and various other supplies, any of which I could use as a weapon. But I can't get to any of those things because I can hardly keep my eyes open, my head spins, and I can't think straight—and I have no idea why. My normal self would have got the hell out of the shed the moment he showed up.

I tremble and convulse, still trying to will sound from my lungs through his smelly hand. My voice is suppressed and useless, and my muzzled terror pleases him.

With that moronic sneer on his face, Ayden explains how things are going to be. "Now, we can do this the easy way or the hard way."

His meaty palm presses my lips against my teeth, and I can't answer. I stare at him, barely moving despite jerking wildly—it's like wrestling with a hanging beef carcass. My face smolders like I'm burning with fever, and I realize it's more than the heat. He's partially blocking my nose. Between that and him squeezing me against the wall, I can hardly get any air.

"You be real still, and you be quiet. If you don't, things are gonna get ugly," he says.

I guess things aren't ugly now. This must be something else. I don't know how to answer, so I nod. At least, I try to. I can't move my head much, but Ayden feels the downward motion of my face against his hand.

"Good," he says. "Now you try anything stupid, and I'll kill you." He reaches around behind his back with his free hand. He pulls out a small switchblade knife. He clicks it open, and for an instant, the blade glints silver in the sun. Then a gust of hot air blows the shed door shut. The small space grows yellow-brown and dark, a cellar-like room that entombs me while my vision adjusts to the change. I nod again.

"Unzip your pants and turn around."

For a few seconds, my mind races in frantic wondering. I run different scenarios haphazardly through my head, envisioning what will happen if I don't comply. My cowardice wins, and I do as he instructs. I unzip my jeans and tug them, along with my panties, down to my ankles. My face burns anew, my cheeks all sweaty and red and wet with tears. I want to sob, but the sound lodges in my throat like a cotton ball. I've stopped trying to scream. I put my hands against the wall to brace myself for what's coming.

But then something happens. It's a pivotal moment, a brief, fortuitous instant when the universe steps in and says, "Here you go. This is your chance to change your mind—if you're still brave enough to do it."

There's an interval of a couple of seconds in which Ayden starts to unzip his own jeans. While I stand there, lightheaded and barely coherent, there's a moment when he isn't actually touching me. Since my cheek is pressed against the particle board wall, besides the sound of the zipper coming down, I don't know everything he's doing. I just know that for a fleeting instant, his hands are off.

My heart plunges, and I drop to the floor. I shield my head with my arm and scoot sideways, where I try to get up and make a run for the door.

"You little bitch," Ayden says. He utters the words half under his breath like he wants to spit.

I haven't made it one foot when he grabs me by the hair and pulls me to my knees with one hand. The cotton ball in my throat breaks free, and I start sobbing. My face contorts in a red, tear-streaked grimace, and terror rips through me like lightning. Terror and disgust. And degradation as thick and repulsive as Ayden's body odor in the swelling heat.

I have to get my mind straight. I have to fight through the confusion and dizziness of this heat exhaustion and figure out what to do. There must be a way to use this chance the universe has given me. To gain an advantage. It doesn't make sense to get trapped all over again.

Ayden yanks, and the muscles bulge in my neck as it bends backward. Here and now, I decide that no matter what he does to me, I won't cooperate. With my scalp sore and stinging where he pulls my hair, I let my body go limp. He'll have to make me stand, or he'll have to commit his sordid act with me lying down. From a self-defense class, I know a move that might get me out of that.

"Have it your way," he says. Still gripping a handful of my hair, he shoves my head against the wall.

Splitting pain shoots through the back of my skull all the way to my temples, and I cry out. He still hasn't let go, and I kneel on the hard floor. Will he stab me now? I don't see the knife anymore.

Ayden's shoulder muscles tense, and I brace myself for another blow. This time, he slaps me across the face. I scream, and my body goes board-stiff before going slack. My already spotty vision worsens for a few seconds, and I blink as I strain to see. Glittery stars everywhere. I cradle my torso protectively with one arm and reach for my head with the other.

"Shut the hell up," he says. With one hand, he shakes me by the hair. He squeezes my face with the other and forces me to look at him. "Shut up! Do you hear me?"

I know he's saying other things, too, even though I can't focus. But I know he is. He's muttering profanity. Calling me names. Giving me instructions. "Lie down," or "You lay there," or maybe it's "Lay down and shut up." I can't say which. I can barely hear him now.

"No, please," I say, choking on my tears. "I'm sorry. I'll call Korey. I'll fix everything. I'm sorry." I would probably tell

Ayden anything now, including admitting to cheating on his brother and other things I didn't do.

Ayden slaps me across the check again. With a crisp *thwap*, the shock jars me rigid. I get another whiff of his grungy sweat and underarm odor before he lets go of my hair so suddenly that my head whips downward. I throw my hands out to stop my face from smacking into the floor.

"I don't give a shit about Korey, you little whore," he says.

I can't see him because now I'm prone with my pants around my ankles. But I picture him leaning over me, leering with his dull, brown eyes set too close together in his round face. He reaches down and grabs me at the hips before pulling me backward toward him. I squeeze my legs and buttocks together, tensing every part of myself. Bracing for impact. But as I lie here, sobbing so hard my drool makes a sticky puddle, I see the nail.

It's a decent-sized nail, not the kind for hanging pictures, but the type used for decking. At this find, a part of me rekindles. Then for a second, a wave of wooziness hits me so hard I almost pass out. My ears ring, and my head throbs. He must have whacked me enough times to mess up my equilibrium. As I worry that I might not be able to make use of this pointed, metal gift, my hope of escape deflates. My consciousness sinks down, down, down, into some dark corner of myself.

Then, with my stomach somersaulting, I whoosh out. It's almost like one of those out-of-body experiences, except I know it isn't. My mind zooms outward and shows me the entire scene and where I fit within it. There I am. And there he is. I imagine I'm looking down on myself—looking down on both of us.

Backwoods Ayden is hulking over me in his crass t-shirt.

His upper lip twitches as he gropes me and watches me squirm. My own face hangs poppy-red, so contorted in grief and pain I hardly recognize myself. Now I watch my hand shoot out like a snake's mouth and grab that nail—that solid, three-inch, gunmetal-gray decking nail—before I twist my body and drive it straight into Ayden's left eye.

Ayden wails. He screams a cry so excruciated and sharp I think I may have killed him. I expect him to spout more profanity, to tell me again all the terrible things I am, but he doesn't. He doesn't utter any words at all. Flailing his arms about wildly, he falls on me several times before attempting to stand up. He staggers backward, his feet pounding the dusty floor like hammers.

After rolling onto my side, for a second, all I can do is stare in silent horror from my place on the floor.

Run. I need to run.

I push myself up and scoot to the corner. Here I crouch down because he's big, and he's in my way. I buried the nail so deeply. I drove it in well. I made it count. Only about a quarter of an inch sticks out from his pupil. If there's any blood, I don't see it. It's nothing like in the movies when blood gushes out everywhere. There's only Ayden's eye and a nail. He puts his hands over it and teeters drunkenly, banging into the plastic shelving unit. The force of his solid bulk makes a shower of various objects tumble off.

That's when the cigarette falls. I didn't see it until now. I was too engrossed with everything else—with Ayden's body and hands and my exposed bottom and the pain in my face. But he came in with the cigarette and never put it out. He set it on the shelf, and I didn't consciously notice, even though I've smelled tobacco smoke this entire time.

Other things occupy that shelf besides the cigarette. A

cordless drill, a watering can, and a plastic container of gasoline for the lawnmower all sit there, right by the smoking
butt that flutters to the floor with Ayden's thrashing. When
Ayden hits the ground in the throes of agony and the
blinding light of retinal detachment, all those things rain
down after him.

Maybe I didn't screw on the cap properly. All I know is
the gasoline and cigarette consummate their marriage in
instant combustion. The floor bursts into flames first. After
that, it's Ayden's jeans. He's still screaming, but now he's
convulsing too. His arms, legs, and really his entire body
writhe in a shivering dance of pain.

With the smell of petroleum and wood in my nostrils, I
leap to my feet. But something else draws my gaze like a
magnet. Ayden's ring, the one he removed when he came in,
rests nearby on the floor. My brain isn't working, but the
jewelry seems significant. Is there something special about
it? He intentionally took it off before putting his hands on
me. Maybe it's a class ring. If so, perhaps it could help the
police identify him.

Another wave of disorientation hits me. I can't pass out. I
can't because if I do, I'll burn to death. For a moment, my
legs won't comply. They give beneath me, and I catch myself
on a plastic bucket. But while I'm halfway to the floor, I reach
out and grab Ayden's thick, gold ring and slide it on my
thumb.

Now run—that's what I need to do—but I can't with my
pants around my ankles. Yanking as hard as I can, I pull up
my jeans, grabbing the panties along with them. I tug them
to my waist, and without zipping, vault across the two-foot
space between Ayden's head and the wall.

My sneakers flit across the dry grass as I surge out into

the dazzling August sun. I inhale the clear outdoor air, so cool and fresh in comparison. I'm free. Seconds tick by with my heart pounding violently, and I slow near the middle of the yard. With my fingers curled around the waist of my jeans, I turn to see the shed. Orange flames devour it— devour the injured man who remains inside the blistering space.

I could shut the heavy door and lock him in. I could.

31

My every nerve crackles with an insane, excited glee while I entertain this dark deed. Then I blink. The thought evaporates, and I'm Aria again. I stand here as a version of myself I don't recognize, all disorientation, blurred vision, and weak limbs. My unzipped jeans sag, and sweat pours down my face. The shed door yawns open like a window to a fiery inferno, but it's not for me to decide what happens next. I run into the house, deadbolt the door, and call the police.

"Was—there's—someone attack me in our sh—shed," I say to the dispatcher. I lean against the living room wall with the sharp smoke odor still in my nostrils.

"Ma'am, can you please repeat that?" the lady asks.

"Yes. Someone attacked me in the fire—I mean, in the backyard. I got away, and the shed caught fire." I groan and run my hand across my head. My fingers find a wet, golf ball-sized lump. "I—I don't feel well. Think I got heat estion—heat exhaustion."

"What's your name?"

"Aria Owen," I say. That's easier.

"What's your address?" she asks.

I tell her. She says she'll send officers and an ambulance and has notified the fire department. While I wait for them to arrive, she asks about the person who attacked me.

"He said he's Ayden Nemeth, my boyf's brother. *Boyfriend's* brother." I stammer out his full description the best I can.

"Have you had anything to drink today?" the woman asks.

"No," I say. My head pounds, and I need to sit down, but I don't want the couch. I lower myself to the carpeted floor. Its stability lessens the dizziness.

"No alcohol today?"

"No, only lemonade." Korey's oily smile invades my mind. He stood there in the hallway, shoving the bottled drink at me as I passed. "I think it had something—maybe something in it."

"Did someone give it to you?" she asks.

"Yes. My boyfriend did, before house—before I left him —his house." Geez. If only I could speak like a human again.

"All right, ma'am. We've got an ambulance on the way. Just sit tight until they and the police arrive, and stay inside with your doors locked," the nice lady says.

"Thank you," I say.

When we hang up, I remember the ring on my thumb. I glance down at my hand to see it streaked with blood. The red smear shines across the gold and whatever that large jewel is in the middle. Something white and blue. My eyes can't focus well enough to make it out. That's okay—all that really matters is having Ayden's blood so the police can run tests on it if they need to. All I have to do is preserve it until I hand it over as evidence.

I stumble into the bathroom and grab the sink to get my balance. I catch my reflection in the mirror. My left cheek is sooty purple, and there's a knot on my scalp, but at least my hair covers it.

My gaze alights on the ceramic cotton ball dish. Painted pink and red flowers with green leaves decorate the lid. I open it, toss the cotton balls in the trash, and drop the bloody ring inside. I replace the top and wash my hands. After drying them, I carry the dish to the living room and set it on the coffee table. I'll give it to one of the officers when they come.

My heart rate finally slows. The drowsiness digs in as I sit on the edge of the couch, my eyelids drooping. No longer having the strength to stay awake, I lie down. My mouth is dry and sour tasting. Within seconds, I'm out cold.

Thud, thud, thud.

Something tugs at my consciousness. Calls to me. Through a deep ocean of rich, encompassing sleep, the sound finds my ears.

Thud, thud, thud.

"Police," says a man's voice.

My eyelids flutter. I blink heavily, and my chest constricts. The police are here. I gasp and sit up, wondering how long it's been.

Thud, thud, thud. An officer's knocking.

"Coming," I say. I stand, and my legs nearly buckle as I stagger to the door. After fumbling with the knob, I get it open.

"Good afternoon, ma'am. I'm Officer Davis," says the

policeman. He's a youngish guy in his thirties with dark hair.

"Officer," I mutter, but my gaze tugs to what's occurring in the backyard behind him. I can't stop gawking.

In a trance, I slip out the door and stand beside the policeman. All I can do is stare. Through the impenetrable brain fog, I visually devour the scene grim I had a part in creating. It's all new again, and it's too shocking to be real.

The fire has spread to the surrounding yard near the greenbelt—thank God it didn't come toward the house. As I watch, two firemen blast the few remaining flames with water from the high-pressure hoses. The charred remnants of our shed are black and smoking now. Scents of gasoline, burnt wood, and melted plastic carry up to me in the hot breeze.

People huddle around something that lies on the ground outside. There are several officers there, so I can't see what. Police officers mill to and fro across the lawn with their radios buzzing. Then the small crowd parts and two EMTs lift a stretcher covered in a white sheet. They carry it briskly around the side of the house, out of my view, toward the front yard. Seconds tick by, maybe minutes, in which I block out all else but this vision. Its intensity turns me to stone.

My phone rings. In a daze, I answer it and talk to Carol, but I'm not really present. Then I come back to myself, and the images before me brighten and fade again. I sag, wanting to tumble and fall into a welcoming, mental blackness.

"Ma'am?" the officer says.

I jerk awake. Was I about to pass out standing up? The policeman stands beside me, his forehead furrowing in concern. I cover my mouth with one hand. He must either think I'm nuts or incredibly rude. "Forgive me. Yes, I'm Aria Owen. Please come in."

He does but stands aside for two paramedics—a man and a woman. The woman has golden brown skin and gives her name as "Asha." I don't catch the man's name—maybe he doesn't say. They have me sit down in one of our wooden kitchen chairs, and the man draws my blood while Asha asks me questions, takes my blood pressure, listens to my heart, examines my head, inspects my eyes with a light, and does a few simple tests to gauge my responsiveness.

"Do you have any drug allergies?" Asha asks. She tugs her navy-blue medical bag closer and rummages in a zipper pocket.

"No, none that I know of." I hold pressure on the cotton ball over the puncture site in the crook of my arm.

"Okay. This will help with the pain," Asha says. She gives me a packet with two Tylenol.

The man hands me a bottle of water, which I guzzle after swallowing the pills. Then he labels three vials of my blood while Asha goes to work cleaning and disinfecting the wound on my scalp. She says it isn't bad, and relief sets in when she tells me they won't shave my head or stick any bandages there. While they continue looking me over, Officer Davis slips out the backdoor.

"Ms. Owen," Asha says, "From what I can see, you don't appear to have a concussion, but you might have been drugged. But because you didn't have alcohol, the effects are much less than they could be—this is a very good thing. You're going to be fine. We'll come to get you after you're done speaking with the police."

"Come get me?" I ask. My head is still spinning like crazy, but my speech has improved a little.

The screen door whines open, and Davis thumps across the tile landing. Radio in hand, he talks in short bursts of code while he lingers on the burgundy rug.

"Yes, we'd like to take you to the ER for a more thorough examination," Asha says.

I frown but don't protest. After the EMTs collect their gear and head out the door, Officer Davis walks over with his gun leather creaking. He gives an apologetic, closed-mouth smile.

"Would you like to sit?" I ask. I indicate the chair on the other side of the table, where I've remained after all the first-aid poking and dabbing.

"Thank you, no," he says. He raises his clipboard. "How are you feeling?"

I blink, and his smooth face blurs a little. "Mostly, I'm just disoriented and sore—and my head is killing me. But I'm okay. I can talk as long as I'm able to keep my eyes open."

"I understand," he says. "I'm very sorry about what happened today. If you're up to it, can you tell me what occurred?"

"Yes, of course." I proceed to do my best. It takes a lot of effort to explain, especially with my head spinning and the thick dopiness clogging my thought process. After I've given every detail I can recall, and he asks a few questions, I look to him for something. I don't know what. A verdict?

"All right, Ms. Owen. Thank you very much for that. Just sit tight and take it easy. I'll be back in a little while."

I nod. Surprisingly, my body no longer shakes, and my pulse has slowed to normal. An almost numbing calmness settles over me. Maybe my adrenaline rush has ceased, or it could have to do with the toxin in my system if that's what happened.

Davis joins the others outside, but I'm not left alone while I wait. A few officers cluster near the door and speak in low voices. Two of them let themselves out, but one remains. After about fifteen minutes, Officer Davis comes back and finds me still at the kitchen table. I glance up at him as I lean back woodenly with my hands in my lap.

"Ms. Owen, I wanted to let you know that we've identified the man who attacked you as Ayden Nemeth. He was pronounced dead on arrival. I also want you to know that at this time, the cause of death is still uncertain. Although it can happen, it's rare for someone to die from a stab wound to the eye. Regardless, the evidence shows you were acting in self-defense. I'm telling you this to put your mind at ease." He gives a firm nod as reinforcement.

My mind still bakes with an overly calm fog. "I see."

"I'm sorry you had to go through that, but at least he won't be able to do something like this again to you or anyone else. Once his family is notified, the Round Rock Police Department can testify on your behalf if there are any legal proceedings. So, you have nothing to worry about there either."

"Thank you," I say. "I really appreciate that.

Asha and the other EMT reappear to take me to the Emergency Room. I grab my purse and follow them out the door into the surreality of the black, smoking backyard. The ceramic dish containing Ayden's bloody ring stays where it lies on the coffee table. I didn't mention it once. I couldn't because I completely forgot about it after I passed out on the couch while waiting for the police.

I HAVE a short stay in the Emergency Room of St. David's Round Rock Medical Center. A CT scan reveals no concussion, which I already suspected due to what Asha, the EMT, told me. As for the nausea and dizziness, however, the doctor informs me I tested positive for Rohypnol. I sit on the papered table in my hospital gown while he explains.

"You've probably heard it called 'roofies'—the date rape drug," he says. The harsh fluorescents gray his olive complexion beneath his shiny, black hair. "It's unlikely to cause you any serious harm, especially since it wasn't combined with alcohol and you're in good health, but you might feel its effects into tomorrow. You might also experience anterograde amnesia, which means that once the effects do subside, you may not be able to remember what happened during the period the drug was active in your system."

The lemonade. Korey.

"And I've found no signs of serious damage from your head wound," he says. "It's a superficial hematoma and will heal on its own."

"That's good." I press a hand on the stiff bed to readjust my position and the paper crinkles. My eyes droop heavily with each blink. At the same time, my pulse has begun rabbiting along again like I've had a Red Bull. I can still smell cigarette smoke and gasoline. I can still hear Ayden screaming.

Looking over at the doctor in his white coat, I ask, "Have you ever seen anything like this before?" I bite my lip.

"Yes," he says. He turns from the counter where he's been noting things in my open chart. "I've seen this and much worse. But you're the first patient I've met who killed her attacker. I know it probably doesn't seem like it now, but you're extremely fortunate. People have wound up in ICU from sexual assault, not to mention needing to prove who did this to them, which isn't always easy."

I nod and glance at the off-white wall. I don't feel fortunate, only exhausted, shaken, and confused.

The doctor continues. "Although he wasn't able to commit the crime he intended, we'll still take certain samples from your body. In this case, we won't have to match DNA to a living person, but the evidence we collect will stay on record and will help if you need to go to court."

"There was no... semen if that's what you mean by taking samples," I say.

The doctor nods. "That's fine. I'll just do the examination. Even though you weren't raped, his actions were violent, happened without your consent, and clothing was removed. That is still considered sexual assault. I want you to understand that. There's a process we go through to ensure nothing is missed—for your safety and that of others."

I inhale. I didn't think of it that way. "Thank you."

The door swings open, and the nurse breezes in, carrying a plastic bundle of what looks like clear, small bags and vials. I discover the whole procedure is indeed a process. The doctor and nurse are thorough in their questioning about the incident, the examination of my body, and they even collect a hair from my clothing that may belong to Ayden.

"Use an ice pack on your head as needed, and it should be back to normal within a few weeks. Get rest and take it easy until you feel better. Unless you have any questions for

me, you're free to go. Just make sure to schedule the follow-
up visit with your primary care physician," the doctor says.

I have lots of questions, unfortunately, none of which the
doctor can answer. Since the blow to my scalp against our
splintery, unclean shed wall did break the skin, he recom-
mends a one-week course of antibiotics. Prescription in
hand, my mind reels more with thoughts of what I did than
the fact of being a near-rape victim leaving the hospital.

THAT NIGHT, after waking up on the couch and talking to
Carol, I take the ceramic dish from the living room and
retreat to my own space. I stand reeling in horror at what I
find when I take off the lid. The bloody eye ring—the "souvenir" of my kill. I pass out and wake up again in the middle
of the night. I pick up my cell phone—no messages from
Korey—and read the time as 3:42 a.m.

The clutter in my head dissipates, and an undiluted
clarity takes its place. Now I remember picking up the ring
from the shed floor. I never took it from Ayden. He slipped it
off before attacking me. Maybe the jewelry had some special
significance, and he didn't want to damage it, but I'll never
know. He accidentally knocked the ring from the shelf with
his thrashing, and I picked it up to give to the police as
evidence. But then later, when I was waiting for the authorities to arrive, I passed out and forgot all about it.

Roofies. That's why I forgot. That's why my recollection
and awareness have been so spotty. And the blood on the

ring? It's my own. I touched my scalp wound before taking the ring from my pocket and storing it.

I pick up the cotton ball dish and carry it to the bathroom, where I ease the door closed behind me and lock it. The police don't need the ring as evidence—they identified Ayden at the scene. I take the gold-ball handle and remove the flower-painted lid. It clinks against the granite countertop when I set it aside. I could mail the ring to Korey. Maybe he or another family member will want it. Or I could give it to the police anyway.

But as I dab cucumber melon hand soap on my palms and wash the blood from the ring, it occurs to me that because I've had it this long, anything I do with it now will make me look guilty. After pinching the ring between my index finger and thumb, I hold it over the toilet. I release my grip, and after a *plink* and a few ripples, the blue eye glares up at me from the bottom of the bowl. I depress the handle, and Ayden's ring vanishes with a whoosh. Then I wash, rinse, and dry the ceramic dish before taking it back to my room.

When I wake up the next morning, the ring is gone, and I have no memory of my realizations or what I did during the middle of the night.

32

PRESENT DAY

My eyelids flutter open, and I sigh, pressing my fingers against the down comforter beneath me. Beyond my open bedroom window in Round Rock, soft darkness floats. A gentle rain patters against the house, and the cool wind shivers the maple tree branches in the front yard. I inhale the earthy scent of wet grass and sit up in bed. I click on the lamp. After grabbing my mobile, I hold it up and stare at my reflection on the black screen.

I'm not a monster. I never was.

TRENT and I are called to appear in Naomi's trial at the Criminal Justice Center in downtown Austin. I've been here before, earlier in the year, after Korey was arrested. The boxy, concrete building on 11th Street has always felt intimidating, but at least I won't also have to attend small claims court for Rance's lawsuit. Being on the hot seat for murder, he never got around to suing Median Realty. Now his mind is on things like procuring a good criminal defense attorney and what spending the rest of his life in prison might feel like. Damn.

Naomi surprises me by pleading guilty to her charges and being open and frank about what she did and why. And what she did turns out to be quite a bit. Austin Chief of Police Riley Sedgeworth's only daughter, Naomi, we learn, has a history of psychological problems. Though the academy knew that she had been institutionalized for a short time five years ago, after counseling and maintaining improved behavior, her father was able to pull some strings and get her accepted into training.

I sit in the courtroom to the right of the defense with Detective Spade, Trent, and my attorney during Naomi's trial. Since she confessed, it's unlikely there will be another hearing after this. She's seated in the stand calmly, though slightly hunched, with her hands folded. Naomi's blonde hair is greasy at the roots and has been hastily put up in a messy bun. Her skin appears dull gray in the fluorescent lighting. The white strip of medical tape still covers her nose, and both eyes bear black-and-blue shiners.

"Ms. Sedgeworth, can you please state your whereabouts on the night of August twenty-second?" my lawyer, Frank Luciani, asks. He's the same attorney who represented me in Korey's trial.

"Yes," Naomi says. "I was on County Road 152 in Williamson County, outside Trent Lemend's house."

"Thank you," Mr. Luciani says. "And what were you doing outside Trent Lemend's home at that time?"

Naomi swallows before answering. "I was upset when

Trent told me Aria was staying over, so I—" She pauses, and her gaze falls. "—I drove out there and stopped in the street with the headlights aimed at the bedroom. I could see a silhouette. I knew it was her."

Well, I guess at least somewhere inside all that crazy lies a conscience. The rest of the story comes out, piece by piece. Naomi parked her car some distance from the house, where County Road 152 meets up with CR 140. Then she walked back to Trent's, and seeing my car parked outside, became furious and hurled rocks at the bedroom. She hoped she'd break the window, maybe even hit me with a well-placed stone, but it was hard to aim well from the road. When she saw the lights from the Williamson County Sheriff's cruiser, she slipped into the mesquite prairie the next property over and hid deep in the brush until the officer left.

Naomi then made her way back to her car and drove halfway between CR 140 and Trent's house. When she saw both our vehicles leave together, she became angry all over again and followed us to the hotel. She admits to disguising her appearance, attacking me in the parking lot, and putting her hands around my neck in the field. But what she reveals next leaves me stunned. Naomi tells the prosecution what she was up to *before* she came at me in the ski mask.

"I drove past the hotel and made a three-way call to my dad and Trent. Before Trent picked up, I told my dad to please wait a moment and listen to our conversation. I also explained that Trent was a fellow cadet in the academy and that after what he had done in the warehouse building in South Austin, his actions were grounds for expulsion. My father didn't see it that way until he heard Trent and me talking, and he could see that Trent was hurting me—he was playing games with my feelings, leading me on. At that point, I got off the phone, and my dad took over the conversation and made Trent explain things. Not just his investigation of the burned building, but his involvement with me. His intentions. And he threatened to have Trent expelled from the academy if he didn't clean up his act."

I would roll my eyes were it not for the fact that Chief of Police Sedgeworth is glaring at me at this very moment. I recall that once I felt embarrassed around Naomi, but now I'm pretty sure our roles have reversed. She keeps her eyes downcast, her posture still drooping. And how must her father feel?

Logan Weber's words flash to mind. "I even know where he goes for a screw occasionally—if you were wondering." I wasn't wondering, thinking it was just another taunt, until now.

"Were you ever in a relationship with Trent Lemend, Ms. Sedgeworth?" Mr. Luciani asks.

Naomi's eyelashes flutter as she restrains herself from crying on the stand. "No. But I wanted to be."

"Had you and Trent Lemend ever engaged in intimate activity of any kind?" the attorney asks.

Naomi folds her arms across her chest, her sour expression like that of someone who just drank straight Everclear. "No. I asked him to. I tried when he came over to my apartment once, but he wouldn't. I tried at his house too."

She swallows, and her cheeks pinken. Shuddering as she draws a breath, she keeps her gaze aimed at the space to the side of the courtroom. She doesn't look at the prosecutor. "Trent told me he was in love with Ms. Owen."

A cannonball drops into my stomach. Are there ever good cannonballs, or are they all bad? At the very least, they're always unexpected, and I wasn't expecting this.

Trent stiffens next to me, and I get a whiff of his faint, woodsy citrus scent. My hands are folded on the table, and I keep my body still. I want to behave as though this piece of testimony is no different than any other. If what Naomi said is true, Trent sure has a strange way of showing it sometimes.

Although I maintain the appearance of attentiveness, I become so embroiled in this juicy morsel I forget to pay attention to the examination. The courtroom, the cherrywood judge's bench, and the defense all melt away as I try to make this fit with everything else I know. Then Naomi's attorney's "objection" breaks into my thoughts, followed by Judge Moreau's "sustained." What was the objection about? I didn't hear the question. My breath hitches, and I straighten.

I learn it was Naomi who shot at Trent and me when we were walking to Tim Corbin's ranch house. "I wasn't trying to hit Ms. Owen or Trent," Naomi tells my attorney. "I didn't even aim at them. I just wanted to scare her. I thought if I could make it dangerous enough to be around Trent, she would stop seeing him."

This much I figured out, but I'm not prepared for what she admits next. She confesses to forging a letter to me in Trent's handwriting and replacing his actual letter—the one he said he sealed in an envelope. "No matter what I did, Ms. Owen wouldn't take the hint."

Relief pours through me at the idea that things finally make sense. I draw a long, deep breath and exhale slowly. There's no telling how many other "little" things like this she did, what she told Trent when they were alone, or how else she manipulated him. Still, I can't get over Naomi's apparent willingness to spill everything. Maybe it's the cathartic effect, and she just wants the whole thing to be over. That makes two of us.

Then, at last, Sedgeworth drops the final bomb. Her death-white face drains of the magenta color it bloomed with only moments ago. "I set the fire in the warehouse building. I made some homemade explosives with a recipe I found online. I set the explosives in the back near some old wiring, hoping it would look like an electrical fire."

"Thank you," Mr. Luciani says. "Can you please state your reasons for committing arson on the property?"

Naomi nods. "I wanted Ms. Owen to get in trouble, to get blamed for not seeing that the inspection was conducted properly, and get fired from her job."

"Had you known Ms. Owen was responsible for the building's inspection?" the attorney asks.

"Not for a fact. But I knew she was a real estate assistant, and scheduling the inspection is one of their duties," Naomi says. Her face remains pale and drawn.

I uncross and recross my legs. My mouth curls into a smile, and I bite my bottom lip to conceal it. The property has no service, so "electrical fire" was ruled out from the beginning.

"Did you do anything else to try and get Ms. Owen in trouble with Median Realty, where she was employed?" my lawyer asks.

After a pause, Naomi says, "Yes. A man named Nick Pearlman was interested in buying that same property." She sniffs. "It seemed like he wanted those old warehouses too much like there was something special about them or he was hiding something. So, when he asked me if I would accept pay to spy on Ms. Owen and the goings-on at the buildings, I said yes. But..." Another sniff. "I told a lie. I told Nick that

Ms. Owen's client paid her under the table to keep a secret. And that I didn't know what it was, but he definitely paid her to keep her mouth shut about something."

"Thank you. And was Ms. Owen or her employment negatively affected by this, that you know of?" Mr. Luciani asks.

"I don't know. I just know that Nick reacted strongly to what I said. I hoped he'd go after her for it, but I don't know if he did."

My heart hammers and I cross my arms before leaning back in my seat. Waves of disbelief roll over me. I can't believe it. Naomi was Nick's contact. A few feet away, Detective Spade's pen weaves back and forth across his notepad. Trent's gaze flicks to me, and I nod. They don't know the whole story with Nick or who he is, but this explains why he was threatening me—why he was so angry.

Mr. Luciani wraps up the questioning by addressing the final incident in which Naomi tailed me from Trent's house and jumped me at Berry Spring's Park. The defense and prosecution also take turns examining Trent, Detective Spade, and me before wrapping everything up. The trial takes a lot out of me, although Korey's was much more demanding and far longer, with multiple hearings. Still, I'm not sad when I finally get to walk out of here.

I stand from the hard chair and stretch my legs. As I hook my purse strap over my arm and begin making my way to the door with the others, Trent pulls me aside. "We should talk."

"Ya think?" almost flies out of my mouth, but I catch it just in time. Smile and nod. That's what I do.

TRENT and I sit in Cianfrani Coffee House in Georgetown across from the old courthouse, just like we did the first time we met after both being in the hospital eight months ago. The place is a familiar and safe retreat from our strange lives. The rain finally showed, and it's still drizzling outside, the blazing August heat subsiding to a humid, southern warmth that carries the smell of wet leaves and granite. From our place on the oversized couch, we can see out the window to 7th Street and catch glimpses of the American flag on the municipal building when the wind stirs it.

Holding my cup of hot tea, I slip off my shoes and sit cross-legged in my black slacks. I give Trent my full attention. I've sure been doing a lot of listening lately.

"Everything Naomi said and did around me, where it concerned you, was under the guise of care or concern," he says. Coffee mug in hand, he shakes his head as he comes to grips with the insanity of it all. "She acted like she was your biggest ally, rooting for you behind the scenes. Sometimes she told me not to say this or that to you because you were still recovering from your trauma. She always told me I needed to think of what was best for you."

I nod but stay silent.

Trent continues. "She's the one who told me you were having an affair with the guy who was threatening you— Nick Pearlman. Said she found it in your case files when she asked her father to do some checking up on you—for your safety, of course."

I snort. "Of course. I bet her 'father's research' didn't tell her that Nick Pearlman isn't even his real name." Shit. I shouldn't have said that.

"It's not? Did Spade finally find something on the guy?" Trent asks. He gets more comfortable, and the leather couch creaks.

Thinking quickly, I say, "No, that's why we think he was using an alias. There's no one by that name his age except someone who died over a year ago."

Trent takes a drink of his coffee. "Naomi was always telling me not to mention her to you—that it would upset you. She told me not to get involved with you, to break off seeing you to any degree, really, because she said I was being selfish, and you were too fragile for any kind of relationship."

I crack a smile. "I believe it."

Trent's mouth falls open. "You find this funny?"

I chuckle and set my tea on the small, round side table. "Kind of, yeah."

At this point, I've been through so much hell my sense of humor is all I have left. The mirth falls away from my expression, and I stare down at my lap. I take a deep breath and look up at Trent again. "Was it true what she said? About how you feel about me?"

Trent's jaw tics the way it does when he's awkwardly uncomfortable or irked about something. He hesitates as he searches my face. "Yeah. It's true."

"Did Naomi tell you not to tell me that?" I ask. The words sound soft and small.

"No," Trent replies. "That was all me."

❧

I TAKE three dresses from the closet and lay them out on the bed. All are autumn-appropriate, but I can't decide between red, blue, or green. Pretty much any bold color looks good on me. After tugging on my pantyhose, I slip into the red one. It has an empire waist with a few large faux garnets in front. It's cute. I grab my new strawberry body spray and spritz my neck once from ten inches away. That's plenty—no need to smell like the farmer's market.

As I push my feet into my black high heels, Margarita pops in and stands back to look at me. "Oh, I like that one!"

"Thanks. I can't even remember the last time I wore it." I turn and glance behind myself in the mirror to check out my back. Not bad.

"Rebecca and Ann are ready downstairs. We can take my car if that's okay," Margarita says. Her tight, dark pink dress suits her.

"Sure," I say. "I'm ready too." I take my small purse from the nightstand.

We trot down the stairs and meet our housemates in the living room. Ann stands a few feet from the entryway fiddling with the clasp of her necklace. I get behind her to lend a hand.

"Aria, I'm so thrilled you're going out with us. I just can't wait. Just think, it's your first time since you moved in. Aren't you excited?" Ann says while I fasten the delicate, silver chain around her neck.

"Ann, shush!" Rebecca says.

I laugh. She thinks if anyone mentions it, I'll change my mind about going. "It's okay. Yeah, I'm really excited. I think it will be fun."

We're going to Alamo Drafthouse for dinner and a movie, and afterward, who knows. I might let them drag me to a club. Rebecca tucks her fists beneath her chin and gives Margarita a silent squee. We lock up the house and file into Margarita's electric blue Toyota RAV4.

I chat a bit on the drive, but after we pull onto Interstate 35, I let the streams of red taillights mesmerize me and lapse into contemplation. This fall, Rance Epstein was convicted of the 1987 murder of Juliana Lange. He got life without parole, and Logan Weber was finally exonerated. I want to show Trent the article on KXAV's website, but I'm not ready to open that can of worms yet.

I have, however, come to a few hypotheses about Logan. You don't need to kidnap a woman and fly her somewhere by helicopter to give her a packet. He likely did that to instill within me the fear factor necessary to carry out my task and lie to the police. The gun helped, too, of course. Would Logan have shot me? I doubt it. Would he have killed Trent? I doubt that even more. Regardless, I'm going to let the dust settle a while longer before telling Trent but especially before reporting Logan. The dust is still in whirlwind status if you ask me.

Naomi was sentenced to twenty years in prison for her various crimes. She would have got more but for her insistence that even when she tried to throttle me in the field and pulled a knife at the park, she had no intention of killing me. The building she burned wasn't occupied and was unused. Still, any future chance at a career in law enforcement is ruined. Unless she's released early, she'll be forty-five years old when she gets out and will have to start her life over. It's a sad ending to a sad tale, I guess, but damn, that girl's crazy.

Margarita cracks the two front windows. The wind whistles through the openings and forces the scent of fresh autumn leaves into the SUV. I glance down at my waist, which has no pockets or belt, only sequins. The flowing hem of the red dress drapes over my knees. Today is the first time I've gone out without my knife and pistol—there's only my pepper spray in my purse. My intuition tells me that taking another life isn't in the cards for me. I'm more than okay with that.

"Aria," a female voice says in some distant background.

Not only did nothing in the past months have to do with Ayden, but Naomi managed to get me to see an aspect of myself no one else had. Despite being as mad as a March hare, she was right about something. She told me that I needed Trent. It nicked me at the time, like a piece of shrapnel under my skin. But it was true.

When I look over my life, with all its morbid tragedy, my difficulties all seem to stem from one thing. I always needed someone. I always thought I needed someone no matter what, and I craved a relationship regardless of what it did to me. I thought that having someone, anyone, was better than having no one, so I wouldn't have to be alone. I needed Korey, and that's why the abusive relationship lasted as long as it did. And I needed Trent, just as Naomi said. I needed him too deeply, too avidly, when he wasn't in the right frame of mind himself to have any kind of relationship with me. Now that I see this, I'm okay with whatever we decide to do in the long run. There's also the fact that he embroiled himself in investigating a suspicious accident at a local farm last week, and I want no part of that. We visit a few times a week, but I'm still staying in Round Rock. Only time will tell.

"Aria?" Rebecca says. She turns in the passenger's seat. "Are you all right? Is the noise too much? We can close the windows if it is."

"I'm better than all right, but thanks for asking. No, I like the highway breeze. Leave them open." I smile. In my peripheral vision, I catch Rebecca exchanging glances with Ann beside me.

"We're almost there," Margarita says from the driver's seat.

"Good. I'm starving," I say.

Everyone laughs like I've said something hilarious, so I just grin back at them. I peer outside. Margarita pulls into the movie theater's parking lot and starts looking for a space. We pass a median near the street where the branches of a row of oak trees sway rhythmically. Several leaves spiral to the ground. From here, I can see the illuminated, red letters of the Alamo Drafthouse sign and a yellow glow spilling across the entryway. A couple walks hand in hand toward the three sets of glass doors. Other patrons gather at the outdoor tables.

All this time, I've been so sure the universe was punishing me—Aria, the monster— for killing Ayden Nemeth. At last, I know this isn't true. If it was punishing me at all, it was for my bad choices in relationships. I guess, in the end, we're our own executioners.

I count myself lucky to have escaped the hangman's noose. I've lived to tell the story, just as Trent lived to tell his own. I unbuckle my seat belt and step out into the clear, crisp evening. Each footfall finds the concrete stable beneath me. The fabric of my light gown flutters with my easy gait as I take in the present moment of walking beneath the sapphire sky amidst bursts of city lights. I'll never again have a slipknot around my neck. I'm not a victim. And I'll never be alone because aloneness isn't so much a condition but a state of mind.

Trent and Aria's story continues with the following books of the series, in order:

Blood in Truth
Flesh and Blood
Blood Is Thicker

Connect with the author:
https://jaconrad.com